ALSO BY DEBBIE JOHNSON

S

i

S

Finding Hope in Starshine Cove

Starting Over in Starshine Cove

A Very Irish Christmas

The Comfort Food Cafe Series

Summer at the Comfort Food Café

Christmas at the Comfort Food Café

Coming Home to the Comfort Food Café

Sunshine at the Comfort Food Café

A Gift from the Comfort Food Café

A Wedding at the Comfort Food Café

Standalone Novels

Maybe One Day

The Moment I Met You

Forever Yours

Falling for You

CHRISTMAS WISHES AND IRISH KISSES

DEBBIE JOHNSON

Storm
PUBLISHING

Ebook ISBN: 978-1-83700-281-8
Paperback ISBN: 978-1-83700-283-2

Cover design: Rose Cooper
Cover images: Shutterstock

Published by Storm Publishing.
For further information, visit:
www.stormpublishing.co

ONE

NEW YORK, ONE YEAR AGO

I am standing in line to see Santa Claus. I am a thirty-seven-year-old woman, and I am standing in line to see Santa Claus. What can I say? It seemed like a good idea at the time.

That was an hour ago, and I think I've made a mistake. This was supposed to be magical, and to start with it was. Santa hangs out in a super cool, pimped-out snow palace. There are polar bears, a steam train and a workshop for the elves. The decorations are dazzling, the music is festive, and I have my very own passport that gets stamped by insanely cheerful helpers as I walk along.

I wandered in here with eyes full of wonder, and a heart full of hope. I was ready for a Christmas miracle – but now I'm just hot and bothered, and people are staring at me. Even the elves seem to be giving me some side-eye. I know I'm probably imagining it, but still, the sensation of being watched is real. I wouldn't be surprised if I glanced down at my chest and saw one of those red laser beams from a sniper rifle. I do a quick check, just in case. Nothing, thankfully.

I think it's just my own brain playing tricks on me. My brain is mischievous like that. It should be nicknamed Loki. Still, maybe it has a point – maybe it's weird that I'm here as an adult on my own. Is it weird? A quick look around shows me I'm the only one, so perhaps. It's all families with children. Again, that should be magical – what could be cuter than seeing a kid excited about meeting Santa? Possibly a Labrador puppy excited about meeting Santa, but I'm not sure dogs are allowed. They might pee on the fake reindeer.

The thing about kids, though, is that they rarely perform as expected, and they get tired and strung out pretty quickly. Some-where, a baby is screaming loud enough to block out the carols, and it does not bring to mind the little baby Jesus lying serenely in his crib. Unless little baby Jesus had a bad case of colic. Right behind me, a harassed mother is trying to explain to her cynical older child why the 'real' Father Christmas lives in Macy's, and in front of me another is dragging her terrified offspring forward as the line moves along. The kid is maybe four and bawling her eyes out. I get it. Old Saint Nick can be a little scary. I feel a wave of sympathy for all the parents, and a familiar wave of yearning.

I don't have children, so I shouldn't be here. What the heck was I thinking?

Too late now, I decide, as we finally approach the grotto. This is it. I'm here. I've put in the hard time, fought off sniper attacks and survived terrorist assaults on my eardrums. I've earned this. This is my chance for some quality alone-time with the fat man in the red suit. I feel utterly ridiculous as I am ushered in by a young man so happy with life that he could explode at any minute – he's a joy grenade waiting to go off. 'Is it just you today?' he asks cheer-fully, as though that is the best damn thing in the whole world.

I nod and attempt a smile. 'Yeah. Is that weird? It is, isn't it?'

He shakes his head and looks horrified at the suggestion. 'Not at all!' he assures me. Huh. I suppose he has to say that.

I look over nervously at Santa. He's sitting on his throne-like seat, and he looks perfect – the suit, the beard, the hair. The twinkle in his eyes. I approach and have no clue what to do next. Do I sit on his lap? I'm not sure even children do that now, and I am a grown-ass adult. I'd probably squash him, maybe even kill him. I'd be The Woman Who Killed Christmas. He pats the seat next to him, and I breathe a sigh of relief at having somebody tell me what to do.

'Well, hello there, and merry Christmas!' he says, his voice suitably jolly and very soothing. I wonder if they have to go on a training course to do this kind of gig. Or if, of course, this is actually the real Santa after all? 'How are you today? Are you excited for Christmas?'

His tone is just too kind. Too fatherly. I grip my purse on my lap, and feel my eyes suddenly fill up with tears. Oh no. Oh, please God, no. Don't let me cry in Santa's grotto! I squeeze my lids real tight, bite my lip, and shake my head. When I open up again, Father Christmas has a combination of concern and horror on his face. I don't blame him. Kids crying because they're freaked out is one thing. Women crying is entirely another. Most men don't know how to handle that, even Santa. To be fair, he recovers quickly, and pats my shoulder with a comforting white-gloved hand. 'There there. I know. It can get a little overwhelming at this time of year. We're all so very busy aren't we?'

I nod and manage a small smile. 'Especially you, Mr Claus.'

'Yes indeed! But I have a lot of help from my elves, and Mrs Claus, and of course my reindeer! Why don't you tell me what you'd like for Christmas?' He adjusts his belt and it jingles. It's a lovely sound, and for a moment it makes me forget reality. It makes me forget that I am lonely, that I am living in a city where I have never felt at home. That I feel like a sad, unlovable leftover. I forget everything apart from that pure, simple sound, and I let myself believe. Even if it's only for a second.

'I want to be with people I love, and who love me back,' I say simply. He looks momentarily surprised, and I add: 'Also, a puppy. And possibly a new phone because I dropped mine in Walmart and the screen is cracked.'

He nods wisely, and soaks it all in. 'Those are very good items for your Christmas list,' he says seriously. 'Especially the first one – because spending time with our loved ones is the most magical thing of all. I'm sure you've been good, and you deserve a little happiness. Now, would you like to take a photo?'

I nod and am told to say 'cookies'. The process is repeated with my phone, and then Santa gives me a hug. It is a magnificent hug, and makes the whole experience worth it. Yes, I am actually so starved of affection that a cuddle from Father Christmas is the only significant physical contact I have had with another human being for months. I try not to cling on and sob into his beard, much as I'd like to stay in his arms listening to him jingle. Loki conjures up a brief image of an alternate reality where I get adopted by Santa, move to the North Pole and live happily ever after.

'Goodbye now, my dear,' he says as I reluctantly stand up to leave. He waves his big white hand at me. 'Remember that Santa loves all his boys and girls, and have a very merry Christmas!'

I stagger away through a Christmas-themed corridor, collecting my Santa button on the way, and head to the escalators. By the time I emerge into the real world of the store, I feel like I'm coming down from an acid trip. Not that I'd know what that feels like from actual experience; I've led a very boring life. I pause behind a rack of Christmas onesies and look at my phone.

Oh, my goodness. That photo is terrible. For a start there is a spider-web of cracks running through the screen, so Santa and I look a little like we're in a horror film and have been cursed by a witch. He is still the perfect Santa, though, with his warm expression and serene air. I, on the other hand, look like I've just escaped from a secure facility. My long brown hair could be a home for sparrows, one eye is open and the other closed, and my smile is a plea for help. This is not the kind of picture you frame or send to friends. It is, in fact, the kind of picture that Santa might use as evidence of how tough his job is and why he deserves a pay rise.

Still, I think, putting the phone away and making my way towards the exit – no regrets. I really needed that hug from Father Christmas. I needed a boost of festive magic, because this year I am not feeling it. Just under a week until the big day, and I haven't watched a Hallmark movie, bought a gift or eaten a single mince pie. In fact, I haven't had a mince pie for over a decade. Americans might have invented the light bulb and put the first men on the moon, but they have yet to discover the miracle of mince pies. I could probably get them at a speciality place for expat Brits, but then I'd end up standing in a room full of Heinz baked beans and Cadbury's Dairy Milk bars and crying from homesickness. I left the UK when I was a teenager, but the place you spend those early formative years somehow always still feels like home, doesn't it? No matter how many tough memories it holds.

I have lived all over the States, but I've spent the last few years in New York. I fell in love with the romance of the place – its energy – during a trip here with my mum. Turns out that the romance and the energy don't feel quite the same when your life consists purely of work and meeting terrible men on dating apps. Well, not all terrible – some just dull, others downright shady, and none of them right for me. Or maybe I'm just not right for anyone. That is the conclusion I'm coming to – a failed marriage in my twenties, and a trail of broken-down relationships since then all point in the same direction.

It's one of the reasons I went to see Santa. I realised as I wandered through the festive city streets, after a scintillating day as an office manager for a building supplies firm, that I had no Christmas spirit. I had no sparkle. I had no *pixie dust*. I was spending Christmas alone, and that did not fill me with joy. I don't even have a tree up in my apartment, because it seems like a waste of time when there's only me that will get to see it. I feel like I'm doing everything alone these days, and it's starting to drag me down. I live in one of the biggest cities in the world, but I feel invisible. Like I might just disappear from my own life.

I want somebody to be close to. I want someone to confide in, to talk about my day with, to be my ally in life. I want somebody to know how I take my coffee, to bring me flowers and hold me close at night. Is this all too much of a Christmas miracle, even for Santa?

It's early evening and fully dark outside. It has been snowing, but it is now mushy underfoot, melting in the roads and dripping from gutters. I stare through the store windows at the busy street, at all the people striding around with a sense of urgency. Couples, families, people clutching bags. Everyone looking so busy and purposeful.

I realise that I really don't want to go home. It is a home in name only – it does not feel like one. When I first moved in, I was a little more enthusiastic. Now, it just feels cold and small, rather than cute and cosy. It's not just the apartment, it's me. I have not been looking after myself, and when you are single, it's pretty damn important to look after yourself. I know that – so why the hell am I living on microwave meals for one? I can cook – I love cooking, and I am a skilled baker! I've always loved spending time in the kitchen, kneading and mixing and whisking. So how come my freezer is full of cardboard boxes that might as well be called Lunch for Losers, or Dinner for Dumbasses?

And why haven't I decorated the place, even with a few strings of fairy lights? Why haven't I bought myself a new phone, or tried going on a date for the last few months?

Because I'm sinking in a pit of melancholy, that's why. My dad has the same tendencies, and I do not like it one bit. I'm going through the motions of living, but I feel like I'm shrivelling up inside. Like I'm giving up on myself.

I need to stop treating myself like this. I cannot press pause on my own life. I think back to what Santa, my new life coach, said. I deserve a little happiness. I decide that he is right, and moping around drowning in self-pity really isn't helping. I need to be more positive. Things can change. I don't have to carry this sense of failure and loneliness with me forever. Christmas always highlights what you're missing – the whole world gangs up and screams at you. It's about children and family and love. For those of us who don't have those things, it can be tough.

But maybe this has been a turning point. Seeing Santa – undoubtedly the real Santa. Maybe my wishes will come true. Maybe I'll walk outside right now and bump into the man of my dreams. I could have my very own meet-cute outside Macy's, and it will be a sweet story to tell our children one day.

Bolstered by the idea, I make my way through the crowds and stand expectantly on the sidewalk. Or, as some of us call it, the pavement. I stand and take a deep breath, and look around. I say a little prayer, looking up at the stars in the night sky. I cross my fingers – and wait for the magic to happen.

Any minute now, I'm sure, a smoking hot billionaire will drive past in his limo and splash me with melted snow-water. Then he will get out of his car to apologise, and our eyes will meet across a crowded street. He will offer to take me to dinner while I dry off, and we will spend the whole evening lost in witty banter and heart-busting flirtation. By dessert, we will be in love. Nice.

Or maybe I'm about to collide with a cyclist, and I will bang my head as I fall. I will be taken to hospital, and he will come with me. When I wake from my short stint in a coma, I will have perfect hair and a full face of make-up, and my teeth will be shiny and white. The smoking hot cyclist will be at my side, holding my hand, gazing into my eyes. He might also secretly be a billionaire, and we will fall in love before you can say 'hairline skull fracture'.

Possibly, the busker on the corner is actually a former member of a chart-topping boy band, playing on the streets to try and rediscover his musical mojo. When I throw a dollar in his guitar case, he will wink at me and my heart will skip a beat. I will recognise him, become his muse, and he will write timeless classic love songs about me. At a guess, I'd say that he will be smoking hot, and a billionaire.

I decide to give the magic a nudge and walk over to the busker. I throw a dollar down, trying not to wince at him slaughtering Elvis's *Blue Christmas*. When he looks up from his guitar, his Santa hat dangling in front of his face, I see that he is maybe a hundred years old. Possibly a thousand. He winks at me, then belches for maybe five solid seconds. I almost pass out from the whisky fumes, and back off rapidly. Okay. Maybe not.

As I scuttle away, a cyclist screeches past, a courier from the look of his uniform, and he misses me by inches. I feel the swoosh of air on my body as he skims by me, swerving to avoid contact. 'Watch yourself, asshole!' he yells, giving me the finger as he rides off into the distance.

Just as I am recovering from the shock of that near-death experience, a huge black SUV with tinted windows drives by. The filthy puddles of rain that have collected at the side of the kerb splash up from its wheels and drench me. The vehicle does not even slow down, and I am left soaked and shivering and wondering where all the polite billionaires have gone. I don't even care about the smoking hot bit right now; I'd settle for someone with manners.

A woman who saw what happened walks towards me and pulls a sympathetic face. 'The world,' she announces firmly, 'is full of jerks. You okay?'

'Yes,' I reply, wringing out my hair. 'Thank you. I'm not sure it's the whole world. I think maybe I'm a jerk magnet.' She pulls a pack of tissues from her bag and passes them over. I dab my face, and smile at her. At last. Someone with manners. She's very pretty, too. Maybe she's a billionaire, and I've been playing for the wrong team all these years. 'Do you want to get a coffee?' I ask, unexpectedly. Like, I had no clue I was going to ask that.

She looks taken aback and shakes her head. 'No, sorry, I'm meeting someone. But keep the pack, and happy holidays to you, okay?' And just like that, she races away. I don't suppose I can blame her. I know from my Santa photo that I'm not looking my best, and now I'm covered in dirty water too. She'll probably tell her pals about the crazy lady she met outside Macy's, wearing a Santa badge and hitting on her.

'I wasn't hitting on you, by the way!' I shout after her. 'I'm just lonely!' She glances back over her shoulder, and a few people stare at me. This is New York though, so nobody really bats an eyelid. I shrug, and trudge on.

I feel weirdly determined now. I might look like a lunatic, and I might feel sad and pathetic, but I will at least try and find some Christmas magic this year. I am not a bad person. I don't kick puppies or steal, or deliberately hurt anyone else. I rescue spiders that are trapped in the tub, and I sponsor a child in Bangladesh, and I always check in on my elderly neighbour, Mrs Baumgarten. None of this qualifies me for sainthood, but it should at least qualify me for the cosmic version of the nice list instead of the naughty list. Shouldn't it?

I know the cosmos doesn't work quite like that, which starts to annoy me. As I make my way through the thronging crowd and the melting snow and the brightly decorated store fronts, I feel a sense of anger growing inside me. The anger turns into strength, and I begin to make some decisions. I start to act rather than react – for the first time in months. I accept the Christmas miracle.

I pause in a store doorway and give myself a pep talk. Out loud, which ensures that everybody gives me plenty of space.

'I deserve to be happy,' I say firmly, putting it out there into the universe. 'I deserve love. I deserve a new phone, and a haircut. And I deserve to bake myself the most spectacular Christmas cake that the world has ever seen. I promise you, Santa, that I will do my very best to make all of those wishes come true.'

And with that, I go shopping – it's as good a place to start as any.

TWO

A YEAR LATER

Tyler holds his glass up towards mine and we clink, laughing as some of the Champagne sloshes over the sides.

'To us!' he says, grinning at me over his glasses. 'And our six-month-iversary!'

'Is that even a thing?' I ask, smiling back at him. Tyler has thick dark hair, and although his glasses give him a vaguely nerdy look, he's a hot nerd. He works out a lot and has a Clark Kent vibe, and even thinking about that makes me wonder what he might look like dressed up in a Superman outfit...

'It is a thing,' he replies, looking hurt. 'Look, I have proof!' He pulls an envelope from his bag and passes it over to me. I can tell it's a card, and I already feel bad because I don't have one to give to him. I tear it open and see that yes, sure enough, it is a card. Bearing the words 'Happy Six Months Anniversary'. I guess it's official then – this is a thing.

'I'm so sorry,' I say, looking up into his blue eyes apologetically. 'I am a terrible girlfriend.'

He reaches out and strokes my face, and I lean my cheek into his palm. If we weren't in public I might actually purr. 'You're not a terrible girlfriend. And anyway, I'm sure you can make it up to me later.'

He winks, and I know it is meant to be flirtatious, but it somehow comes out comedic instead. When we first met, I really wasn't sure about him. He was good-looking, and seemed decent, but until I got to know him better I thought he was joking about literally everything. And that's fine – who doesn't love a good sense of humour? But even when he was talking about serious issues, like his mom's cancer battle or his grandad's experiences in France in World War II, he always seemed like he was only a wink and a nudge away from laughter.

I know now that it's just a social tic. He can feel awkward easily, and one of the ways he has dealt with that since childhood is to joke around. The physical remnants of that creep into all his interactions, and I've learned to interpret them better with time.

'Well, I'll do my best,' I say, enjoying the look of surprise on his face as I slide my foot up his leg under the table. 'A six-month anniversary is a thing. Everybody knows that. We have to mark the occasion.'

He leans forward to kiss me, just a gentle touch of the lips, and I tell myself yet again how lucky I am. The world of online dating is probably a carousel of crap for everyone, but in a city like New York, it's even worse. It took a lot of courage to try again, and I'd kissed my share of frogs before I found this particular prince. In fact I was on the verge of shutting down the apps, and was about to do that, when his message landed. Not only was he geeky-hot, but he has dogs. Three yellow Labradors, to be precise. The dogs swung things his way, and I decided to give this one more shot.

I'm still with him a whole half-year later, but I'd be lying if I said I was all in. Even after I vowed last Christmas to be open to love, part of me is still cynical, still scared I guess. Lessons you learn when you are young are hard to unlearn; they seem to take root in your emotional DNA.

My parents split up when I was sixteen, and it was Messy with a capital M. I still don't know what caused it, but my mum and dad went from being normal and boring to all-out warfare overnight.

There was a terrible period of screaming rows and fights, me lying in my room confused as I listened to plates get thrown downstairs. My normally calm mum became shrill and angry, crying in that way women do when they're furious. My dad gave as good as he got. It was a terrible, traumatic time in our lives, and something in me seemed to get broken in the process.

The warfare lasted for months, and I was caught in the middle, dazed and confused. My parents ran an inn in Cornwall, the place where I grew up, and maybe they stayed together because of that. Or because of me. Who knows? Eventually, Mum met and married Ethan, a cardiologist who came to stay at the B&B. I was dragged kicking and screaming from my home, my father, my friends, and relocated to the States, where I felt like a freak. The perfect storm for a teenage girl.

My ex-husband, a man who I married when I was twenty-four just because he asked, told me I was 'emotionally unavailable', and I suspect he was right. I think I probably need a world of therapy, but I'm still just a bit too British at heart to consider it.

Though Tyler, sitting there opposite me in all his glory, might be enough to make me change my mind. Doesn't he deserve someone more whole than me? More fixed than me? In fact, don't I?

That's too big a question for a pleasant night like this, I tell myself.

'You know,' I say to him, 'at first, I was worried that those pictures of you with the pooches were fake. I mean, how could someone who looked like you, and who had such beautiful dogs, be single?'

'I know,' he says seriously, nodding. 'It is hard to believe, isn't it? I think it's the glasses. Or my boring job. Or maybe my, uh, personality?'

'True. You are rotten, really. You're lucky I gave you a chance.'

'I am, but I also know you weren't really interested in me. You just wanted to get your hands on my puppies. Which when I say it like that, sounds pretty suspect!'

I laugh and sip my Champagne. Six months of Tyler and his puppies. Amusingly, he wouldn't actually introduce me to the dogs until we'd been on quite a few dates. They were like his babies, and he needed to be sure before I was allowed into the inner circle. They were worth waiting for, though.

After that fateful visit to see Santa, I fulfilled my promise – I made real changes to my life. I left my job and instead joined a temping agency, reducing my working days to four a week. On the Friday and the weekends, I now bake – and people even pay me to do it. At the moment, it's a side hustle, but who knows?

I got the haircut, and the new phone, and I put more effort into making my apartment feel like a home. As for the love – I'm doing my best. I am giving it a good shot and trying to open up more to Tyler. I like him a lot, but I haven't said the L-word yet. There is an emotional block inside me still, one that means I can't quite let myself go. I am a work in progress, I guess, and I have always been honest with him about that. I have never promised more than I can give.

I know he wants more. I know he is being patient, and I cannot expect him to wait around forever. But life has taught me never to let my entire sense of wellbeing rest on a man, no matter how good he is. It's not fair to the man, apart from anything else. My ex cheated on me, and although those wounds have faded so much they are barely there, the scar tissue still lies beneath the surface.

'What are you thinking about?' Tyler asks. I blink away my thoughts and decide on a white lie. The real answer – Oh, I'm just wondering if I'll ever be capable of committing to anybody – would be a bit of a downer on our night out.

'I was just wondering,' I say, 'if you'd ever consider dressing up as Superman?'

'Well, that depends on the circumstances. I mean, I have a meeting tomorrow with the CEO and a tax auditor – so obviously, yes, I'd wear it then. Is that what you meant?' He does the silly wink again and makes me laugh.

'Yes. That's exactly the kind of situation I had in mind... as long as you kept it on later. When you came round to my place.'

He raises his eyebrows. 'Anything you say, Lois.'

I am pondering these possibilities when my phone rings. I glance at the number and see that it is my father, which is deeply unusual. We rarely speak on the phone, and I immediately feel a prickle of concern, especially when I realise it's after eleven at night there. I mouth a silent 'sorry' to Superman and answer, walking away to the outside of the bar where it's a little quieter. 'Dad?' I ask. 'Is everything all right?'

'Hello, dear girl!' he says, bridging the thousands of miles between us. 'Is life treating you kindly?'

On the rare occasions that he writes to me, he always starts his conversations with the same line. Sometimes I am darling girl, sometimes a completely new and made-up pet name, but he always asks if life is treating me kindly. He is only seventy-five, my dad, which is not old by modern standards – but he is old-fashioned. It's actually a point of pride with him, the way he clings to the way things used to be, back in what he would undoubtedly think of as better days.

I frown, confused by the whole thing. 'Um, yeah, I'm okay, Dad. Why are you calling?'

'Just to hear the sound of your voice, darling! It's been too long since we had a proper chat. Is that so bad, for a father to want to speak to his only child?'

Now, that's an odd question – because we have never really done 'proper chats'. We have never really spent hours on the phone catching up and exchanging the dull details of our lives. That's simply not the relationship we have ever had. I know my dad loves me, and I love him, but we are just not close in that way.

When my mum met Ethan and moved me to the States, I begged my dad to let me stay – but he shook his head sadly and told me 'It wouldn't be for the best.' I remember being so angry that nobody was listening to what I wanted and feeling so hurt that he wasn't fighting for me. We have never discussed it, because that is simply not the way he functions – I have not seen him in the flesh for over ten years now, and although we are not in any way estranged, we are also not the kinds of people who call 'for a chat'.

'It's not bad, no, Dad, but it is unusual. Are you sure everything is all right with you? Where are you?'

'Oh, I'm in the usual spot, love, in my study. Dark out there but I can see the moonlight reflecting down in the bay. The owls are calling. I can hear the waves too. A beautiful evening. How about you?'

My dad's study is at the top of the eighteenth-century inn he still runs, and by day the little room has stunning views all across the sandy bay to the Atlantic Ocean. Depending on the time of year it is a dazzling patchwork of glittering blue, the froth of the waves curling white onto the sand. That sound – the waves rushing in and sucking out, or crashing against the rocks – is always linked with my childhood. Cornwall is one of the most beautiful corners of England, and for me it is also the past. A place littered with happy memories, childhood magic and emotional landmines.

'Well, I'm in Manhattan,' I say, looking around at the bustling streets and the busy bars, the roads packed with traffic. 'It's a little different than St Tilda. I can't hear any owls, but I'm sure there are some in Central Park. Foxes too. Are you okay?'

'Of course I am! I'm about to turn in for the night, Eleanor, and I just had an urge to hear your voice. I forget how American you sound these days!'

'I really don't,' I reply, smiling. 'Everyone here immediately knows I'm originally British, but the last time I was in the UK, they all thought I was American.'

'Well, isn't that marvellous – you can fit in everywhere!'

Or nowhere, I think, because in my experience that's been the case. I've never quite felt like I've fitted in, and it's only recently that I've stopped caring about that.

'How is work?' I ask. 'Lots of bookings?'

'Oh yes, packed to the rafters. I really must retire one of these days. Maybe I shall travel to the New World and visit you, my angel.'

'You'd be very welcome,' I say, still unsettled by this whole conversation. My father has never been here to visit, and I have only been back to England a few times, meeting up with him in London. He's never seemed comfortable with the idea of reunions, and I have often wondered if it was too painful for him – to see me briefly but to have lost me. Or maybe I'm over-thinking it and, as he always claims, he simply doesn't like to travel. 'I could show you the sights. You could meet my friends.'

I am convinced that something is wrong. I am suddenly desperate for him to visit, or for me to go back to St Tilda. To be near him again.

'Anyone special?' he asks, casually. I have told my mum about Tyler, but not my dad. Why haven't I told my dad? When is the last time we spoke about anything more serious than the weather and work?

'Maybe,' I say coyly. 'I have a nice guy waiting for me right now, in fact.'

'Ah. I should hope so. You're really quite the catch. Are you happy with him, sweetheart? Do you think there's a future in it?'

'I am happy, yes, Dad. As for a future... well, who knows? None of us can predict that, can we?'

I'm evading the question really, not just with my father. But also with Tyler. We are at the six-month mark. He has been dropping hints about how much time we spend at each other's places, and how big his house over in New Jersey is, and how much I love the dogs. I have a suspicion he wants us to move in together, and I'm not sure how I feel about that yet. About uprooting my life, giving up my apartment, moving across state lines. The fact that I'm not sure tells me I'm probably not ready, so I'm ignoring his hints, and taking it day by day. Is he special, though, like my father asks? Yes. He is definitely that.

'Very true, my angel, very true. Right, then, Eleanor, I shall say goodnight. You do know I love you, don't you? I fear my stiff upper lip has always got in the way of me saying that to you enough.'

Damn. There is definitely something wrong. My dad is from an old English family who fell on hard times. He grew up rattling around the stately home that had been in de Vere hands for centuries but had reached the point where the roof was coming in and all the land had been sold. His family were rich in class but poor in cash, which is why he ended up working in the hotel business instead of running their country estate and organising pheasant shoots. That was what his father did, and his before that, and various members of the de Vere clan were well-known enough to have obituaries in national newspapers. By the time my dad, Peter, was born, only the accents, the attitude and an abundance of tweed clothing remained.

The house was eventually donated to a heritage charity, and he became the first de Vere to have to actually work for a living. His background helped in his line of work – the plummy English voice matched with his twinkling eyes and roguish smile. His upper-class childhood also left him with a taste for the finer things in life, and an aristocratic repulsion for talking about his feelings. That's what is making this so scary.

'I know, Dad. I love you too,' I say. I'm about to press him for more but he hangs up, leaving me staring at my phone, a sense of dread settling on my shoulders. No matter how many times he said he was fine, something just didn't ring true. It's time to call in the cavalry.

I wave at Tyler through the window, letting him know I haven't absconded, and he puts his arms out straight in front of him. One fist clenched, like Superman flying. I'm still laughing when my mum answers. She and Ethan retired to Florida a few years ago, and they live an active and sociable life that puts most people in their twenties to shame.

'Is there anything wrong with Dad?' I ask, without preamble.

'Gosh, Ellie, sunshine of my life, fruit of my loins, it's so nice to hear from you! And I'm great, thanks for asking!'

'Sorry! I'm sorry! It's just that he *called* me.'

A pause. A breath. 'He actually called you? He never does that!'

'I know! And he sounded... off. I can't quite say why, but he sounded off. I'm worried.'

'Leave it with me,' she says soothingly, kicking straight into mega-mum mode. 'I'm sure it's nothing, but let me send a smoke signal to my St Tilda spies, all right? It might take me a while, it's late there, but I'm sure I'll find someone awake. No point in me calling him, he'll just lie and say he's fine. He'd have been one of those people doing the tango in the *Titanic* ballroom as the damn thing sank. Now, you go back to whatever it was you were doing, and try not to freak out.'

'Have you met me?' I ask, trying to inject some humour into my voice. I'm making a joke of it, but it's true – I can over-react. I used to be a feisty teenager with no fear of the world at all, but those days are long gone. I wouldn't be doing the tango on the *Titanic*. I'd probably have slept in the lifeboats just in case, and you know what? That would have been a smart move.

We say our farewells and I go back inside to Tyler. 'Everything okay?' he asks, taking one look at my face and seeing the signs of distress.

'I hope so,' I reply, sipping my cocktail. 'It was my dad, and then it was my mum, and now she's calling her spies.' He looks confused, which is entirely understandable. 'So,' I explain, 'you know how my parents split up when I was a teenager, and we moved here when I was sixteen?'

'I do,' he confirms. 'And the way you say your cute English words is one of the many things I adore about you. Go on, say it... please?'

I can't help smiling at his pleading tone. 'Okay, since you asked so nicely. *Aubergine!*'

He claps his hands together in glee. 'Damn! I love that. You even make an eggplant sound sexy. So, what gives then, with your pop?'

'Probably nothing. But he never calls me, you know? He sends emails. Very occasionally he texts, and sometimes I get a letter through the post. But he never calls. Said he just wanted to hear my voice, and then at the end he told me he loved me.'

'Okay. That sounds kind of... fatherly?'

'It does, but it's not normal for him. It had a weird energy. Like, an end-of-the-world kind of energy. Or, and this is possible, he'd just drunk a bottle of port and felt maudlin. Now I come to think of it, his speech was a little on the slurred side.'

'Maudlin. Port. It all sounds very Gothic. I'm sure he's okay, babe. He was well enough to call you at least, which is a good thing?' Tyler takes my hand in his and squeezes it reassuringly. I lose myself in his eyes for a moment, and let my mind wander back to the Man of Steel.

'Tell me about him,' he says. 'Tell me about your life back then. You never talk about your childhood much.'

I gulp down some wine, almost choking. He raises an eyebrow at me. 'That bad, babe?'

'No. Not really. In fact, the early part was wonderful. Cornwall is wonderful – it's this little bit of England, right on the coast, like nowhere else on earth. It has its own climate, and history, and flag... and it's beautiful, Tyler. So beautiful. I had a pretty idyllic childhood, for most of it.'

'You were never lonely, having no siblings?'

I was, I vaguely remember, when I was very little. But then Liam Byrne and his family moved to St Tilda – all the way from Ireland, which seemed very exotic. Mr Byrne had relocated for work and brought his wild tribe of kids and his force-of-nature wife with him. Liam became my best friend, and they became my second family. I feel a familiar twinge of deeply rooted pain, and shut down that train of thought before it crushes me. Even thinking about Liam, thinking about those times, hurts me so much that I have mastered the art of closing it off. If Liam crosses my mind, I immediately chase him away. It's too hard, too mixed up with my parents splitting up, too connected to being forced to leave.

'Not really,' I reply simply. 'I had friends. We were like a pack of feral dogs, especially when we got older. We roamed the beaches and the bays, did stupid things, snuck booze from the inn, pretended we liked smoking even though we all secretly hated it... those last few summers were so special. I'd help my parents out in the inn, usually at breakfast. Then the day would be mine, and Cornwall was my playground. Campfires, swimming in the ocean, picnics on the cliff tops... Every day seemed to last forever. I still remember the smells, you know? The suncream, the cut grass, the wildflower meadows. The scent of sea salt drying into my hair.'

Even thinking about it, I can almost hear the gulls and the oystercatchers calling, feel the sun on my skin. Taste the freedom.

'It sounds amazing,' Tyler replies, smiling gently, his hand still on mine. 'I wish I could have known teenaged Ellie.'

'No, you don't – she was trouble! And she was also pretty sad by the time she left. I didn't want to go. I had other plans.'

I clung on desperately, trying every trick in the book to get my own way. I begged my dad to fight for me, and told my mum she'd have to knock me unconscious to make me go. Tears, emotional blackmail, all-out anger – I threw the lot at them, and none of it worked.

I'd planned on going to university in Bristol, and being close enough to home that I could still visit. I loved it there, and I loved my friends. I loved Liam, even though things had turned sour between us. I wanted to sort that out, to go back to the way we'd been since we were seven years old, but I never got the chance. Before I was mature enough to find my way back to our friendship, I was thousands of miles away from him, in a strange land.

'But you liked it here in the US, didn't you? Once you settled in?'

'I did, but that took a long time. I was sixteen, and I was not an easy sixteen. I was messed up and angry, and I never really came to terms with what had happened. With hindsight, as an adult, I knew my parents' marriage was over, but it took her meeting Ethan to force a change. He was doing a walk around the coast and stayed at the inn. Their eyes met over a crowded break-fast room, and the rest was history – a history I had no part in shaping. I was furious and confused, and I took it out on my mum, on Ethan, on anyone who tried to get close to me. Plus we moved around – California, Chicago, Atlanta. I was always the new girl.'

Tyler is an astute guy, and I can practically see him putting two and two together. The way my childhood so abruptly ended, the way I was dramatically pulled out of a life I loved. Moving from place to place, starting over, not trusting the process. Never feeling at home. It doesn't take a psychology degree to join the dots – maybe I can't commit because I still don't trust the process. And maybe I've never quite felt at home since I was that earlier incarna-tion of myself.

I don't want to talk about it. I don't want to analyse myself or my complicated relationship with my dad. Luckily, I'm saved by the bell. My phone rings, and I see my mum's name on the screen. I pick it up and answer, biting my lip as I hear her voice.

'So, please don't over-react, sweetheart, but it seems that your father had a small stroke. He was in hospital for a few days and has been home since Monday. Doris tells me it isn't anything to panic about, and that he made her promise not to mention it. She also added that he is being stubborn and pretending nothing has happened. They're all trying to chip in and help, but you know how he can be – too proud to know when he should let his upper lip be a little less stiff.'

That's almost exactly what he said earlier – about his stiff upper lip getting in the way. My heart melts at the thought of him sitting there, alone in his attic room, fighting the sadness that I know has always haunted him.

'A stroke?' I echo, my worst fears confirmed. I talk to my mum for a few more minutes, and Ethan comes on the line with a few facts. I can tell he is using his very best 'keep calm and carry on' doctor voice, trying to stop me going off at the deep end by stressing that strokes are not necessarily the disaster our minds first conjure up. I am grateful to him, but I also feel dangerously close to that deep end.

By the end of the phone call, Tyler has clearly picked up on what's happened. He pays the bill and wraps my coat around my shoulders as we stand to leave. He drops a gentle kiss on my head and says: 'What do you want to do?'

'I think,' I say, feeling my way through it, 'that I need to go home. I need to go and help my dad.'

THREE

The following evening, I am at the airport. I spoke to my dad again this morning and he still didn't mention anything at all about the stroke. He is the most stubborn of old goats, it seems. His refusal to even tell me made me more determined, and I booked onto the next available flight.

I've told the temping agency that I am away for an unspecified amount of time, and set the email of my baking business up to reply to queries with a message explaining I'm temporarily unavailable. I'm glad I got to finish off my last project at least – a giant sponge diplodocus for a dinosaur-crazy eight-year-old's birthday party. That was a lot of fun.

Now, I am here, ready to fly to another country, and my own past. I am nervous, but it is the right thing to do – and right now, my nerves are completely over-shadowed by Tyler's. We're standing together near the check-in desks, and he is clearly stressed. His hands are shoved in his pockets, and his eyes are darting around as though he's looking for an escape route.

'Are you all right?' I ask, seeing how pale he looks. 'I know you don't like flying, but does even being in an airport get you this wound up?'

Tyler had asked if I wanted him to come with me to the UK,

which I appreciated as the noble gesture it was. The man is truly terrified of flying, which is a slight glitch in the whole superhero thing. He has never even left North America because of his phobia, and says he never really felt the need – it's big enough and varied enough that you can feel like you're in a whole different world just by using trains and driving. He's travelled extensively in Mexico and Canada, and all over the USA, visiting every state apart from Hawaii and Alaska.

Offering to come with me was touching, but it also didn't feel quite right. Maybe there will be a time to meet my parents, but this isn't it – this will be challenge enough for me, never mind adding in a boyfriend who may or may not have a meltdown on the plane journey over. Besides, I'm just not ready for that step yet – it would be relatively easy to introduce him to my mum and Ethan, but I haven't. For the time being, I am happy taking it slow and steady, building up my ability to trust in love. Looking back at last Christmas and my tearful encounter with Santa, my unsatisfying job and equally unsatisfying encounters with men from dating apps had left me strung out and close to the edge. I felt empty, hollowed out, lonely. And I had no faith in my ability to ever not feel any of those things.

I have worked hard in the last year to become, as they say on TV shows, a better version of myself. Tyler has helped with that, but I am still not quite as committed as he, and maybe I, would like.

'Um, yeah actually,' he replies, gazing around at the usual airport sights – the digital boards showing the departures and arrivals, groups of harassed-looking people, armed guards, long lines. 'Even being here has this effect on me. I'm sorry. It's not an attractive quality is it? Definitely putting a dent in my alpha male image...'

I smile and stand on tiptoes to kiss him on the cheek. 'Alpha males are over-rated, babe. You have other qualities.'

'You mean my boudoir skills?' he replies, raising his eyebrows at me and then winking. 'I know, I know, I'm an amazing lover...'

'You ain't too shabby in the sack, pal, that's for sure. Now, why don't you get going? I'm fine here.'

In truth, I actually love airports. I always get to them way earlier than I need to, because I love the whole vibe. The hustle and bustle, browsing all the different shops, looking at all the amazing-sounding destinations that come up on the boards. Give me a café to sit in while I people watch, and I could spend the whole day in an airport. Tyler, poor man, clearly does not feel the same.

'Okay, Ellie, I think I might, if you're sure you're okay? That suitcase is pretty damn big though... you might need my macho muscles to carry it for you.' He winks again, and I have to laugh.

'That would be true if not for the fact that it's on wheels, and even a little lady like me is capable of pushing it – I'm fine, honestly! Thanks for driving me, that was a huge help. I'll miss you, and the dogs. And now I won't be able to bake you those special cinnamon Christmas cookies in the shape of stars I thought you'd love...'

'You can do them when you're home. I'm good with a late Christmas. We'll miss you too. I... uh, I actually wanted to ask you something before you leave...'

He looks even more nervous now, and my own knuckles turn white as I grip the handle of my luggage. 'You're not about to go down on one knee and propose like we're in a rom com are you?' I ask. The thought makes me breathless, and not in a good way.

He grimaces, then laughs. 'Ah, no – I wasn't going to do that! But now I feel like what I am going to say is a real anti-climax in comparison! I was going to say that I think we should give some serious thought, when you're back, to moving in together. I... look, I know you're still not sure, Ellie. No, don't protest, we both know it's true – and I get it, I really do. Life has really done a number on you, and I know you dated a string of assholes. But I'm not one of them, and I want to be clear about that. I love you, Ellie, and I want to take the next step. There. Cards on the table.'

He makes a gesture, like he's laying down cards, and I stare at him, silently. New Jersey is not that far away. Thousands of people commute from there into the city every single day. It would not be a huge upheaval, I know. But I also know that even if Tyler lived in the next block to me, I might still feel this strange and annoying reluctance. I call it reluctance. I think a better term right now would be *massive paralysing panic*.

I suck in a big gulp of air and try to reply. But each time I open my mouth to speak, no words emerge – instead, I just make a kind of weird 'bleeurgh' noise, more of a grunt than a sentence. I get redder and redder as I just about manage to form his name in front of the grunt. I feel like I'm actually choking here, and wonder if someone might run over and offer to perform the Heimlich manoeuvre on me as I splutter.

Tyler stares at me, and shakes his head. He lays one hand on my shoulder and squeezes gently. 'Just breathe, Ellie. Come on now. In through the nose and out through the mouth...'

He does it with me, and after a few deep breaths I regain control over my senses. 'So,' he says, grinning, and thankfully looking amused rather than devastated. 'I think that went well, don't you? That was a much less spectacular panic attack than I expected...'

'I'm sorry,' I say, slapping myself on the forehead. 'I'm rubbish. You know that already. And even if it's cheesy, you get that the whole "it's not you it's me" line is totally real here don't you? I think you're great, and I hate the thought of not being with you – but I still don't know how I feel about sharing my life and my space. That probably makes me an asshole, but I don't want to lie. Look, I'm going away to literally the other side of the world – I suppose this gives us both the opportunity to think about things? You as well as me. I mean, I'm not exactly the catch of the century...'

'I don't need to think any more,' he says. 'You are bat-shit crazy and I know that. It's all been factored in.'

'Did you set up a spreadsheet?'

'Don't be silly. I coded my own algorithm. Look, you've always been up front with me, and I owe you the same. I want you to move in with me – when you're ready. There's no deadline on that. This isn't an ultimatum, it's a declaration. I wanted to get it out there in the open properly, rather than dropping hints – we're not kids, either of us, so what's the point in playing games? Just promise me you'll consider it.'

I pull his head down towards mine, and hold his face between my palms. 'I will most definitely consider it. Now shut up and kiss me – give me something to remember you by on this long and boring flight!'

He follows those instructions to the letter, and when he finally waves me goodbye, he leaves me with a spring in my step and a smile on my face.

FOUR

The flight was long, and the recovery time I spent in London was nowhere near enough to clear my jet lag. That was followed up by a train journey to Cornwall, which took most of the day because there was a light dusting of snow. I'd forgotten how everything seems to stop in England when there is even a hint of extreme weather. I have no clue why, as it happens every single year.

Despite the stop-start nature of the trip, and the apparently random need to swap trains three times due to 'adverse weather conditions', it is a beautiful journey. The last part of it in particular – as we make our way through Devon and Cornwall to arrive at Penzance – is gorgeous. I stare out of the window at the white fields and the frost-coated trees, pale yellow sunlight reflecting from the rivers and streams. We work our way through the familiar places, the magical names falling from my lips – Lostwithiel, St Austell, Truro. This corner of the world is special in so many ways, and I find myself smiling as we surge ever deeper into the county.

St Tilda, the village where I grew up, is on the far west coast of England. The nearest places of note are St Ives, a beautiful town perched on the edge of the sea, and Lizard Point, the most southerly part of mainland England. It's hard to capture how dramatic the scenery is, with jagged cliff faces tumbling into the ocean, bays and beaches, never-ending vistas and a surreal quality to the light that has made it a place beloved of artists and writers. Plus, you know, the millions of tourists who flock here all year round.

The village itself doesn't have a train station. It barely has a bus stop, although that of course may have changed. Maybe these days it has two, or none at all. So many exciting new things to discover, I think, as I wheel my luggage to the taxi rank. A seagull promptly makes a streaky grey deposit on my suitcase, and I remind myself that it's supposed to be lucky.

I ask the driver to take me to the village via the coastal road, even though it will take twice as long and cost twice as much. He gives me a look through his mirror, and follows it up with a shrug that seems to say 'well, it's your money, love'. I have an urge to explain that I'm not actually a crazy American tourist, but that I was born here. I have no idea why, because it really doesn't matter what the cab driver thinks of me. He seems to agree, and puts on some aggressive techno music so loud my eardrums almost rupture.

It's not the most idyllic of ways to see the coast, listening to the kind of jerky dance music that makes me think of zombies at a rave. But even that can't quite detract from the raw beauty of the landscape. The waves pounding in and splashing up foam, the seabirds circling overhead, the sense of wonder that it all stirs up inside me. I never wanted to leave this place; seeing it again, I understand why.

The drive gives me time to re-acclimatise to being here, the chance to ease myself back into what will be an environment both alien and achingly familiar. My dad doesn't even know I'm coming, so it also gives me the opportunity to prepare for that. I knew that if I asked permission, he would say no – he would be too proud to admit that he needed help, and too stubborn to accept that I wanted to visit from love rather than a misguided sense of duty. My dad's worst nightmare is being dependent on other people. I am simply going to turn up, and present myself as a fait accompli.

Hard to tell someone they can't fly over from New York to stay with you when they've already done it.

I know it's the right way to approach this, but that doesn't mean it's easy. I had hours on the plane to think about him, and about our relationship. I am nervous about seeing him again. As a teenager, I felt like he rejected me when he let me leave with my mum. I was hurt and angry, for a long time, with both him and my mother. I think I may even have accused her of kidnapping me at one point.

Since then, I have only seen him twice – both when I flew to London. Why is that? Why didn't I come home for summers? Why didn't he come to the States? Why have we kept each other at arm's length for so long? I guess there's no simple answer to that question, and over the years I have found it easier to just accept it. That was more straightforward when I was in New York, living my New York life. Now I am here, in St Tilda, at the edge of the world. I will see my dad soon, but first I need to take a few moments to deal with this new reality.

The cab drops me off outside the inn, and my eyes run greedily over the familiar outlines of the building. The St Tilda Inn is at the back of the village, perched on the side of a cliff. It dates back to the early 1700s, all whitewashed walls and imposing stone. Some of the roof is thatched, and there is a slightly later extension as the place expanded. The windows are all mullioned, and it is set in its own patch of emerald green land. Dad used to keep a small kitchen garden to grow his own fruit and veg, and there are benches set up near the edge of the cliff for the more adventurous to sit on and watch the maritime world go by.

On a wild day, the spray from the waves reaches up to lay wet fingers on the grass, and you can spot seals and even whales when the season is right. A steep path is cut into the cliff, leading down to the perfect horseshoe cove at the bottom. It's always been easy to imagine this place in days gone by; it looks just like something from a Daphne du Maurier story about smugglers. A magnificent place for a moody teen to grow up. I never yearned for nightclubs or bars, because I had all of this.

Despite the cold, I stare at the view for a few moments. Late afternoon, winter, the sun already sliding away in a final blaze of subdued glory. I always loved watching the sun set here, but now it takes my breath away. The day is clear but cold, and I feel the chilled touch of the ocean breeze against my skin. My eyes water, or maybe I'm crying – either way tears flow down my cheeks, and I feel a rush of pure emotion. I can't decipher quite what it is that I am feeling, but it is powerful. The sense of being home, of being here in this amazing place. Of confronting a past that wasn't always easy, and a world of memories that I think I'd suppressed. There is a lot to unravel, and it is overwhelming.

I turn back to the inn. Christmas lights are strung along the edge of the rooftops, swaying in the breeze and starting to sparkle in the dusk. Smoke curls from the chimneys, conjuring up images of a warm, cosy fireplace. A dense Christmas wreath hangs on the door, filled with pine cones and bright red berries. All of the pub's windows are lit up, and as the day darkens even more, they will shine out like beacons, calling weary travellers to the door. Well, that's probably how it worked in the olden days – now I guess people use booking apps instead. I make my way around to the back of the building, where there is a door for staff. I find a man out there in the white outfit of a kitchen worker. He's sitting on a plastic chair having a cigarette, his head nodding in time to music that only he can hear.

He looks up in surprise as I tap him on the shoulder, and his eyes widen when he looks up at me. 'Shit!' he says, dropping his smoke. 'Is that you, Ellie?'

I stare back at him, narrowing my gaze as I try and figure out who he is. I've not been here in over two decades, and it is disconcerting to be recognised. 'Um... yeah. Do I know you?'

'Course you do!' he says with a grin, getting to his feet. 'Though fair's fair, I was only four last time we met... I think you called me a dickhead and then puked up on my shoes...'

'That sounds horribly plausible,' I reply, feeling a blush develop. I really was bloody awful back then. I'd like to say it was all down to my domestic situation, but I have the sneaking suspicion that I would have been awful anyway. There was a wild streak to my nature that died out when we left. I miss it.

I stare at the man, knowing that he must be in his mid-twenties and not seeing any trace of a child I once knew.

'It'd probably help if you imagine me covered in snot, and wearing hand-me-down clothes that were always too big for me...' he says, a twinkle in his eye. I suddenly realise who he is and almost fall over from the surprise.

'Sean! No, it can't be. Sean Byrne? No way! You're... well, you're a lot taller for a start.'

'Well, I was like Liam – a short-arse until I was sixteen!'

He laughs and pulls me in for a hug. I wasn't quite expecting that, but what the hell? Technically I've known him since he was born – he is the youngest of the Byrne siblings. My friend Liam's parents thought their baby days were behind them, but fate had other ideas. Sean was a 'late-in-life miracle', arriving with a ten-year gap between the others when his mum was forty-eight. It made us all go cross-eyed at the thought of such very, very old people still having sex.

'I remember you getting brought home from the hospital,' I say, looking up at him. He's well over six foot now. 'You were the first newborn baby I'd ever held, and frankly I thought you were disgusting. Do you still live here then? I can't believe you still live here... what about everyone else?'

Everyone else, I think. Apart from Liam. Please don't tell me about him, I think. I'm just not ready.

'Well now,' he replies, leading me back inside the inn, carrying my case over the steps for me. 'That would take a while, and I have spuds to be peeling. Maybe we could meet up for a drink later. Your daddy didn't mention he was expecting you.'

The trace of an Irish accent is still there, lurking around beneath the surface, even though Sean was born in Cornwall. His home was a little patch of Ireland though, transplanted when Brian and Bernadette moved here for Brian's job, and they all picked some of it up. These days there are probably Byrne grandchildren running around confusing tourists by speaking with an Irish accent.

'My daddy doesn't know!' I tell him, whispering it and looking around. We're in the back rooms of the building, and very little has changed. There's been a lick of paint, and as I look through into the kitchens I see some new appliances, but the smell and the feel of the place is exactly the same. It's so odd. It's almost like I never left. 'I know he's not been well, so I thought I'd come home and, uh, you know, surprise him.'

'Aye. You mean, you knew if you told him, the stubborn old arse would come up with an excuse to stop you?'

'Exactly that. Sean, gosh, it's so nice to see you... I can't believe how much time has passed. How can you be a grown man when you were only four a few months ago?'

He flexes his arms to make his biceps pop, and grins. 'As you can see, very much a grown man! Let me know if you fancy that drink now, won't you? I'll be here this evening, or if not then pop in to see us all. Mam and Dad will be tickled to see you again. Your dad always tells us what you're up to, and shows us photos and the like, but they'd love to have you round for a cuppa.'

I nod, feeling a combination of pleasure and worry at the idea. So much of my past is tied up with this place, and the concept of just popping in to see the Byrne clan is both wonderful and over-whelming. Then again, it was always overwhelming. I always left their home like I was on a sugar rush, completely over-stimulated, and only part of that was due to the never-ending supply of boiled sweets that the kids always seemed to have. Chocolate limes and cola cubes were basic food groups there.

'Are you still at the same house?' I ask. They lived in a three-bedroomed terraced house that was a very cramped home to Bernadette and Brian, and their many children. It always smelled of food and the coal fire and unwashed boys. Only one of their children, Cara, was a girl, and she pretty much pretended she was a boy to make life easier for everyone. I smile at the memory, of the noise and the constant fighting and the even more constant laughter.

'Oh no, we're all in a new one up the hill... our Liam had it built for us. You'll have heard he moved to Australia?'

I nod, because I had heard – but I have no clue what happened to him after that, or to any of them. I blanked out everything from that part of my life because I missed it too much. I remember being about nineteen and in college, and hearing tales of Liam leaving for Sydney on some kind of tech scholarship. Even years after I left, it still hurt to hear about what I'd lost. I told my dad I didn't want to hear any more village news and issued a similar ban to my mum. If I couldn't be there, I wanted to put it all behind me. Especially Liam. It wasn't mature, but I felt like it was the only way to survive the hurt of it all – and part of me still feels like that.

Now, standing here with Sean so genuinely pleased to see me, I also feel a bit ashamed of myself. I pretended they didn't exist, and even thinking about Liam still makes me feel embarrassed and uncomfortable. We haven't spoken since we were sixteen, and frankly I'm glad that he lives on the other side of the world, childish as that might seem. I have questions, of course – like how and why he bought them a new house – but all that can wait. For now, I need to see my dad. One step at a time.

'Right. Well, I'm not sure how long I'll be staying, Sean, but we'll definitely have that catch-up.'

'I hope so. You're looking beautiful, by the way, Ellie – American life has suited you, I'd say!'

He kisses me on the cheek and walks back into the kitchens. Is he flirting with me? Is Sean Byrne flirting with me? I'm old enough to be... no, actually, I am not anywhere near old enough to be his mother. It just feels like it because he's still an irritating child in my mind.

I leave my case in the back rooms and walk through into the public part of the building. My dad might be behind the bar, or on reception, or nowhere here at all. He always used to love the part of his job that involved talking to people, but he has just had a stroke. That might not be something he has rushed back into doing.

This is always a quiet time of day here. There are only four bedrooms for people to stay in, and check-in is usually done by three. There are two parts to the inn, one slightly posher and smaller, where we served up breakfast. I wander inside, my fingers tracing the dark wood panelling on the walls, inhaling the still-familiar scents. Breakfast was hours ago, but I swear I can still smell the bacon, the toast, the coffee. The carpet is new, I notice, and all of the light fittings have been changed. The furniture is the same though – quality lasts, I suppose, and these tables and chairs have been around for a lot longer than I have. The whole room has been festooned with fairy lights, twinkling silver and gold in the dimness, making it feel magical.

I walk through to the bigger side of the bar, the one that is simply a village pub. It is dressed for Christmas, the little window ledges decorated with boughs of holly, the long wooden bar draped with a beautiful garland. It's quiet right now, but most nights it always ended up packed. Locals and tourists all settled into this warm and cosy space with its beamed ceiling and slightly sloping floors. The age of the inn shows in here, accentuated with old-fashioned décor that makes it seem timeless. It feels exactly what it is – a room where folk have been gathering for hundreds of years to share shelter, food, drink, companionship. A place where people come together, where friendships are made, where bonds are formed. Where fights are settled, where romance blossoms, where gossip is to be had. The very best of a British pub.

Again, there are new carpets, and some new fabrics in the little tucked-away booths, but basically it is still the same. The aromas are slightly different in here – beer, whisky, wine. A delicious undercurrent of fresh pine from the enormous Christmas tree. Just under two weeks to go until the Big Day.

I grin when I see that the same battered fairy with one wing left is still perched on top of it. A few of my younger efforts are still visible on the branches – a penguin made from the inside of a toilet paper roll, a polar bear created with cotton wool and cardboard that now looks a bit the worse for wear.

I nod at the one person in here, sitting with a pint at a small table, his back to the crowded bookshelves in the corner. They're draped with red and gold tinsel but still crammed. The little lending library always had a life of its own, stacked with dog-eared paperbacks that people swapped out, along with maps and guides. A pile of board games sits on the shelf below, showing their age now – the boxes and the lettering telling me that at least some of them are the same ones that I grew up with. Chess and draughts and an old peg board for scoring card games. I vividly recall the intense matches that used to go on, collections of men and women huddled around the tables, the ale flowing, the laughter and chat as they faced each other in endless rounds of gin rummy and cribbage.

I pick up the cast-iron poker from the fireplace and give the fire a prod. A wooden Nativity scene is playing out on the huge mantelpiece, and I almost fear for their little wooden bodies as the logs crackle and spark. That gorgeous smell, and the little wisps of smoke that escape the chimney, make me smile. It was always freezing in here first thing in the morning at this time of year, and so toasty-warm by the evening. I'm now used to American architecture, buildings that are air conditioned and heated to perfection, and the quirks of a place like this make it feel like a different world.

I approach the bar, noticing that sprigs of mistletoe are hanging at strategic points. That could lead to what the Byrne family would call 'shenanigans'.

I ring the little brass bell that has stood on the smooth wooden counter for as long as I remember, noticing that it has had a Christmas make-over – a little red and green tartan bow added to the handle. Within seconds, Sean appears from the kitchens.

'Good day to you, miss!' he says cheekily. 'And what can I be getting you? I'll have to see some ID if it's alcohol, mind! We don't tolerate under-age drinking in the St Tilda Inn.'

'Ha ha, very funny. I was drinking in the St Tilda Inn when I was fourteen...'

'That was you and Liam stealing the jugs of ale though, so it doesn't count. You okay for a drink, Mr Owen, while I'm here?' He shouts the second sentence over my shoulder, and the man reading a book holds up his almost-empty pint glass. Sean nods and starts to pull a Guinness.

'Did you actually want anything, Ellie?' he asks as he leaves the Guinness to rest. Always important to leave a Guinness to rest before you add the creamy head, I remember my dad telling me when I was a little girl, perched on the bar, fascinated by everything that he did.

'I'll take a water, Sean, if you don't mind?'

He pops open a bottle for me, and says he'll 'add it to my tab'.

'Is Dad upstairs?' I ask, after I take a refreshing drink. 'I thought he might be working again. Not that he should be.'

'I've no idea, to be honest, I only came on shift an hour ago. And as for the working, of course he shouldn't be – but try telling him that. It's just that we don't open to general customers until later, these days, Ellie. Mr Owen here is a staying guest, so he's different. Your dad has been in the bar every night since he got home from the hospital, including the very day he arrived. Said he might as well get stuck in, because there was no point in him otherwise. I think his exact words were "I'm neither use nor ornament if I can't work my own bar", at which juncture he looked at his reflection in the mirror, and said actually he was still fair ornamental for his age. I told him he was just mental, and everything seemed to go back to normal...'

'That sounds like him,' I reply, frowning. The joking, the mock-vanity, all detracting from what he must have actually been feeling. A small stroke it might have been, but still a significant event and a blunt reminder of his own mortality.

He should be resting, but I always knew he wouldn't. Saying that there is 'no point in him' isn't good, it has an air of melancholy to it, and my father is prone to melancholy. At least that's what he always called it, because he thought it sounded more romantic than what it probably is – borderline depression. I know he will have been surrounded by people from the village since I left, and that running the inn is by its nature a sociable job, but that doesn't mean he hasn't been lonely. There has been no mention of other relationships, and his tone during our intermittent communications has always held that slight edge of regret and sadness.

I feel a rush of guilt that suddenly knocks me for six. I was angry with him when I left, because I was sixteen and hurting. Over the years that has settled, but maybe not completely disappeared. I should have come home sooner. I should have made more effort. I met up with him in London once I became an adult and capable of independent travel, but I have never come back here. He never asked me to, and he also never came to visit me in the States – but still, especially as he aged, maybe I should have done it anyway. I didn't need to be invited – I should have just got over myself and come.

My dad is a complicated man, though, and nothing with him is ever simple. He is charming and charismatic, and he has a style of presenting things that makes it simply impossible to disagree with him. I always knew he loved me, but he also never applied even a hint of pressure for us to see each other more. In fact, I always got the impression that he found it all easier if I stayed away – was that just a fake-out because he didn't want to ask? Didn't want to feel like a burden? I should have tried harder. He is no longer a young man, and in some ways I am glad I found out about what happened – without my mum making discreet inquiries, we probably never would have known.

I tell myself that I am here now, and there is nothing I can do to change the past. Relationships are complex, especially with a man like my father. He appears so larger than life, so open, but in reality he is extremely private, even with his own family. My mum has never bad-mouthed him to me, but she did once say that he was so expressive and outgoing on the surface because it shielded him from anyone getting to see his real feelings. That makes sense to me

– he could be this big, bold personality one minute in company, and then you'd catch him alone, staring out of the window with a look of deep introspection on his face. He is my father, but I wonder how well I know him – how well anyone knows him.

There are two flights of stairs in the inn. One is public and leads up to the rooms that are rented out, and one is private, taking you up to the part of the building we called home. It isn't huge, but it was always enough – especially when the whole of nature is your playground, and you are only indoors when you absolutely have to be.

While the public areas show signs of renewal, the steps up to the apartment are exactly the same. Not even a new carpet here, and as my hands grip the wooden rail and I climb the steep stairs, it feels so strangely normal. Like I climbed them only yesterday. The feel of the wood beneath my fingers is exactly the same, and my feet automatically avoid the middle of the fourth step up because I know it creaks. Loud enough to alert a parent to a teenager sneaking back home after being out too late.

I suck in a breath when I reach the landing, and smile at the framed photos on the walls. There's still one from my wedding, even though my dad didn't come to it, and the marriage is over. There are photos of me as a child with both my parents, and some of his family and his time with my mum before I was born. I notice, with an air of sadness, that there is only one picture of him that was taken after I left, and that one is of me and him when we met up in London eleven years ago. I know his life didn't end when Mum and I moved to the States, but he certainly didn't seem to feel the need to celebrate it.

In the living room there is a new couch and TV. The curtains are different, but everything else remains the same. The big oak bookcases, the battered pine dining table, the big windows with their views down to the bay. I run my fingers over the walls, feeling the familiar bumps of the plasterwork and paper. I can't believe I'm here, and I am fighting back the tears. I planned this trip in such a hurry, I never stopped to consider how it would feel – I was so busy thinking about my dad and the logistics that the emotional aspect has taken me by surprise.

There are no decorations up in here and no tree, which I find a little sad. Did we used to have a tree, I try and recall, or did we just focus on downstairs? I frown as I think about it but then a vivid image of Liam and myself being allowed to decorate the upstairs comes to mind. There was a tree, a small plastic one, and by the time we finished with it none of the branches were visible at all. Now, though, there isn't even that. Is it the same every year, or is it because he has been poorly? The inn looks festive and charming but upstairs shows no signs of Christmas at all.

I go through into the kitchen and see that it has had a refurb. New cupboards, different counter tops. I see the signs of a solitary lifestyle – the single mug left by the kettle, the solitary plate left to drain. I open the door to the pantry – way too many tins of soup. Nothing in the fridge apart from some expensive-looking Stilton cheese, which is about right for my dad. I'll make sure he eats better while I'm here; that's one way I can definitely look after him. I'll make him soup from scratch and spoil him with desserts. He loves old-fashioned puddings like jam roly-poly and steamed sponge with golden syrup and custard, which I know he won't be able to resist.

I'm starting to wonder where he is, and if he's even at home at all. He did always like an evening walk down on the beach, and watching the sun set was one of his favourite things to do. The steps down to the cove are steep and rough, and I really hope he's not pushing himself too hard.

It's just as possible, though, that he's simply in his bedroom, having a sleep, or up in his study in the attic. I notice a half-empty glass of water on the counter, next to small flurry of pill packets and sachets. I pick them up but have no clue what the names mean. Is it even okay for me to look? Do I have the right to walk back into his life and invade his privacy?

I google them anyway, deciding the moral quandary can wait. I discover that they are medications for high blood pressure, for cholesterol, and an anti-coagulant to prevent blood clots. All of them are freshly prescribed.

I carefully place them back down and wipe an unexpected tear from my eye. I feel like I left my dad as a man in the prime of his life, and I have returned to find him old and sick, living off tinned soup. He must hate this, I know. Feeling weak and frail, needing help, not having his usual energy and zest for life.

I walk out into the hallway, staying quiet in case he is napping – he needs his rest, after all. I tiptoe along towards his bedroom, intending to take a sneaky peep inside and check if he is there. I take a deep breath first, part of me afraid of what I will see. How will I cope with seeing the new him? With seeing this new and reduced version of my dad? I need to be prepared for it, for the fact that he will not look like himself. I need to not react badly and upset him even more. I am here to help him, and judging by all those drugs it seems like I arrived at exactly at the right time.

I'm finally ready, and I gently turn the handle, about to carefully pop my head inside. As I do, I hear the unexpected sound of a woman giggling. Is he in there watching TV maybe? Having a rest but unable to sleep?

Suddenly, the door gets tugged open so quickly that I lose my balance and fall right into the woman who is giggling. A real-life woman. There is quite a lot of her, and it is all on display.

'Shit!' she yells, trying to hide her plentiful bosoms with her hands, but then realising her nether regions are on display and attempting to cross her legs. This results in her wobbling over, grabbing hold of my shoulders to steady herself, and her boobs flying free once more. I clasp my eyes firmly shut and hold my hands up in the air, desperate to avoid making unnecessary contact. 'Shit!' I also shout, both of us obviously shocked.

'I'll keep my eyes closed!' I say. 'Put some clothes on!'

I hear a frantic rustling, and my dad's voice. 'Ellie? Is that you? What the hell are you doing here?'

FIVE

'Um, can I open my eyes?' I say, risking a peek between my fingers. The mystery woman has rapidly thrown on a robe, and is standing uncertainly at the foot of the bed. The bed where my poor, sick father is lying, looking like a man who has just been getting jiggy with it.

'Well,' he says, his rich, deep voice sounding amused, 'this isn't awkward at all! Ellie, uh, meet Sandra. Sandra, meet Ellie.' He runs his fingers through his thick hair, now peppered with silver, and smiles at me.

'Nice to meet you, Ellie,' Sandra says, dashing out of the room. 'I'll leave you to it!'

I had expected my father to be in his sick bed, and would normally have walked over to give him a kiss, but frankly, I'm not sure I want to right now. We all know as adults that our parents have sex, but being confronted with it in the flesh is a completely different matter. I am horrified, and embarrassed, and want to wash my eyeballs in soap and scalding water. This reunion isn't going the way I planned at all.

'Darling child,' he says, seeing my bright red cheeks, 'I'm so sorry – bit of a pickle, eh? Obviously, I wasn't expecting you...'

'Obviously. Would you like to, um, get dressed? Or are you not feeling well enough to get up?'

He raises an eyebrow at me, and I have to laugh. There are way too many answers to that, and he is clearly not feeling all that unwell right now.

'Well, dear, I would probably have had a little snooze for the next hour or so... but yes, why don't you put the kettle on, and I'll join you in a few minutes?'

I nod and close the door behind me. I rub my hands over my face in relief at being away from the scene of the crime. Not that having sex is a crime – but it definitely feels that way when it's your own dad committing the deed. I head to the kitchen, and find Sandra already in there, the kettle boiling away. She gives me a little finger wave, and a toothy grin. 'Sorry,' she says, 'I left all my clothes in there! You're his daughter, aren't you?'

'I am, yes. I thought he might need some help around the place, so I decided to come back and surprise him...'

'Well, I'd definitely say you surprised him! And that's nice – coming back, all the way from New York. He'd never admit it, but he could do with a hand. Coffee, tea... triple vodka?'

'Ha! I won't rule the vodka out, but for now, yeah, coffee would be great. So, are you my dad's... uh, I don't know what to say here! Girlfriend?'

As Sandra is clearly in her sixties, that seems a strange term, but I'm coming up blank. I didn't even know she existed until five minutes ago. She laughs at my discomfort, making our drinks.

'Girlfriend? I'm not so sure about that, Ellie. I live over in Penborne, you know it?'

I nod. It's an even smaller place than St Tilda. At least it used to be.

'So, not exactly a lively dating scene in this part of the world,' she continues, 'and I knew your dad from coming into the pub. My hubbie Bill died a couple of years ago, and Peter was single, and... well, I suppose we started keeping each other company. It's not a big deal – neither of us is in love. It's more of a friends with benefits kind of thing, you know? I loved that film...'

'Me too,' I echo, sipping too-hot coffee and knowing that I'll never enjoy Justin Timberlake and Mila Kunis in quite the same way ever again. I mean, rationally I know that older people have needs, both physical and emotional. It's not just the young and the gorgeous who make these arrangements. But still... I try to hide my slight shiver.

'Bit much, I know,' she says understandingly. 'I have a daughter your age and she'd throw up in her mouth if she knew about this. But she lives in London, so my secret is safe!' She lets out a loud super-villain laugh, and her whole body jiggles with merriment.

'What's her name? Maybe I'll message her and rat you out!'

Her eyes widen and her curls bounce around her face as she laughs, pointing at me. 'Oooh, you, you're wicked, just like your dad... speak of the devil.'

Right on cue, he walks into the kitchen, dressed in his trade-mark cord trousers and a smart shirt. I swear to God they are the exact same items of clothing I last saw him in. I'm not going to ask though, because he'll just make a speech about how quality counts, and good tailoring is worth paying the extra pennies for.

He walks over to me and immediately wraps me up in a hug. I'm still holding my coffee, but Sandra thoughtfully takes it from me so I can hug him back. I find myself sniffing his shirt, inhaling the sheer dad-ness of him. I haven't seen him for so long, and nobody has ever hugged me quite like my dad. I realise I am crying and when he finally lets me go, I have made a damp splodge on the fabric. 'Sorry,' I say, gesturing towards it.

'Nothing to be sorry about, Eleanor, it is so wonderful to see you! I'm sorry for the, ah, unexpected encounter with Sandra.'

'No worries,' I say, wiping my eyes and inspecting him. 'I guess it's my own fault for not giving you any warning. How are you? Really?'

I am assuming that as he was naked in bed with a lady friend, he wasn't feeling too awful – but for all I know, they were simply having a cuddle or talking about the weather. While nude. I'm certainly not going to ask whether any cardiovascular effort was involved, that's for sure.

I look at his face; he has aged since we were last together. He is still handsome, but the lines are deeper, the eyes wearier. More grey in his hair, even though it suits him. I realise that he is doing the same to me, carrying out his own inspection.

I am suddenly awkward, feeling a strange streak of tension. Sandra's boobs were a good ice breaker, and that first Dad hug was magnificent, but now the initial rush of emotion has worn off we are both looking at each with carefully held expressions. Neither of us knows the etiquette.

'All things considered, I'm not too bad, my sweet,' he says. 'I shan't lie – it was a fairly terrifying experience, and nobody likes being in hospital do they? But the doctors in their wisdom have told me to see it as a wake-up call and warned me I need to make some "lifestyle changes". Sounds ghastly, doesn't it?'

'Yeah, Dad, it does – so no more cigars, huh?'

'No more cigars and less stress. And, alas, a bacon ban! I find myself wondering if a life without bacon is even worth living...'

I'm guessing that he'll also be monitored for the other fun stuff, high cholesterol and his blood pressure, but that would clearly be a depressing conversation for him right now. Once we've settled into this visit, I'll find out more and talk to Ethan about it. He's retired but he'll be able to give me some guidance at least.

'Well, I'll go on a bacon ban with you, Dad. And I'm here to help out in any way you need, in the pub, over Christmas. I might not have technically worked behind the bar when I was a kid, but I grew up watching you do it.'

'Yes. And from memory, you were certainly adept enough to swipe those jugs of lager for you and your friends to imbibe, weren't you?'

I keep my face blank. 'I have no clue what you're talking about.'

Sandra laughs at our to-and-fro, then announces that she's

going to make herself presentable. As she leaves, she gives my dad a quick peck on the cheek, and he smacks her backside. She squeals and runs out of the room. I shake my head, and he mouths a quick 'sorry'.

'Why don't you go and sit down, and I'll make you some tea?' I ask. 'Do you want anything to eat? I noticed you're not short of soup...'

'I am partial to a nice soup. And there really is no need to be looking after me, Eleanor. I'm absolutely fine! You really shouldn't have felt obliged to come all this way—'

'I didn't feel obliged,' I reply, not entirely truthfully. 'I wanted to come. It's been too long. Life has done that thing life will do, and years have passed in what feels like days. Don't be a pain in the ass, Dad, just let me help!'

'I think you'll find it's "arse", dear, not "ass" – that would be a type of donkey.'

'You're a type of donkey – you're about as stubborn as one for sure. Now, will you please go and sit down?'

He holds his hands up in surrender and leaves me be. I find his traditional Earl Grey, but notice that there is no sugar bowl full of little lumps like there used to be. Just some sachets of sweetener. It's either a health kick, which seems unlikely, or he's also diabetic. That would not surprise me, given his age and the fact that he always had a sweet tooth. I shall have to adjust my recipes accordingly.

My father is an active man, has always walked and swum in the sea, but he never liked to deny himself anything he enjoyed. And as I hear Sandra yell a cheery farewell, I realise that he still doesn't. That whole incident was embarrassing, but really, isn't it better that he has companionship? And that there's still enough fight in him to be naughty? There is no harm in it, I tell myself. We're all adults here. That's my story and I'm sticking to it. And at least it was better, on the whole, than finding him lying in his sick bed wasting away.

I finish the tea and notice three miniature bottles in one of the cupboards. A vodka, a gin and a whisky. Presumably for emergencies. I pocket the gin just in case I have an emergency of my own later. Huh, I think, deciding to put the vodka in my other pocket – home for ten minutes and I'm already stealing booze.

I carry the tea through, and find him sitting in his usual armchair, a big smile on his face. There is better light in here, and I can see the signs of age and illness more clearly. A paleness to his skin, puffiness beneath the eyes. A very slight tremor in his hand as he accepts the mug.

'So,' he says, 'shall we start again? Darling, I'm delighted to see you. There was really no need to come all this way, but having said that, it is an absolute treat to have you here. When are you leaving?'

I raise my eyebrows at him. 'Really?'

'I didn't mean it like it sounded! Obviously, you're welcome to stay as long as you'd like. I do have a slightly complicated situation going on, but nothing that can't be managed.'

'Like what?' I ask, frowning.

'Like nothing that matters right now, Ellie. Let's just relax and enjoy being together again. I'm due downstairs behind the bar in couple of hours, though, and I wouldn't mind a quick nap. And yes, I know, I just got out of bed, but—'

'Leave it there, please!' I protest, throwing my hands over my ears in a show of great maturity. 'I don't want to hear! La la la la la!'

He's laughing when I finally dare listen again, and I add: 'I think I might go for a little walk around the village, then, Dad. See what's what.'

'Good idea – but I doubt you'll see much that's different. There's a self-serve check-out in the garage shop, but nobody uses it.'

'Wow, that sounds exciting – I think I need to see that for myself! Will you be all right on your own for a while?'

'Darling, I've been all right on my own for years. Now shoo!'

I know he doesn't mean to make me feel guilty with that comment. I know it is actually the opposite – it's an assertion of independence. But still, I feel a flush of regret that I have left this so long. Meeting him in London for a couple of days, taking in a show and visiting the National Gallery, wasn't real like this. It was too easy for him to put on a front, to present the image that he wanted to present. Here, it is different. He might have a Sandra in his life, but he is also an elderly man living alone in a draughty old building, trying to run a business as his health fails.

That all changes now, I decide. I will stay for as long as he needs me and be as useful as I possibly can. And along the way, maybe my father and I can get to know each other again – the way we are now, not the way we were back then.

SIX

I decide to unpack first and wheel my case along the hallway. As I pass the open door to his bedroom, my dad calls out: 'Ellie! I have something for you!'

'Is it a naked woman?' I ask hesitantly.

'No, dear, I only have the stamina for one of those per day. It's this. I meant to send it to you through the post, but events rather overtook me. A little light reading for you.'

He passes me a big brown envelope, kisses me on the forehead, and says he will see me later. I glance at the package and shake my head. It's addressed to Professor Doctor Prima Ballerina Eleanor Ponsonby-Smythe. The only one of those titles that's true is the Eleanor, although everybody calls me Ellie. I am not a professor or a doctor, have never danced professionally, and my surname is Dexter. What can I say? He gets carried away.

I carry it with me along to my bedroom, wondering what changes there will have been in the last couple of decades.

The answer is: not many, but there is the exciting addition of a basketball hoop machine, one of those you see at amusement arcades where you throw for points, and then you have a gazillion little paper tickets and have spent so much cash you could have bought a car. Instead you trade them in for a set of pencils or a small stuffed dinosaur at the arcade shop.

I have no idea why it is here or if it works, and decide that is a question for another time. Other than that, the room is eerily like a time capsule. There is still lilac paint on one wall, black on the other. My transition from little girl to angsty teen was not a graceful one, and if I'd stayed here longer, I suspect the whole room including ceiling and floors would have been black as well. At the time of course I thought I was a wild rebel, going crazy – in reality, I now realise that a lot of teenagers go through their 'paint it black' phase. At least there wasn't a pentagram on the floorboards. There wasn't when I left but, as I've learned in the last hour, my dad has a life I know nothing about.

My bed is still the same single I had as a child, but the duvet is folded up with no covers. Time capsules are one thing, but mouldy bedding is another, so I'm quite happy to root around in the airing cupboard and find some clean sheets. My old ones are still there, soft to the touch from washing, tucked away beneath my extra blankets and the crocheted shawl Liam's mum made for me one year. I can't believe I left that here – I always loved it so much. Bernadette didn't have a lot of spare cash or time, but she always made me something, every Christmas.

I tug out the shawl, sniff the soft multi-coloured wool in shades of red and orange, everything always made from whatever she had left over. She'd carve out an hour each day away from kids and chores, and sit in her chair while she listened to Frank Sinatra records. She'd crochet and knit and sew, her fingers moving like the wind as she sang along to the tunes. I smile, and decide I will give the shawl a wash to get rid of the vaguely musty smell, and I will wear it while I'm here. No matter what happened between me and Liam, it wasn't his family's fault.

I change the bedding, and sit down, looking at the room. Posters of the White Stripes and the Strokes jostle for space with movie promos, and tucked away in one corner is my Josh Hartnett shrine. I laugh as I pick up the framed photo of him in *Pearl*

Harbor. I was convinced I was going to marry Josh Hartnett, and even his terrible haircut in *The Faculty* didn't put me off.

My desk is still here, now piled up with giant packs of toilet paper. My old cork notice board is propped up against the wall, pins plunged and holding up the ghosts of photos past. I took most of them with me, angry-crying as I slipped them inside my bag, convinced I'd never make friends again. I left behind the ones of me and Liam, and I stare at them now, thinking how petty it seems. How long ago it was. But at the time, I was hurting. I was a wounded animal.

I tug the pictures down, three of them, curled with age, the colours faded. It seems like a different world, one where you actually printed out photos instead of having them on your phone. I'm glad it was, or I'd have deleted them and they'd have been gone forever.

One shot is of Liam down at the beach, in his baggy jeans and his Cypress Hill T-shirt, his floppy fringe grown over his forehead to try and hide his acne. He was so self-conscious about it, not least because his siblings tormented him mercilessly. There's also one of him jumping off the cliffs, blurry and in motion as he plummets to the sea. He was always smaller than his brothers, and tried to make up for it by being a daredevil. He'd always be the first to jump off a cliff, or skateboard off the back of a cement mixer, or try to do parkour around St Tilda's rooftops.

There was – possibly still is – an abandoned manor house about a mile outside the village. I'm sure it was amazing in its heyday, but it was long uninhabited by our teenage years, and full of enticing prospects – crumbling walls, overgrown gardens, rotting floorboards, little turret rooms. Teen heaven. I was always a tiny bit worried it might be haunted, but Liam loved it – he had no fear at all, even when he fell through a hole in the ground and ended up on his arse in the cellar, covered in plasterboard. He just laughed and shook himself down. Really, it's amazing that the human race has survived, given how stupid teenagers are.

I remember the day this photo was taken. A gang of us was

down at the bay, cheering him on as he leapt, but inside I was terrified. My heart was pounding and I was so scared that he would hurt himself. He was my best friend, and I knew – just *knew* – that I couldn't live without him. It turned out that I could, but life was definitely a lot less fun without him in it.

The last photo is of me and him, lying flat out on the grass of the village green. We're both grinning, and both wearing tops that say 'My Parents Went to Tenerife and All I Got Was This Lousy T-shirt'. Our parents hadn't been to Tenerife – his never had enough money for holidays, and mine never had enough time. We'd bought them in a charity shop on a trip to Penzance, and thought we were super-cool rebels. He's holding two fingers up at the camera, but I'm not – my mum would have killed me.

I smile, and put them back on the corkboard, leaning it back against the wall. I remember these walls in earlier years, when my tastes were more innocent – My Little Pony being a particular favourite. I mooch along my bookshelf, see the likes of Harry Potter and Eragon, along with a battered copy of Donna Tartt's *The Secret History*. I read that when I was fifteen, and it made me feel super grown-up and sophisticated.

The drawers are mainly empty, but a few of my old clothes are still hanging in the wardrobe. Most of my belongings were packed up and shipped to the States, along with me and my mum. I hated it so much. I hated being dragged away from here, and I sobbed with every single thing I placed into a packing crate. It must have been so tough for my dad, too – he certainly doesn't seem to have been in a rush to change anything. The room is still basically the same. It stirs up a lot of feelings, and I'm not sure where to put them all. I guess I need another packing crate.

I pull back the curtains, and see that it has gone dark, the moonlight reflecting off the bay. This room always had the most luscious view, and I spent hours curled up in that cushioned window seat, wearing that shawl, watching the seasons change. I toy with the idea of doing exactly that right now, but my sleep patterns still aren't back to normal, and I know I'll be better off staying active – for all kinds of reasons.

I have such mixed feelings about this room. Many of them happy and silly, but not all of them. That summer, when the world imploded and my parents went to war, I'd huddle beneath the covers with my earbuds in, listening to music to drown them out. I still can't hear certain songs from that era without getting lost in a time loop – in particular, Coldplay's 'A Rush of Blood to the Head' album or *Beautiful* by Christina Aguilera. The minute they reach my brain, I'm right back there, crying beneath my bed covers, feeling like my world has been torn apart. And now I'm back here, hoping my adult self doesn't get ambushed by my teenaged angst.

It's not just my room that makes me feel like that, if I'm honest. It's everywhere. The living room is where they screamed at each other. The kitchen is where she threw the plates. The little breakfast area downstairs is where my mum first met Ethan, where I first noticed how kind he was, how interested in her. The way he made her smile when all my dad did was make her cry.

Outside, where the taxi dropped me today, was the exact same spot I last saw my father here in St Tilda. I still recall him as the man he was when we left   tall, handsome, charming. But also broken by that stage, hugging me before I climbed into the car to the airport. Clinging on just as hard as me, saying goodbye in a way that felt horribly permanent. It's real even now – the smell of his clothes, the lingering aroma of cigars, his big arms wrapped around me. It was hard, so very hard. Even my mother understood that, tears glistening in her eyes as I was finally peeled away from him.

I grew to love the States, amazed by its sheer scale and variety, and the way you got so many different climates and time zones in one country. I still love it – but I'm not sure I ever really recovered from that traumatic wrench. I was sixteen. Everything is in flux anyway at that age, isn't it? Throw in a whole new lifestyle, a different culture, and saying goodbye to everything I'd ever known... Well, it wasn't easy. It took me a long time to forgive my mother for taking me, and my father for letting her.

I shake my head and tell myself off. I cannot avoid facing the past, but I can at least not wallow in it. I send Tyler a quick message telling him I'm here safely, then finally pick up the package my dad gave me. There is a little weight to it, and I spend some time feeling its bulk and trying to guess what it is. Eventually I shrug and open it up.

A pile of papers spills out, the first of them handwritten in old-fashioned ink pen by my father on the fancy stationery he always orders in from a little shop in Mayfair. One of those leftovers from his childhood, I suppose – he can be a terrible snob about the smallest of things. He used to happily shop for bargains at the wholesale stores, but always insist that the towels in the hotel rooms were the absolute highest quality. He drove around in an ancient Aston Martin, refusing to upgrade to a more practical or modern car, and bought one good bottle of wine a week – a bottle that would cost as much as a dozen normal vintages. I suppose he is an eccentric man, full of quirks, and I understand as a grown-up why he holds on to those quirks so hard. Sometimes it's all we have left.

'Dearest girl,' it begins, 'I hope that life is treating you kindly...' His traditional greeting, and one that feels odd to read as I sit only a few rooms away from him.

I found this absolute treasure trove of delights when I was clearing out some boxes. Your darling mother must have tucked them away, in that way that mothers will, knowing that one day they would be unearthed like precious artefacts in an archaeological dig! There were a few other things as well, including some of your baby teeth, but I wasn't quite sure how that would work – sending body parts over international borders and all that. I had a fear that somebody in your zealous customs office would possibly blow it up, or send the CIA to vet me! Anyway. I hope you enjoy reading these – what a wonderful child you were. So full of fight and spirit, always up for an adventure, always keeping everyone on their toes! I'm so dread-fully sorry about that last one, though, sweetheart. I ummed and aahed about including it, and whether perhaps it might not be better to simply throw it on the fire, but at the end of the day it is part of your history too. And these days, of course, we do at least know that it all worked out well in the end! Enjoy, Eleanor – and wishing you a very merry Christmas.

I am curious now, and as I glance through the other sheets, I recognise my own handwriting too. I cast my eyes over them, and laugh out loud when I realise what I'm looking it. They are my old letters to Father Christmas, the lists that I would make every year.

Wow. She would never let me put them in the post box – we had to go to the village Post Office to send them 'special delivery'.

Doris, the lady who worked behind the counter, would always smile and wink and say she'd get that sent straight off to Santa's workshop. I'd be given a lollipop from the big tub she always had, and away we'd go. The cunning plan was clearly always in place, and Doris must have given them all back to my mother every year. Amazing, really, how much effort and subterfuge goes into making Christmas magical for kids.

Before I start, I screw the top off the vodka and swallow some down. That warning about my last Christmas letter sounded a bit ominous, and I have vague memories of writing it one night after drinking some illegal lager scammed from behind the bar. I'd have been sixteen, and way past believing in Father Christmas – but my life was also a mess, and I needed a way to express that beyond slamming doors and telling my poor mum that she 'just didn't understand'.

The first letters are from when I was very small. The lists are short and I have drawn pictures in between the words, so it looks a bit like hieroglyphics – or maybe a non-digital version of emojis. I asked for a puppy on every single one, and a variety of toys that make me smile. Pens and art supplies, a baking set, a doll, a cuddly hamster... who asks for a cuddly hamster? Me, I suppose.

The first letter that is properly written is from 1996, when I'd have been nine. The handwriting is much tidier, and I have clearly used a pencil and eraser because you can see where I've rubbed words out to correct the spelling. Possibly I started to suspect that Santa was fussy about such things. I smooth it out on my lap, the paper crinkled and yellowing. It's quite long, and I've put a lot of effort into it.

Dear Santa,

I have a been a very good girl all year. Apart from when I kicked Lewis in the bottom and made him fall on his face in dog poo. Miss Jones said that was naughty. Mummy said he deserved it because he called my friend Liam a bad name and you should always stick up for your friends. Plus I didn't know there was dog poo, did I, so that's not really my fault. Liam isn't a smelly dwarf and Lewis shouldn't have said that. And he doesn't speak weird, he's just from Ireland. His house is very small and he has five brothers and a sister and only one bathroom so he doesn't have as many showers as we do. Maybe he is a bit pongy sometimes, but it's rude to call him names isn't it? So I was secretly glad when Lewis landed in the dog poo. He was very smelly after that. Anyway, if I am still on the nice list, I would really really really like any of these things for Christmas:
1. A puppy. Any kind at all, but I do like spotty dogs like in 101 Dalmatians

2. A Tickle Me Elmo

3. Some writing pads and pens so I can write stories

4. A Baby Born doll

5. A Stretch Armstrong toy (this is for me to give to Liam, he always wanted one)

Thank you very much and I hope you have a nice Christmas.

Eleanor de Vere

I am wiping tears of laughter from my face by the end of that, especially the bit about dog poo. I was always protective of Liam – he was like the brother I never had. Looking back, it must have been so hard for him. He joined our school when he was seven, straight from County Wexford. He came from a huge Irish family, and people were so rude to them. He was called a 'gyppo' on a regular basis and mocked constantly, both for being small for his age and on account of his accent.

I also remember that the Stretch Armstrong toy did turn up under the tree that year, and was promptly given to Liam as soon as I was allowed to run across the village green to his house. The chaos and noise in there was always overwhelming, especially to an only child, but I always felt safe and welcome. I suppose my mum must have bought the Stretch toy for him, unless there really is a Santa.

I move on through the letters, seeing requests for Tamagotchis and Furbys and those tennis games you play in the garden where the ball is on a string. Every year, I still asked for a puppy, and a gift for Liam.

I seemed to start questioning Santa's existence when I was eleven. I am astonished that I lasted that long – it seems old to still be making Christmas lists – but maybe it was that only child thing. I remember Liam being more cynical, because of his huge amount of siblings and cousins, but I also remember him protecting me from that. His older brother Callum once laughed at me for believing in the tooth fairy, and Liam punched him on the nose. Then Callum chased him all around the village, and by the time he caught him, their dad had got wind of the fight and stepped in to stop it. He did that in his traditional way – by dragging them both off by their ears and forcing them to shake hands.

I don't write any more genuine Christmas lists after 1999, and even in that one, I was basically calling Santa out and sneakily accusing my mum of doing it all behind my back. Poor Mum!

I feel quite emotional myself by the time I reach the last letter. I have finished the vodka, and now I open the gin. It's been weird seeing the person I was before brought so vividly to life. Fun, but also sad – the carefree days, and my friendship with Liam, all finished so abruptly.

I place the letters I've read back in the envelope, and take a deep breath before I delve into the next. I have no idea why my mum would have kept this one, or why it would have ended up with the others. In fact I don't even know how she got hold of it, because for sure at the age of sixteen I wasn't visiting Doris in the Post Office to send off my letter to the North Pole. Doris in the Post Office viewed me as a child of Satan by that stage, because she'd caught me trying a cigarette behind the bus stop. I attempted to eat it so she wouldn't notice and ended up burning my lips.

The paper I've written on is obviously torn from an old school book, and it's all creased, like it's been thrown in the garbage in a ball. Did she rescue this from my waste paper basket? I guess she must have. Mothers are resilient and clever creatures, and never to be under-estimated. I wasn't talking to her, so she was forced to carry out snoop attacks.

My handwriting is a mess, with splodges and scrawls and words scribbled out. Even the scribbles look angry. If sheets of paper could give off energy, this one would definitely be in a bad mood. I see that a few of the scribbles are covering up swear words – even as a blazingly furious teenager, it seems I was too embarrassed to write the 'f' word in full, and instead I've scratched them out and replaced letters with asterisks. I might have hated the world the night I wrote it, but I was still a bit worried about using bad language. It's cute in its own way – or at least it would be if I didn't remember exactly how bad I felt.

Dear Santa,

You massive big arse of a man! You don't even exist, do you? It's all made up. It's all a lie. Because parents are liars. They use you to control us. If we're not good, we don't get presents. It is <u>complete</u> bullshit. It makes me so mad to look back over all the years I wasted believing in you. You can f*ck right off with your elves and your reindeer and your stupid list. Nothing is true and nobody cares what kids want anyway. Nobody listens to us. Prove me wrong, you big red b*stard – here is my Christmas list! I WANT:

1. A bloody puppy – why did I never get a puppy?

2. For Ethan Wallis to not exist

3. For America not to exist

4. For me and Liam to be okay again

5. To stay with my dad

I bet I don't get any of those, you lying scumbag,

From Ellie de Vere

I stare at the angry writing and the little stains that I suspect were caused by tears. Ironically, I did get a puppy. Ethan gave me a card that included a photo of a litter of Golden Retriever pups, telling me that one of them was mine. Ethan was – in fact still is – a deeply kind man, and he knew how hard it all was for me. I tried to stay mad with him, and I was very conflicted. I mean, how could I be happy about leaving my dad? Was it okay to even still want a puppy? Big questions when you're sixteen and think you know everything, despite the daily reminders that you know nothing at all.

The puppy turned out to be a little lady called Sunshine, and she was the one saving grace of those first few years in the States. I didn't make friends easily at my new school, mainly because I didn't want to be there. I was prickly and different, and defensive about being different, and it took me a long time to settle in. For a while Sunshine was the only light in my world. I still fill up a little when I think about her, even though she lived a long and happy life.

I place that final letter in the envelope, wipe away the tears that have snuck up on me, and sip my gin. Precious artefacts, like my dad said – but also reminders of so much that I had forgotten. Your own past sometimes slips away from you, and the memories are bittersweet. Thinking about home, thinking about Liam, thinking about the younger me. Where did all that fight go, I wonder? All that spirit?

I put the letters away and call my mum. She's five hours behind us in Florida. I swig a quick gulp of gin, but she answers immediately and catches me spluttering.

'Ellie? Is that you? Are you choking?'

'No! Sorry, Mum! You answered so fast...'

'Yes, well, I was about to start my ninetieth game of bocce this week and was desperate for an excuse to disappear. How are you, darling? How is he?'

'I'm good, and he seems okay,' I reply, deciding against telling her about Sandra just now. 'I just wanted to say I love you. And thank you for always buying a Christmas present for Liam when we were little.'

She laughs lightly. 'You're very welcome. Liam's family were marvellous, but I did always like getting him something that was just for him, you know? That he didn't have to share. Where is all of this coming from? Are you drinking? Hitting your dad's whisky bottle?'

Damn. How do mums do that?

'No! It's gin, actually. Dad found all of my old Christmas lists. They were sweet, and so were you. I'm sorry I was such a cow when I was sixteen. Did you get that last one out of the garbage?'

There's a pause, and I hear the sound of her pouring a glass of something in the background. 'I think you threw it at my head actually, when I asked you if you wanted any toast... and yes, you were a bit of a moo, weren't you?' she replies. 'But I totally got it, I really did. I know it's impossible to imagine when you're that age, but I was a teenage girl myself once, back in the Ice Age. I remembered what it felt like, having no power over your own life, and the way my own mum never seemed to understand me. I must confess I was a bit of a cow too, and I had nowhere near as many reasons to be as you did. Your whole life was getting messed with just because of grown-ups and their bullshit.'

My mum rarely swears, she is a classy lady, and my eyebrows shoot up on my face at hearing her utter that word. 'Mum! I'm shocked... but yes. I suppose so. I didn't even understand it, you know? Why it was happening?'

I leave that door open, waiting to see if she will walk through it. She has never talked to me about that time, and why she left my father. In turn, he has also maintained silence – although it was much easier for him because he lived on the other side of the world. I'd begged my mum to let me stay there with him, and when she insisted that was not going to happen, I hated her for it. I hated her quite vocally and loudly too. I shudder a little at the thought, and understand now as an adult that she was also going through an upheaval. But like most kids, especially teenagers, I was selfish and really didn't care.

'Mum? Are you still there?' I ask, wondering for a moment if she's hung up on me.

'Yes. I'm sorry it was... Well, I'm sorry. Let's leave it at that shall we? No use raking over the past is there, sweetheart? It all worked out well in the end.'

My dad said those exact same words in his letter. I suppose they comfort themselves with that line, find consolation in the fact that even though my life was turned upside down, it all 'worked out well in the end'.

'It did, Mum, yes,' I say. 'Anyway. I just wanted to check in. I'm off for a stroll around the village now.'

'Oooh, do send me pictures – I believe there's a self-service till at the garage shop now!'

SEVEN

I head back downstairs, wrapped up warm against the chill of the winter night, and find a torch left in the back porch window just like it used to be.

I soon discover that I don't really need it – my feet have retained their muscle memory. Even in the starlight, I easily pick my way along the path that cuts through the gardens, the sound of waves breaking in the bay murmuring behind me. It all feels eerily familiar, even though I left here so long ago.

I follow the path through to the centre of the village and pause as I reach the oval green in the middle. A huge oak tree stands right in the heart, the branches bare now, but in warmer months covered in leaves and offering welcome shade. Now, it is draped in colourful bulbs for Christmas, casting a merry glow on the snow-covered grass.

The green is surrounded by the homes and businesses that make up the beating heart of St Tilda – but there are so few it has a very low heart rate. In fact it's pretty much asleep. It's just after five pm, and lights are still shining from a few buildings. I walk around the cobbled street that circles the green, remembering who lived in each house and wondering if they still do. I see the Post Office, now a small supermarket as well, and quickly pick up pace just in case Doris is still working there.

The little gift shop has closed down, which isn't really a surprise. We do get tourists, and the inn does okay, but we're not top of anybody's list when they visit this part of the world. The pandemic a few years ago took its toll around the world, and I know it was tough for my dad as well. Nothing seems to have replaced the shop, but a brand new boutique has opened next to it. The shop is closed, but the window display shows some very fancy threads. I have no idea how it survives in a place like this, where women are far more likely to be wearing jeans and wellies than sleeveless gowns with matching evening gloves.

I see the doctor's surgery, though the name has changed to a Dr Khan – unsurprisingly, as Dr Mountford was about a hundred back when I lived here. His cure for everything was a long walk and a glass of water, I recall, which worked just fine until that time Liam had broken his ankle somersaulting off a hay bale, and ended up walking on the fracture for over a week before his mum took him to town for an X-ray. Then he got a giant boot that he hated with a passion.

I'm happy to see that Maggie's bakery is still trading, even if it's closed right now. I wonder how old Maggie is these days, because she seemed elderly back then. I think any assessment of age is pretty skewed when you're a teenager though – everyone over forty seems ancient. I'm approaching that myself and suddenly it seems relatively young. Maggie was always lovely; she used to save the wonky pies and cakes for Liam to take home with him, saying she couldn't sell them but didn't want them to go to waste. We'd usually sneak off and gorge on a couple ourselves before depositing them on Bernadette's kitchen table.

I used to hang out with her when I was little, and she taught me the basics of baking – I still hear her voice sometimes when I'm working on a project myself.

I'm still lost in the memories when the door to the fancy clothes shop opens, and a super-stylish woman steps out. She's wearing spike-heeled boots over skinny jeans, and has perfectly coiffed red hair draped over the shoulders of her faux-fur coat. I live in New York, where there is a lot of glamour, but here in St Tilda she sticks out like a sore thumb. I wonder who she is, and when she moved here.

She locks up and walks towards me. She's humming away to herself – something from the works of One Direction if I'm not mistaken – and then comes to a sudden halt when she spots me lingering outside the cake shop. The story of my life.

'Jesus, Mary and Joseph! Is that you, Ellie de Vere?'

For the second time today, I find myself at a disadvantage. Have I really changed so little? In some ways it's a compliment, I suppose. I still have long dark hair, and my perfectly average height and perfectly average build haven't altered much. Inside, I'm a totally different human being – but on the outside, apparently not so much.

'Um... yes?' I reply hesitantly. 'Unless I owe you money. In which case, no.'

'You owe me a hug!' she says, high-heeling towards me with alarming speed and wrapping her arms around me. She smells glorious, like the most expensive perfume from the poshest of shops. I inhale her hair slightly, feeling a bit giddy at the assault on my senses.

'It's me, Cara, you bloody idiot!' she announces, when she finally pulls away and I still look confused.

I stare at her, doing a double take. That can't be right. Cara Byrne is Liam's little sister, and she does not look like this. Cara Byrne has short ginger hair, wiry muscles, and dresses in her big brothers' cast-offs. She doesn't wear heels, and she smells of Lynx Africa on a good day, and old socks on a bad day.

'No way!' I say, grinning at her. 'My God, what happened? Were you kidnapped by aliens?'

She laughs, and flicks her gorgeous hair for effect. 'Yes. They took me to the Planet Make-over. I suppose I just grew up, Ellie. When you left I was, what, thirteen? Not long after that, our mammy insisted I needed my own room, and poor Dad was up in the attic putting in the floorboards and suchlike... and that was when it all began to change. I realised I didn't have to hang round with the hooligans all the time, and that I could use the showers at school, and I could buy a bra without fear of one of the swines putting it on his head and running around the house pretending to be a pilot from the olden days...'

'Well, you look fantastic, Cara. I really can't believe it. I've already bumped into Sean, and I didn't recognise him either.'

'Did he tell you to come up and see our mum and dad?'

'He did. And I will. I'm not sure how long I'm here, but I'll make sure I call in and say hello. I believe you have a new house?'

'We do,' she says, 'or at least they do, and very nice it is too. More than one bathroom for a start, plus bedrooms downstairs 'cause Daddy isn't too good on his feet these days. I live with my husband and kids just down the coast. I run the wee shop here, keeps me busy and turns a profit.'

I probably don't do a good job of keeping the surprise off my face, and she punches me lightly on the shoulder. I'm glad to see that the old Cara isn't entirely gone – she was forever scrapping, with her brothers, kids from school, pretty much anyone who ever crossed her path.

'What, you don't think a little place like St Tilda is busy enough for a fashion empire?'

'Frankly, no. I looked in your window. Nice stuff, but not exactly practical.'

'Ah, well, you see – I have a loyal customer base who come from all over just to buy from me! I built it up online, sourcing one-off items, and eventually sold the online company on for a fair few quid. I opened the shop instead, because I'd be bored sick without something to do other than look after little ones and watch telly. How about you, Ellie? What are you up to these days? Still America is it?'

'Still America, yes. New York. I... um...' I'm realising that I don't know quite how to describe the last few decades of my life and decide to go with a quick summary. 'Married, then divorced, then single, now not. I work doing temporary contracts as an office manager, but my real love is baking, and I'm trying to make a go of that.'

Her face lights up. 'I still remember that birthday cake you made for Liam's fifteenth. It was in the shape of a gravestone, but it tasted of lemons!'

I laugh at the memory. 'It was a *Buffy the Vampire Slayer* inspired cake! And he liked lemons.'

I feel awkward talking about Liam, and I'm relieved when she continues.

'What other news, Ellie? I know your daddy would have told us if you had kids, but what about pets, tattoos, significant others?'

I clench inside at the mention of kids. You get asked about it a lot as a woman of my age, and it always gets to me. It's nobody else's business, and feels intrusive to have my biological clock referred to in conversation. And more to the point, it makes me sad – I would like kids, but it just never seemed like the right time with the right person. Or maybe it's down to me, because Tyler is most definitely good father material, and I'm still not picturing that in my future.

'No kids, no, or tattoos. Technically no pets of my own, but I share my boyfriend's three Labradors. He's called Tyler and he looks like Superman.'

'Which version?' she asks seriously. 'Christopher Reeve, Henry Cavill, *Smallville*, that fella who was in *Lois and Clark*... I need specifics now!'

'How come you know so many different Supermen?'

'My ten-year-old is obsessed, as is the hubbie. So, which would it be?'

I think about it, and nod decisively. 'Definitely Henry Cavill. But more when he's Clark Kent, you know, kind of goofy but hot?'

'I do know! So, congrats on that, then. Living the dream right there, so you are. You'll have heard that our Liam moved from Australia to Dublin? Terrible shame, it was.'

I shake my head. No. I had not heard that. I feel slightly unnerved at the fact that he is getting closer. Also unsure as to why it was a terrible shame – I'm sure Dublin is a very nice place. 'I hadn't. I kind of lost touch with everything. I just came home to help my dad.'

She pulls a sympathetic face and pats my arm. 'That's a good thing to have done. He needs the help whether he admits to it or not. Right, I must be getting home now, but I'll be seeing you soon – you'll have to come and visit, meet the brats!'

I promise her that I will, and continue my stroll. The weather is harsh, but New York winters aren't exactly tropical so I'm well prepared. It is an enjoyable thing to do, noting the small changes in the place, then feeling amazed at how small those changes are. Big cities are in a constant state of change, always evolving and developing. Here in St Tilda, it feels like time has stood still.

I head to the back of the village, to the less picturesque area where the bus stop lives – and, I see, the new additions of big recycling bins. The bus stop is a small wooden structure with a seat inside. It's where us wild and crazy teens would hang out – the nearest thing St Tilda had to a seedy underbelly. As I walk I see that hasn't changed. A small gang of kids are lolling about. I see the glow of cigarettes or, from the fragrant scent in the air, something slightly more exotic. Huh. They're obviously much better at being wild and crazy than I was.

The chatter and giggling stops as I go by, and I try not to laugh – they're all trying so very hard to look tough, but they don't give off a single threatening vibe. One of them – a stunning-looking girl with dyed black hair and a nose ring – is lounging fully flat on the wooden bench, smoking almost defiantly. Unlike the others, she makes eye contact, then leaves the cigarette in her mouth so she has her hand free – with which she proceeds to give me the finger.

I can't help it at that point; I actually do burst out laughing. She narrows her eyes at me, obviously not happy with that reaction, and I give them all a little wave as I walk away. Oh my. The fashions might change, but the attitude doesn't. I had exactly the same surly outlook, the feeling that I was trapped. I felt trapped right up until the moment I was told I had to leave. Then, it was like a switch flicked on inside me, and I realised just how special it was here.

What St Tilda lacked in nightclubs and gigs and cool shops it more than made up for in natural beauty, in a sense of community, in friendship. I had more freedom running wild here than I have had in the rest of my life. Those kids hanging around the bus stop don't realise how lucky they are, but I suppose it was ever thus with teenagers.

I'm still smiling at the encounter as I head back to the inn. It's time to roll up my sleeves, and get stuck in. I'm here to help my dad, and that starts tonight.

EIGHT

A few hours later, I realise that I am officially hopeless. Help my dad? I was deluding myself – he's better off without me!

I started the evening shift with great gusto, determined to be a useful soldier and to make my father's life easier. I'd been an unofficial member of the pub staff for years as a kid, helping him change barrels, learning how to pull the perfect pint, operating the glass machine. I was confident that it would all come flooding back to me as I stepped behind the bar.

For a start, I hadn't accounted for the fancy new till – or 'my archnemesis', as it is now known. Every item is listed individually, including every different drink, every mixer, every bag of nuts or basket of chips or bottle of wine. It feels like I spent most of the night staring at the screen, searching. Then my dad would wander over and point it out, patting me sympathetically on the shoulder when it was right there in front of my damn eyes the whole time.

I also understand now that when I was a kid, he was really just letting me play. There are several different types of ale – the stuff that's in barrels, the stuff that's in casks, the stuff that comes as a limited-edition guest range. And each of the darn things needs to be pulled in a slightly different way. Not only is my arm aching from the constant pulling, but I swear I ended up throwing away half of it. Too much head, not enough, no fizz, too much fizz... you would not believe the number of ways that pulling a pint can go wrong.

The wine and spirits were easier, apart from putting them through the archnemesis, but the food orders were so complicated I eventually gave up on using the till and wrote them down on a little notepad for Sean instead. That did result in me ordering several meals twice and forgetting pretty much all of the special requests – no salad, extra tomato, whatever. I started to hate people who made special requests, which was totally unfair. Especially coming from me, a woman who goes into meltdown if there's a cucumber on her plate. Cucumbers are my other enemies.

As well as messing up the food orders, I dropped pints, smashed glasses, and almost knocked my dad over repeatedly within the small confines of the bar. Basically, you name it, I did it. Worst. Barmaid. Ever. I need to get that printed up on a T-shirt.

Food service stops at eight, at which point Sean blessedly offers to swap with me – he takes over on the bar, and I agree to retreat to the kitchens to do the clear-up. I cast a final glance at the seven million customers all angrily demanding service and realise that it's actually pretty quiet. It might have felt like a zombie invasion but it isn't even that busy, when you're looking at it from the other side of the bar.

'Don't worry, darling,' my dad shouts as I leave, 'it gets easier with practice!' I swear he looks relieved as I go.

I walk into the kitchens and take a few deep breaths as I survey the abandoned plates, mounds of dishes, and scraps of food on the floor. I then rush to the toilet, because I haven't had the chance to go for what feels like a week. I glance at myself in the mirror as I wash my hands afterwards and see that I am as much of a disaster zone as the kitchen. A lot of people recognised me today, and it was incredibly strange to see so many familiar faces – and now, staring at my own, I get that it must have been strange for them as well. I left here at sixteen, and now I am back. Plus after that ordeal, I am not looking at my best.

I'd started off with tidy hair in a ponytail, with make-up and lip gloss and a fresh top from my suitcase. Now, only a few hours later, I look like a scary clown in a Halloween fun house. The kind that chases you with a chainsaw. My mascara has slid down under my eyes, and my hair has escaped from its band and is stuck to the sides of my shiny, sweaty face. The lip gloss is long gone, and even my neck and chest are red and splodgy. As if I've actually had an allergic reaction to the whole experience. It reminds me of my Santa photo from Macy's – I have exactly the same shell-shocked expression.

That, I tell myself, was the start of a much better year for me, so it's not necessarily a bad thing. Besides, I'm now officially relegated to kitchen duties, so it really doesn't matter what I look like at all. There is nobody here to see me, or to care. Like Saint Bridget Jones, I am all by myself.

Smiling at the thought of Bridget drunk-singing into her rolled-up magazine while she necks wine, I dance my way back into the main room, slamming the door open with my ass. I start the hot tap running and grab up an empty beer bottle from the island. If it's good enough for Bridget, it's good enough for me, and I start singing into the neck of the Bud bottle. Nothing like a good sing to clear away the cobwebs.

'ALL BY MYSELF!' I yell, spinning around and waving my arms, like I'm on stage at Wembley. I have the voice of a tone-deaf angel, but what I lack in skill I make up for in enthusiasm. I combine my power-house performance with scraping leftover lasagne into the food bin, and I'm soon feeling better – I might look like crap, and I might be a terrible barmaid, but who cares? Tomorrow is another day, and if the last year has taught me anything, it's to grab the fun times whenever and however you can. Living alone has also taught me that the whole 'dance like nobody's watching' thing is very real. These days, I try to do pretty much everything like nobody's watching.

I finish my scraping and decide to take my impromptu concert to the next level – I pull up The Killers doing *Mr Brightside* on my phone. I bop around the kitchen as I screech, punching the air and doing a few karate-style high kicks. It's only when I decide to take a leap from the small step stool during the chorus that things go wrong. I land directly on a sneakily camouflaged dollop of mashed potato, and my leap becomes a spectacular slide that leaves me half in the splits on the floor. It's an ungainly and painful position, and I am feeling less than bright as I self-triage.

I feel even worse when I hear a voice say: 'Are you okay? What happened? Let me help...'

'I'm all right, nothing broken, just severely bruised pride!' I swipe a clot of mash off my leg as I speak. 'I was dancing. Bit too enthusiastically apparently. Got carried away.'

'Nothing's changed then!' he says, and I finally look up properly at the man standing over me. He grins, and holds out a hand.

It takes me a minute. Possibly two. I stare at him, my mouth dropping to the catching flies position, my brain feeling like a steam train is tunnelling through it. He is almost unrecognisable from the boy I knew. The scrawny kid with acne has become... damn. There's no other word for it – he has become incredibly hot.

I take his hand, and he tugs me to my feet. I look up at him, which in itself is a novelty. At sixteen he was barely the same height as me; now he is towering over my five foot five, and he hasn't only grown upwards. He's filled out in ways I could never have imagined, and there is no sign of a single spot on his sun-kissed skin. His hair is the same brown with flecks of auburn, but short and stylish, and his clothes are a million miles from the scruffy skater boy who was always tripping over his jeans. The eyes, though... the eyes are the same. A deep shade of hazel with flickers of gold.

'Liam,' I finally say, once I've finished examining the new him. I can tell he's been doing the same, his gaze taking it all in. I'm suddenly far more aware of my sweaty hair and my beer-stained top.

'Ellie. You've got mashed spud on your arse,' he says, gesturing down.

'Oh... fudge!' I curse, swiping it off. I tuck some stray strands of hair behind my ears and try to calm down. This is not how I'd pictured seeing Liam again. Not that I really had pictured that – I'd locked him away in a little mental box and thrown away the key.

I look back up and he has an amused smile on his face. 'Now you have mashed spud in your hair. Stay still, let me get it out for you.'

I bite my lip and close my eyes, trying not to jump out of my skin when he makes contact. Liam Byrne is touching my hair, and his fingers are brushing the side of my face. Liam Byrne, who is very much not a teenage misfit any longer. It makes me tingle, because it is like being touched by someone who is familiar and at the same time an undeniably gorgeous stranger.

He holds his fingers up and grimaces. 'Yum,' he says, and grabs up some kitchen towel. I notice a plain gold wedding band, and try not to react on the outside. Liam is married. To someone I don't know. Obviously, considering the fact that we've not seen each other for so long, that should not come as a surprise – and yet it does somehow. He is married, and might have children, and that is odd. Odd but good, I decide. I'm glad that he has someone. I'm glad he found his person.

I tilt my head to one side and manage to smile. 'Back when we were kids, you'd have eaten that.'

'You're not wrong. I was always hungry. My tastes are a bit more refined these days.'

'So I see,' I reply, looking him up and down. 'Posh clothes, nice cologne, a proper haircut... what is it with you Byrne kids being late bloomers? I saw Cara earlier too.'

He nods and grins. 'I know, she told me you were here. What can I say? We changed. It happens. You, though... Jesus, Ellie, how is it that you look exactly the same? Except without the angry scowl?'

I pull my face and narrow my eyes, folding my arms over my chest and letting my lip do the little sneer it used to wear permanently.

'Ah! There she is!' he says, sounding delighted as he laughs. I can't help but join in, despite how weird this is. Just like the rest of him, his voice is both the same and different – there are hints of the different places he has lived, but beneath it that same Irish lilt that always marked him out as an alien when he joined our school.

I am suddenly flooded with memories, all rugby tackling me at once. The first time I saw him, the summer before we went into the same class. He was kicking a football around the village green, wearing shorts that almost came down to his ankles, passed on from his big brothers. 'Ach, he'll grow into it!' was a common refrain in his house.

I remember the first time he came to the pub for his tea, and he couldn't believe I had a room of my own. The first time we got drunk together, and Liam was sick all over both of us. His dad made us stand in the back yard and hosed us down with the pipe. The endless firsts we experienced together – starting high school, skiving off high school, the cigarettes that made us choke, the bus trips and walks on the cliffs and swims in the sea and the constant, unceasing talking. Mainly the talking – it felt like we talked non-stop for years on end.

Liam and I shared everything from the age of seven until we were sixteen. Such incredibly formative times in our lives, going from being little kids into young adults. He was my ally in life, my best pal, my other half – my soul mate. We never, ever ran out of things to say to each other. Until the time we did. Until a combination of immaturity and teenage hormones drove a wedge between us.

I wonder if he is feeling the same as I am right now – embarrassed, excited, and below all of that... relieved? Yes. I'm relieved to see him again. It feels like I'm actually home now and I should let the dark parts of our past go. Earlier today I was thinking I was glad he was on the other side of the world. Now he is standing in front of me, I can't help wanting to tell him every single thing that has happened to me since I last saw him. Just like we used to at the end of every school day, but with a bit more to catch up on.

I am also made of questions – literally bursting with them. I want to know every single thing that has happened to him since we were last together. Which would be quite a lot of things, I'd imagine. I have the urge to immediately launch into an interrogation, but I bite my tongue. I tell myself to slow down, to give myself the chance to steady. To calm. To not explode with this unsettling mix of excitement and dread.

For all I know, this isn't a big deal to him. Maybe he's just thinking it's nice to see an old friend. Maybe he has barely even thought about me over the years. I'm sure I'm over-estimating my own importance, and don't want to completely overwhelm him.

'This is weird, isn't it?' he says, his gold-flecked eyes running over me.

'Yeah. Totally. But we are mature and responsible adults these days.'

'Says the woman who just fell on her backside dancing to The Killers in a pub kitchen.'

'There is that.' I'm unable to stop smiling now. 'Maybe my inner child sensed you were nearby and acted accordingly.'

'Right,' he says, raising his eyebrows cynically. 'So it's all my fault, is it?'

'It is, yes. I'll be swigging red wine and painting my toenails black before you know it. Want to help me clear up?'

I am keeping the tone light, but this feels intense. Why is Liam here? Why isn't he in Dublin, or Australia, or Timbuktu? Why does he look a bit sad and tired, despite his new state of handsomeness? Why is my heart crashing against my chest like I'm out of breath?

I need to be active, to be doing something other than staring at him and getting ambushed by my memories. He nods, and immediately gets stuck in. I leave the music on, and we both sing along to Nirvana and Green Day and then bizarrely Whitney Houston. I have eclectic tastes. He already knows that, of course, because so much of what I like now was already in place back then. He doesn't bat an eyelid as we segue from punk to *I Will Always Love You*.

'You were always a better singer than me,' I say as he stacks the dishwasher.

'That's not saying much. A zombie warthog giving birth is a better singer than you.'

'Oi!' I respond, throwing a tea towel at his head and laughing.

'Don't you mean oink?' he says, throwing it back.

And just like that, I am sixteen again. The good bit of being sixteen. Like on the night of my birthday party, where my dad let all my friends come to the pub, and pretended not to see the hip flasks of vodka doing the rounds. It was before my mum and dad fell apart, before Liam and I fell apart – before everything fell apart.

I remember lying on the grass outside with him afterwards, both of us staring up at the stars in the night sky and waiting for the world to stop spinning. Everyone else had gone home, but we were still out there at one in the morning, determined to last the whole night. Planning to talk for hours, and give our own names to the constellations. We'd got as far as making Orion into Brian before we inevitably started making Uranus jokes. Eventually we fell asleep, the waves our lullaby, the stars our blanket.

When we woke up with the dawn light, we were both covered in sleeping bags my mum had snuck out and tucked around us. The sea birds were calling and we were both wet from dew. We didn't care. We were young, and life was an adventure.

I miss that, I realise. I miss life being an adventure. Things have improved for me over the last year, but I am still smaller and more scared than I used to be. I can't commit to Tyler, and I don't know if that's because he's not the right person, or simply because I'm a coward and afraid to try again. I'd like some of sixteen-year-old Ellie's fearlessness back again.

'So,' Liam says as we finally finish the job, 'do you want to sneak a six pack of Guinness and drink it on the beach? I'd suggest a smoke, but neither of us really ever liked them did we? We were just trying to be cool.'

'I know. I'm glad it didn't stick.' I lean back against the kitchen counter and watch him as he pours himself a glass of water.

'I can't believe how different you look,' I say, letting my eyes run over him. He shrugs, obviously a bit more used to the new him than me.

'I had a full body transplant,' he replies, gesturing down at himself. 'Picked it out of a catalogue.'

'Well, you picked a good one...' I say, immediately blushing at the appreciative tone in my voice. I can't flirt with Liam. I didn't intend to, either, it just came out that way. 'Though I liked you just the way you were,' I add hastily. Which, I realise as soon as the words are out, makes it even more awkward.

His eyes meet mine, and I see such kindness in them. Such understanding. This is what Liam always was: someone who just 'got' me. Even after all these years, his expression tells me that maybe he still does. At least about this.

He points at me and says. 'Your face is so red right now. You look like a giant tomato. You're just a great big enormous tomato that has legs. Astronauts on space stations are pointing and saying "What the hell is that?" in a dozen different languages.'

I laugh and pretend to be offended, but I am grateful for the escape route. Insulting each other is much safer territory.

'Well at least I don't smell of farts!'

'What?' he says, looking shocked. 'I don't smell of farts! I smell of Tom Ford!'

'Not to me you don't. To me, you'll always smell of farts. It's like they're ingrained into you. Soaked into your skin. Part of the very essence of your being. Eau de Liam.'

'God, I so wish I could just squeeze one out right now, it would be so funny...'

He contorts his face, obviously putting some real effort into it, but thankfully nothing emerges. He looks sad and says: 'I feel like such a failure.'

'Don't worry,' I reply, patting his arm, 'it happens to all men. Now, I think we're done in here... and I need a drink. If you're lucky I'll get you one on the house – I know the owner.'

He glances at his watch, and I find myself loving that he wears a watch. It feels so old fashioned, and the watch itself is gorgeous. Like something James Bond would wear. He shakes his head, and I see a flicker of regret on his face. 'No, sorry, I'd better be getting back. How long are you here for?'

'No idea,' I say, biting back my disappointment. I realise that I don't have a clue if he is here just for Christmas, if he has his wife with him, if he has kids. I tell myself that is fine. I have spent years not wanting to know any of that, and it was my choice to blank him out of my life. 'I'll stay until my dad is back on his feet. Until he's okay to run the place on his own.'

His hazel eyes meet mine, and he frowns slightly. Or maybe I imagined it, because as quick as it appeared, it disappeared. He just nods, and the mood suddenly feels awkward again.

'Well, it really was great to see you. I'd love to catch up properly, if you have time while you're here? And I know my parents would love to see you. If that isn't enough to tempt you, there's also a puppy...'

I am immediately interested. 'You know I'm a sucker for a puppy, Liam Byrne.'

'I know. You'd have ridden away with the clown from *IT* if he had a puppy in his clown car.'

'This is true. And yes, of course – we can catch up. It'll only take about five minutes at my end, but I'm guessing yours might be more interesting. Right, off you feck then!'

I make a shooing gesture with my tea towel, and we both laugh at my impression of his mum. He closes the distance between us, and I freeze as I realise he is coming in for a hug. His arms wrap around me, and after the initial panic, I relax. I let myself feel small and warm and safe. I always felt safe with Liam, but the small is a new thing. I can't help inhaling a little as my face lies against his chest. That really is very good cologne.

I pull away, wrinkle up my nose in disgust. 'Fart boy.'

'Tomato face.'

'Off you feck!'

He finally leaves, and I slump back against the kitchen sink. What the hell just happened?

NINE

It is after midnight, and I am still working. Last orders in the pub is at eleven, but it takes anything up to an hour to chase the stragglers out. I remember my dad having a very loose relationship with the concept of 'last orders' anyway, and impromptu parties often sprung up unplanned and unannounced. The locals were also friends, and would beg for a 'lock-in'; my father was usually happy to oblige.

He was in his element, really, in a place like this. The companionship, the humour, the warmth of the village coming together under his roof. He was the perfect host. On weekends, they'd let me stay up late and join in, and when I was little I'd sit on the bar with endless glasses of lemonade and bags of Kettle Chips. Other nights, I'd lie in bed and listen to the fun going on downstairs and feel left out – always looking forward to the days when I'd be old enough to do what I wanted.

Now I am old enough to do what I want, and as most grown-ups discover pretty quickly, it's nowhere near as much fun as you think it's going to be when you're a kid. In fact you seem to do even less things that you *want* to do, and more things that you *have* to do. There are bills to pay, and you have responsibilities, both to yourself and others. Nobody is looking after you anymore.

I guess that's supposed to change if you have a partner, but somehow I can't see myself ever fully allowing someone to look after me, because what happens when they cheat or walk away? That's a horribly pessimistic outlook, but I can't shake it off. My ex-husband was a cheat, and although that happened many years ago, I still remember the way it sucked me dry of all my self-confidence. Then there were my adventures on dating apps, which provided me with ample proof of how relationships can go sour. Tyler should offset some of that cynicism, but I think it runs deeper – it also stems back to seeing my parents' once stable marriage blow up.

In some ways, being away from the US is good for me. I need to give some serious thought to Tyler's suggestion that I move in with him. I like him, and we have fun together, and I'm happy with things as they are between us. For me, it's perfect – we allow each other our own space but also have someone to share life with, and of course to have lovely sexy times and cutesy cuddles with. Why do things have to change?

I suppose they have to change because what is perfect for me isn't perfect for him, and I know he wants more. He said there's no deadline on that change but I'm not sure our relationship can survive the imbalance. Or if it's even fair to expect it to – at what point does it stop being him giving me time, and become me stringing him along? It's a lot to consider, and being here gives me some leeway.

My dad is quiet and pale by the end of the evening, which really isn't like him. I chase him up to his bed despite his protests and tell him I can handle everything else that needs doing. He looks sceptical. 'Dad, just get some rest, and let me clear up – I promise you I won't touch the cash register!'

I used the American term on purpose, knowing that he would immediately correct me. 'That would be the till, Eleanor!'

'That would be my archnemesis, Father. Anyway, I'll steer clear of the damn thing. It hates me. You can cash up tomorrow. But I can clear up and get things ready for breakfast. How many guests are in?'

'Five in the doubles, and three in the family room. They have a five-year-old with them. We've changed the times though – from eight instead of seven.'

I nod. That at least is a blessed relief. 'Does anybody come in to help?'

He shakes his head. 'Not tomorrow. Maggie and Sandra have taken turns, but tomorrow was my first day back to doing it myself. Which, by the way, I am perfectly capable of!'

His voice lifts a little, but I can see the slight tremor in his hand, and how tired his eyes are. He has put on a good show tonight, for me and for the customers, but he's not fooling anyone now. Except possibly himself.

'I know you're capable, Dad, but let me help, will you? I've come a long way to help – and yes, I know, before you protest, you didn't ask me to. But I'm here and I'm staying, and I'm also capable. So please, have a lie-in, for feck's sake!'

He smiles and raises his eyebrows. 'How was it? Seeing Liam again? I never figured out what went wrong between you two. You used to be thick as thieves, and then he was persona non grata and I wasn't even allowed to talk about him...'

'We just grew up, Dad. People change. And it was fine – seeing him. It was... uh, it was nice. Now, go, leave me to it.'

He looks as though he wants to ask more, clearly not accepting my simplistic explanation. But something in the set of my face must tell him I don't want to discuss this, and he nods. My dad and I have built our entire relationship as adults on not discussing things, and I don't think that is going to be easy for either of us to change.

Reluctantly he gives in, disappearing into the back rooms, and I turn to look at the disaster zone that is the pub. I take a deep breath and get started. I get the glass washer on the go, cleaning one load as I gather up the empties that are scattered on the tables and the wooden surface of the bar. I smile at the Christmas tree as I walk by with an armful of lager bottles. It's so cute that my old decorations are still up – a reminder of simpler times, when my dad and I were completely relaxed in each other's company.

It takes a good hour to do the cleaning, and this part does come back to me – washing the drip trays beneath the beer pumps, cleaning the nozzles on the pumps themselves, spraying down the tables and stacking the chairs. We used to have a cleaning lady who came in most days, but Dad has told me he does it himself now. I pick up as much detritus as I can and throw it away, but I'll be up early to run the vacuum around too.

I rake over the coals in the fires to make sure I'm not going to accidentally burn the place down on my first night here, and start on breakfast prep. I lay the tables, adding the condiments and sugar bowls, and check that the fridge is fully stocked with everything I'll need. I spend a bit of time in the kitchen getting bowls and plates ready to go, knowing that tomorrow morning's me will be grateful to tonight's me.

I do a last walk-through, tidying up the Christmas garlands and checking that the little baby Jesus is happy in his Nativity scene crib, then switch off the lights and climb exhausted up the stairs. This was hard work when it was me and my mum and dad doing it. How he has managed alone I have no idea. I know he used to have more staff for sure, but from what I've gathered this evening, the only actual regular employee now is Sean. The late nights, early mornings, the sheer amount of graft involved in running even a small place – I'm not surprised his health has suffered.

I wearily brush my teeth and fall into bed. Just as I snuggle beneath the sheets, a message arrives from Tyler. It's a picture of him and the three Labs – Pippa, Polly and Miley Cyrus. The latter is only a year old, and was supposed to be called something to match the others, like Penny or Posy. Instead, as Tyler says, she barrelled into their lives like a wrecking ball, and the nickname stuck.

I smile as I look at the photo. It's five hours earlier back in New Jersey, and he'll be about to take them all out for their evening walk. He lives in a nice neighbourhood in a three-bed house, and has a big yard for the dogs to play in. It's not exactly a terrible world that he's invited me to share.

I yawn as I type out a quick reply, sending him some kisses. 'They were for the dogs,' I add. He quickly responds. 'You don't want to kiss Miley right now. She just rolled in fox poop.'

I laugh, picturing the dog's guilty expression. 'Stop it with the sexy talk,' I answer. 'Wiped out now, babe, will call you properly tomorrow xxxx. Those kisses were for you.'

I set my alarm for seven, so I can get clean the breakfast room properly before the guests come down, and set my phone aside. It is so strange being here, in my childhood bedroom. Staring up at the familiar ceiling, with its stick-on glow-in-the-dark stars. Not all of them have survived, and what used to be a smooth swirling line that it took me and Liam ages to do is now just a random smattering of eerie light.

I close my eyes, listening to the sound of the waves. It's gentle tonight, a constant mild backdrop of the water splashing into land. On stormy nights when the tide is high, it's much louder. Our little bay is curved like a half moon, a golden patch of sand surrounded by rugged cliffs filled with wildflowers and colonies of sea birds. The sound of the ocean slamming in with force is one I'll never forget, and always reminds me of how powerful nature is.

It takes a little getting used to after New York, where the evening lullaby comes with the gentle whisper of breaking glass and sirens and other city noises that I am now accustomed to. In fact, despite how tired I am, I struggle to sleep. My body is exhausted, but my mind is whirring along at a million miles an hour. Why do minds do that? Why doesn't your brain – which is actually part of your body – co-operate when you're so tired? By rights I should crash out now, and grab the few hours' sleep I can.

Instead I am tossing and turning, and every minute I spend awake makes me more and more stressed about how wiped out I'm going to be in the morning. Which, obviously, makes it even tougher for me to switch off. Eventually, I need to go to the loo again, and then I need a glass of water, and by that point sleep seems out of my grasp.

I settle back into my little single bed and decide not to fight it. I've discovered over the years of on-and-off insomnia that fighting is the worst thing to do. Instead, I just accept that tomorrow will be a shitstorm, and there's nothing I can do about it. I let my stupid mind wander, and the random thoughts of the day ping around my skull like dodgem cars, crashing into each other.

How long has my dad been seeing Sandra? Is there a chance they might get married and then I wouldn't worry so much about him? And why doesn't he have a cleaner or extra bar staff anymore? Does Maggie still make those amazing fruit scones? Should I start baking fresh bread for the breakfasts, because it's the best smell in the world? What is Tyler doing tonight? How long will I be here? And what about Liam?

As soon as that last thought lands, the others fade away. Liam. That's what's actually bothering me. I might as well be honest with myself. I stare at the moonlight filtering in through the curtains and listen out for the owl that lives in the trees nearby. Nothing. Even the owl is steering clear.

I sit up, sip some water, and rub my sore eyes. I have tried so hard not to think about Liam over the years. Too hurtful, too sad, too embarrassing. I cut him out, blanked him from my mind. Made him a creature of dread and legend. Now, tonight, I came face to face with the monster – and he wasn't a monster at all. Of course he wasn't. He never was – he just became a symbol of that broken time in my life.

Tonight, he wasn't a symbol, he was... Liam. No matter how buff he looked or how much he'd grown, beneath all the physical changes he was still just the goofy boy I used to think of as my soul mate. Neither of us talked about the past very much, or in fact the present – we just messed around. We sang and danced and made stupid jokes about farting. Both of us almost forty, both of us still behaving like kids.

The last time I spoke to Liam, it was this time of year. In fact it was Christmas Day, when I was sixteen. It was not a good time in my life. It was probably the messiest I have ever been. Being a teenage girl is always messy; your body and mind – and the world's perception of you – is in a state of constant change. Your own perception is even more fluid.

Added to that unappealing blend of hormones and natural boundary-pushing was my home situation. My parents had turned into strangers, and looking back I think that all upset me so much more than I was able to acknowledge. My mum and dad had never been the kind of people who had rows or swore at each other. Suddenly, though, they were – and they stayed like that for months and months. When Mum met Ethan, things changed very quickly. The rows stopped, but a different type of upheaval began. The kind that involved me moving to another country, and my dad looking like he was being crushed by the weight of his own sorrow. Me trapped between them.

I was a kid. I didn't really understand any of it. I just felt insecure and helpless, and those feelings manifested in my small rebellions. Staying out later than I should, drinking too much, refusing to help in the B&B. Some of this had already started, and was harmless and natural enough at my age – but the changes at home accelerated it.

Like most girls at that stage, I was interested in sex. I'd never done it, and in fact I'd only ever kissed a couple of boys, and found the whole process a bit icky. Too much tongue, too much groping, too much everything. I couldn't figure out what the fuss was about, and even wondered if I might be gay – except I didn't find girls especially attractive either. Looking back it's just funny – those poor teenage boys, no clue what they were doing, and me thinking 'huh, really?' I was convinced that Josh Hartnett would be much better at it.

If I'd carried on living where I lived and leading my normal life, I'm sure I'd have figured it all out – but there was the great schism. When my mum told me we were leaving for California, I basically lost the plot. She broke the news maybe ten days before

Christmas, and I was furious. With her, with my dad, with everything. Nobody was listening to me when I said I wouldn't go, and nobody seemed to give a damn what I thought about it at all. I felt irrelevant and invisible.

A few days after that I broke into the pub cellar and stole a whole crate of Budweiser. Well, technically I didn't break in – the place wasn't locked. I waited until Mum and Dad were in bed (in their separate rooms by then), and snuck down in my pyjamas and Converse. I could barely carry the crate, and remember the clinking noises of the glass as I made my escape. I'd arranged to meet Liam down at the beach, and he was bringing the essentials – sleeping bags, torches, snacks and cigarettes that neither of us wanted to smoke. He used to pinch them from his older brother Patrick.

I wrapped up in an extra layer of fleece, added my hat and gloves, and clinked my way down the steep steps to the bay. I'm lucky I didn't die, in all honesty – I wouldn't do it now. I'd be too scared that I'd slip in the dark and impale myself on a Budweiser bottle. What an undignified way to go.

He'd galloped up the steps as soon as he heard me coming and helped me carry the case down to the sand. We weren't complete idiots, we did know the tide wasn't due to come in and trap us, and it all felt deliciously naughty – the theft, the sneaking around, setting up our little camp in the early hours of the morning. We zipped the sleeping bags together to create one big one and sat snuggled up together as we got to work on the beers.

I often look back and wonder if I was an especially bad teenager. I certainly seemed to drink quite a lot, but part of that at least was because I had relatively easy access to alcohol. Once I moved to the US, where they were much more strict on IDs and technically didn't let you touch booze until you were twenty-one, I wasn't as interested. Probably a big save for my liver.

That night, to start with at least, was so perfect. Me, Liam, the sea. There was a full moon, and it seemed to paint the rippling water in shimmering shades of silver. It was cold but not freezing, and we were well wrapped up, only our faces showing. We laughed and talked and sang along to our favourite music. We planned our future, one where we were independent and no grown-ups could tell us how to live.

We would go to college and then he would start his own business building computers, which was the only thing he was interested in. We would both go to Bristol uni, and share a house, and have so much fun. Eventually we might even get a puppy. He would meet and marry Sarah Michelle Gellar, and I would be wooed by Josh Hartnett, and we would be friends forever.

It was a version of a conversation we had shared over and over again – but this time, it felt totally impossible. Even as I was saying the words, I knew that none of it would happen. Because I was moving to the States, and Liam was staying here and, let's face it, neither of us was ever going to marry a movie star.

'It's all crap, though, isn't it?' I'd said. I'd drunk so much by then that I was already sounding a bit slurred. 'It's all crap because I won't be here. I'll be on the other side of the world, and you'll forget all about me.'

'Don't say that!' he'd replied, passing me another bottle of beer which I very much didn't need. 'It's not all crap. It might just happen differently than we planned. And I will never forget about you, Ellie. You're my lobster!'

'That isn't even real. That's just a stupid thing off *Friends*. I'll move away, and you'll find a new lobster, and I'll never make another friend like you...'

I was crying by that stage, all snot and tears, the sheer frustration of my position combining with the booze to overwhelm me. Liam put his arm around me, and let me cry on his shoulder, doing as good a job of comforting me as most sixteen-year-old boys could. He stroked my back and held my hand and kissed the tears from my cheeks. I think it was that final gesture that pushed me over the edge. He was kind and sweet and there, and I was so unhappy – desperate to feel anything other than that swirling pit of emotional nausea.

After all these years, it is still vivid. It still stings. It still makes me blush, even as I lie alone in my own bed as a grown woman. It was all too much for me – the waves, the booze, the boy. The way he always seemed to know me so much better than anybody else, and the horror of leaving it all behind.

I grabbed hold of his face and kissed him. Properly kissed him. At first he went rigid in shock, which was totally fair enough – there had never been even a hint of anything romantic between us. He was about as experienced as I was – in other words, not very – and neither of us had ever expressed an interest in our friendship being anything more than it was.

I pulled him down on top of me, because that's what I thought I should do. Like most kids that age, I'd watched too many movies and films, and had no idea of how awkward the actual act of physical union could be. Even kissing someone was a logistical nightmare – the clashing teeth, the swiping noses, the bumping foreheads. So I did what I'd seen on screen, and dragged him into my arms. It must have been comical really – he was the same size as me then, and undoubtedly terrified at this unexpected contact.

'Let's do it,' I'd whispered, tugging at his clothes. 'We might not see each other again. We're both old enough. Let's get it out of the way...' So romantic.

I recall grabbing his hand and shoving it underneath my pyjama top – the momentary thrill as his fingers touched my breasts, and the feel of his body pressed against me, responding exactly how most sixteen-year-old boys would at getting to second base without even trying. Drunk as we were, that kiss with Liam was already a million times better than any of the kisses I'd endured before. I actually started to feel excited, genuinely curious, tingling in places I didn't know could tingle.

I rubbed up against him in a way I assumed was sexy, having no clue at all what I was doing but knowing I didn't want it to stop. I was young, I was naïve, and I was drunk. He was all of those things too, but obviously not as tipsy as me – because he suddenly rolled off me and pushed me away.

I tried to pull him back, determined to do this insane thing, but he shouted at me to stop. He climbed to his feet, and I stared up at him, feeling sick, rejected. Humiliated. 'No,' he said, 'this isn't right. It's not... not what you really want. You're just pissed and sad.'

I staggered upright, wobbling from side to side, and tried to kiss him again. 'I do want it!' He shoved me away more firmly then, and I fell flat on my backside.

'No, Ellie, you don't – and I don't either! This is weird now... I'm going home, okay? You should too. Come on, let's go.'

He tried to help me back up, but I screamed at him to feck off. I was feeling so bad by that point, emotionally and physically. Liam, the boy I trusted most in the whole world, didn't want me. Therefore I must be unwantable. Unlovable. Unlikeable. Maybe that was why my dad didn't even want me to stay here with him, because I was such a loser...

I made him go, lashing out and kicking at his ankles until he had no choice. Then I threw up in a carrier bag, and spent the night alone on the beach. Freezing cold, drunk, and broken hearted. I didn't really get any sleep, and when dawn finally came I felt like a different person. As the booze started to clear my system, I was flooded with regret and with self-loathing. A part of me wanted to just walk into the ocean and end all of this pain, all of this sadness. I was no use to anyone, especially myself.

I cried so much my eyes glued together, and I realised I'd made a terrible mistake. I'd thrown myself at Liam. I'd tried to persuade him to have sex with me, and he said no. Why the hell had I done that? What was my problem? Why was I such an idiot? And was I so repulsive that no boy would ever be interested in me? It didn't help that I had actually enjoyed the contact, while he seemed disgusted by it.

I'd staggered back up the steps and forced myself to go to his house. Bernadette was already up and making breakfast for the tribe and ushered me inside without asking a single question. It was considered normal for me to turn up looking like crap at six in the morning.

Liam was crashed out on the sofa in their small living room, curled up in a ball under one of her woollen creations. I wanted to apologise. I wanted to beg him to forgive me. I wanted everything to feel okay again.

I nudged him awake, and he scurried away in horror when he saw it was me. 'Liam. Sorry. Please don't be a dick. I was just drunk, okay?'

He'd rubbed his eyes, looked at me warily. 'Yeah, I know that, Ellie. But what the feck? You totally freaked me out. I, uh... look, it'll all be okay, but I need a bit of time, all right? Just leave me alone for a bit while I sort my head out will you? I just need a bit of time off.'

This was the first time ever in the history of our whole lives together that he had asked me to leave him alone. From seven years old until now, we had been joined at the hip, allies in life. Soul mates. And now, I could tell by the look on his face, that was all over.

I just mumbled a reply and left, my cheeks burning and my heart breaking and everything in my entire life crumbling around me.

Quite obviously, I could never, ever talk to him or see him ever again. I had now lost my best friend on top of everything else.

It sounds insane, but even now I still feel how hard those feelings hit me. It's still visceral and real, and immense – it was like being flattened by a ten-ton truck. It was so bewildering and painful, and I never really let it go. I was upset and mortified enough for that sense of embarrassment to take permanent hold. It became so deep-rooted that I am still affected by it now. I avoided Liam as much as I could after that, convinced that if we were alone in the same room ever again, I would simply explode with misery.

I refused to go to school, and when I did see him, I wouldn't make eye contact or speak to him. It was an immature response, but I was only a child really. It must have hurt him too, this sudden ending, but I simply couldn't bear being near him because it made me feel even worse.

He tried to explain himself, to make things right, but he didn't ever quite understand – it was nothing that he could make right. My shame came from the way I had behaved as much as the way he responded. Nothing would ever make it right, I knew – and that is a feeling that has stuck with me for all these years. It's why when I moved, I shut out all memories of my time here, of our closeness. Why I never wanted to hear the name Liam Byrne ever again. It was easier to pretend he had never existed than to face my own humiliation.

He called me, on Christmas Day that year, and it was the last time we spoke. I told him to stop bothering me, that he was 'doing my head in'. I said I was leaving for America anyway, and none of it mattered – he should just forget all about me. That I planned on forgetting all about him as well. I pushed and pushed, and eventually he'd yelled: 'Fine! You can piss off then, you moody cow!'

I cringe now, seeing how transparent it all was – lashing out at him like that. I hated myself and everything else, and I poured it into my response to Liam. I did my very best to stick to my word though, and forget all about him. I numbed myself to him, and everything he represented. More than two decades have passed since then, and I have never once spoken to him since. When he called me a moody cow, they were the last words we shared. Until tonight. Or last night, I correct myself, realising that it is almost three am.

Last night, Liam Byrne walked back into my life – and it went so much better than I could ever have imagined. If I'd known he was here, I'd have been so stressed out. I would still have come to help my dad, but I would have been dreading it, and possibly walked around the village in disguise in an attempt to avoid a reunion.

Never would I have believed that it would actually have all gone so well. That despite a few moments of awkwardness, we would fall straight back into our old patterns. Against the odds, I spent most of that time together laughing and smiling.

I have, I realise, been an almighty dick. There really is no other way of seeing it. It's not that I held on to a grudge – I never blamed him for what happened, and have many times since been extremely grateful that he made the choice he made that night. It was the honourable choice, and not one that many boys his age would have made.

But while I have not held on to a grudge, I have held on to the pain and the shame. The sense of rejection. All of my feelings about Liam became dominated by that one awful night, rather than the joy of the previous years. For that, I could slap myself.

Still, I'm here now. He's here now. Let's wait and see what happens.

TEN

I woke up before my alarm, realising that there was no way I was going to drift off again. I gave up trying, and came downstairs to whip up some fresh breakfast muffins and some simple chocolate chip cookies. The cupboards are not exactly fully stocked, but there was enough for that at least. The repetitive tasks of baking were restorative, as usual, but I'm still not at my best – in fact I'm running on adrenaline and two hours' sleep.

My dad is a natural at engaging with the guests, and I am not. I do my best, though, and they are at least quite interested in my almost-American accent. The five-year-old asks me if I know Bruce Wayne, and I tell him we go to the same dentist, just to see the look of astonishment on his face. Mr Owen, the man I'd met the day before in the pub, just nods politely and reads his book – the ideal customer.

I manage the cooking with ease, serving up multiple full English breakfasts, topping up toast and coffee, replenishing the little buffet table with cereals and big jugs of juice. The muffins go down well, and I vow to carry on adding little home-baked treats to the menu. It will be good for my state of mind to spend some productive time in the kitchen.

I'm clearing up when I hear Dad's voice coming from the

breakfast room, and straight away it's followed by delighted laughter from the guests. It's a familiar routine, and it makes me smile even as I'm putting on rubber gloves and plunging the blocked sink.

He wanders in after spending a few minutes chatting to them. He's dressed in his usual 'casual country gent' attire, smart navy blue cords and white and blue check button-up shirt. His hair is freshly washed, and he looks bright-eyed and bushy tailed. I check for signs of fatigue or illness, but come up blessedly blank.

'Do stop staring at me, dear,' he announces sternly. 'I had a very minor stroke, from which I am expected to make a full recovery. You're looking at me as though you're measuring me up for a coffin.'

'Ha,' I say, passing him the plunger, 'there won't be a coffin. I'm just going to strap you to the ride-on lawn mower and point it at the cliffs. Burial at sea.'

'Sounds marvellous. Maybe you could fire a flaming arrow at me as I go. You might need to rethink though, because I don't have that mower anymore. It was older than me, and when it broke down there were no spare parts to fix it. In the summer I get Clive the Tree to do it for me in exchange for free Guinness.'

'Crikey. Is Clive the Tree still working?'

Clive was definitely in his late fifties or early sixties when I left, and the thought of someone of his advanced years being up trees with a chainsaw is alarming.

'Not full-time. His son Bobby the Tree has taken over the business. Clive just likes to keep his hand in around the village. He does all his work on a barter system – free cakes from Maggie's bakery, beer here, that kind of thing.'

'Does he get free ball gowns from Cara's shop as well?'

'Well, what a man gets up to in his spare time is his own business. Now, why don't you go and... be somewhere else for a while? I'll do the cleaning.'

As we've been talking he has effortlessly unblocked the sink – years of practice – but I'm not ready to disappear just yet.

'Tell you what, how about we cut a deal, Pop?'

I lay on the Americanisms thick, partly because I know it makes him cringe, but while he's doing that, he's also not worrying about anything more important.

'I am your father, not your "pop". Pop is a fizzy drink.'

'You mean a soda?'

'I mean please go away. Shall we meet for luncheon? In Maggie's café?'

This is news to me, and distracts me from all other issues. Forget my dad, forget Liam, forget everything – this is big! 'Maggie has a café?'

'She does. It's in a big glass conservatory extension at the back of the bakery. Very nice it is too. Would one o'clock suit you?'

'Sure,' I reply, standing up on my tiptoes to drop a kiss on his cheek. 'Sounds great. I'll get some more stuff done here and then see where the world takes me.'

He grimaces but holds up his hands in surrender. I leave him filling the dishwasher and go back out into the breakfast room. Everyone apart from the family has left, and the little boy is looking from me to his mum suspiciously. I start to gather up their plates, and he says: 'My mummy says she bets Batman doesn't have any fillings. Is that true?'

His mum suppresses a laugh, and I reply very seriously: 'That is totally true. Mr Wayne is renowned for his fantastic dental hygiene. He brushes and flosses all the time and really looks after his teeth.'

The kid looks impressed, and as they leave I hear him asking if he can go back up to the hotel room to use his toothbrush. Ellie Dexter, fighting cavities one fib at a time.

I clear and wipe down the tables, then get the vacuum out of the big store cupboard to run it around both rooms. It takes an age, and my back is slightly sore by the time I finish. I put all the tables and chairs back down ready for the evening and go back in to see my dad.

'What's the score with the rooms?' I ask. 'Do we still do house-keeping every day?'

'No, new system these days. If they're staying for less than a week, they simply request changes of bedding, extra towels, that kind of thing, when they need them. We go in every two days to clean, empty bins, unless asked not to. Only Tintagel and Lizard are due to be done today – and I am perfectly fine to do them!'

I wink at him and scoot out of the room. I'll definitely be doing those rooms, I think, grabbing up the master key from behind reception and heading up the stairs. All of the guest suites are named after famous local landmarks, and I knock on the door of Tintagel. No answer, and a quick peek inside shows that it's empty. I find the cleaning products in the store room, and set to work. This is one of the jobs I used to help my mum with, and again the muscle memory kicks in as I clean the bathroom and tidy up the bed. I find that I'm enjoying it – it's one of those zen activities where you can give your thinking mind a break and concentrate instead on the relatively simple task right in front of you.

When I'm done, I go back to our own part of the building to have a shower. I drop my mum a quick message as well, because I know she'll be wondering how I'm getting on. This must be strange for her as well. Signs of my dad are obviously everywhere in the apartment, but the remnants of my mother's life here are fainter. A few ornaments in the main room; a painting that she bought from an auction and left behind. Not a lot of physical evidence that she ever even lived here.

Physical evidence is one thing, I think, as I get dressed and walk out into the big lounge – but for me, the emotional evidence is everywhere. The table where she used to sit with me when I was a little girl, craft materials scattered, both of us happy with our paints and glitter and glue-sticks. The same table where later on, she'd help me with my homework. The original TV is gone, but that corner of the room is still magical – it was where we used to watch her collection of DVDs. Her two favourite films were *When Harry*

Met Sally and *Gladiator* – so different but both brilliant in their own way.

I smile as I remember sitting in this room with her, eating popcorn as we watched movies: *A Bug's Life, Titanic, Toy Story, Pearl Harbor*, the entire works of Hugh Grant... even when I entered my 'difficult' period, we still bonded over watching movies. We were talking about it a few years ago, and she said: 'When you were about fifteen, everything I did annoyed you. You literally once told me off for breathing too loud. But that same night, we sat and watched *The Lord of the Rings* together, and you didn't roll your eyes at me once. It was more magical than Gandalf.'

Now, her presence in this place is held in my mind only. There is one photo of her – a group shot of the three of us when I was a baby – but it feels like an ancient artefact, a thing out of time. She has had a great life with Ethan, and there is nothing to feel sad about on her behalf – but I still do, a little. Or maybe I'm sad for me, or my dad, or all of us. It always felt like something precious and sacred was shattered here, and I never even understood why.

I shake off the approaching melancholy and decide to go for a walk. After lacing up my hiking boots, I head out to explore. I cross the gardens and my feet automatically take me to the steps that lead down to the bay. I pause at the top, as ever awestruck by the view. It's a cold but clear day, the sky a vivid blue, a light dusting of frost and snow clinging to the grass. I can see one person down there on the sand, and hope I don't disturb their solitude as I make my way carefully down the stone steps. At least I'm not carrying a crate of beer bottles this time.

I am relieved when I make it down safely, and stand on the beach for a moment, simply appreciating the place. I always loved the colours here – the light is so pure, the shades of sand and sea so bold. The puffed-up white chests of the terns and gulls dot the cliff-sides, and their cries blend with the constant sound of the waves. It's a breezy day, and they crash and roll onto the beach, throwing up froth and slamming over the rocks.

I see footprints in the sand leading to the one other person who is down here, sitting cross-legged near the shoreline. Black hair flows down her back, and I realise she is the same girl I saw at the bus stop – the one who so charmingly gave me the finger. She's up early for a teenager, or maybe she just never went to bed.

I don't want to disturb her, as I am definitely in the category of Grown-Up Who Doesn't Understand My Pain. Instead, I walk off to one side and explore the little rock pools at the base of the cliffs. I spent many happy hours making friends with crabs and other little sea monsters when I was a kid. I walk as silently as I can on the slightly frost-crunchy sand.

I alter my course to give her space, noticing that she has headphones on – of course. I could make as much noise as I liked and she probably wouldn't hear me. As I look on, she removes her big padded puffer jacket and lays it at her side. She stands to her feet from the cross-legged position, in that limber way that the young take for granted, and remains there for a few moments with her hands on her hips. I'm shivering just looking at her, her dark hair blowing around her head like a shadow storm, a flimsy T-shirt on beneath her coat.

She starts walking towards the waves, her stride determined, eating up the distance. The water laps at her feet, and is soon up to her ankles. She pauses, seems to take a deep breath, and plunges on even further. What the hell is she doing? As I stare, dumb-founded, the waves roll up to her knees, and an especially strong breaker soaks her from head to toe. Her black hair is plastered against her skull, the headphones dripping. Surely, now she will turn back. She will have got it out of her system, exorcised whatever demon needs chasing away. The shock of that icy-cold drenching will have snapped her out of her reverie.

No. She just keeps walking. I have a moment of absolute horror, followed by a few seconds of indecision. Then I yell, as loud as I can, screaming at her to stop. There is no response, of course, no outward sign that she has heard me. Between the wind, the waves and the headphones, she seems to have no clue that she isn't completely alone down here on this secluded beach.

I run towards her, watching her stride further and further out to sea. She isn't swimming, or jumping, or making any movements that imply this is exercise or fun. I have the dreadful feeling deep in the pit of my stomach that this is something more. I have been that teenage girl sitting on the beach, staring out at the water and wondering if it might be a better option than dealing with the pains and sorrows of my life.

I speed up just as her head goes under, her black hair spreading out on the surface of the water, a rippling circle of dark strands. I throw my phone down onto her jacket, and go in. I feel the shock of the freezing waves as I gallop forward, forcing myself on with pure adrenaline. Should I have taken my boots off? People in films always seem to stop and take their boots off. There didn't feel like there was time for that, so I press on, my feet sinking into the seabed.

In a few strides I am there by her side, splashing through the water, grabbing hold of her shoulders and pulling her head up. She spits a mouthful of sea at me and slaps my hands away. She looks shocked and angry, suddenly kicking and treading water instead of simply letting herself sink. We're both soaking, both staring at each other, both obviously wondering what the hell is going on.

'Leave me alone!' she yells over the sound of the ocean. 'I'm swimming!'

I pull her headphones off, randomly thinking she's going to need some new ones. 'Not here you're not. It's too dangerous to swim when the weather's like this. Come on now, let's go back. If you don't, I'm staying with you.'

'Just feck off, will you? This is none of your business!'

Feck off. Even in these strained circumstances that tells me she might be part of the Byrne clan, which comes as no surprise. There are probably thousands of them by now.

'I will not feck off, no – if you're swimming, I'm swimming! You're stuck with me!'

She glares at me, her blue eyes furious, her nostrils flaring. The nose ring is matched by a lip ring, and one of those that go through the eyebrow as well.

'I mean it,' I shout, kicking my legs to keep myself afloat. She is a little taller than me and isn't struggling so much. It would be ironic if she simply swam back to shore and I was the one swept to sea. 'And I'm not that good a swimmer – I'm your responsibility now!'

Her glare intensifies, but whatever she sees in my eyes seems to convince her that I mean it. She screams, full throttle, the anguished and frustrated sound rising over the hiss and roar of the waves. She slaps her hands down hard on the water. Without a word she turns and makes her way back to the bay. She does it effortlessly, letting the waves sweep her along, not showing an ounce of fear. I follow behind, a lot less gracefully, a combination of swimming, hopping and falling over. I can barely feel my legs anymore, and the boots now feel like I've got lead weights attached to my feet. I am beyond grateful when I am firmly back on wet land, shaking and trembling from both the cold and the shock.

The girl looks the same, and some of her fight has clearly drained from her. Her skin is so pale it's almost translucent, and her lips are blue. She could have been out here for hours, and she was in the water for longer than I was. I need to get her indoors and dried off.

'Where do you live?' I ask, doing half-hearted star jumps in an attempt to keep my blood flowing. I grab my phone and her jacket, and do my best to shove her arms into it. We're both trembling, and I'm starting to wonder if I should just be calling for help at this stage. She shakes her head and mumbles something, rubbing her hands together. Now she's out of the water it's like she's a different person – younger, more vulnerable. Less angry, and more sad.

'Come on,' I say firmly, pushing her towards the steps. 'I live at the inn. We can both get dry and have a hot drink. Then I can get you home.'

She lets me guide her, her sodden cargo pants sticking to her legs as she clambers up the stone stairs cut into the side of the cliff. 'You live with Peter?' she mutters.

'Yes, I'm his daughter, Ellie.'

She glances back at me, a look of surprise on her face. 'Eyes front!' I snap. 'It's no joke falling down these steps, take it from someone who has!'

We make it up to the top safely, but she stalls as we walk across the grass to the pub entrance. She turns to look at me properly, her huge eyes filling with tears. She bites her lip ring, and screws her lids shut, obviously embarrassed. Which goes without saying at her age, really – you're always embarrassed about something.

'It's okay,' I assure her. 'Dad is busy downstairs getting the bar sorted. We can go in the back way. Nobody will see you.'

She nods, and for a moment I think she might even say thank you. The moment passes quickly, and she follows me around to the back of the building. Smoke is coming from the chimneys, and the light dusting of snow has settled on the thatch. It looks super-pretty, like something from a film, and I might have stopped to appreciate it if not for the fact that I'm freezing my arse off.

We go upstairs, and I lead her back to my room. I give her my robe and tell her to dry off in the bathroom. I do the same in my dad's, cautiously checking first, just in case he's in the sack with Sharon Stone or something.

I feel better as soon as I've peeled off my jeans, and when the shaking stops, I head to the kitchen to make drinks. Hot chocolates for us both, I decide, as well as a couple of the cookies I made earlier. I carry them back through into my room, knocking on the door before I go in. I find her bundled up in the robe, a towel turbaned around her head. Her damp jacket is thrown on the floor, and her headphones abandoned next to it. She's staring at the photos that are pinned to the cork notice board. I remember her 'feck off', and my conclusion that she was part of the Byrne family.

She reaches out, touches the picture of me and Liam in our Tenerife T-shirts. 'This is you...' she murmurs. 'And Liam? Is this Liam?'

'Yep. When he was half the size he is now. See that one of him jumping off the cliff there? He was always doing stuff like that.'

She looks at me, her eyebrows raised in surprise. 'Really? Because he's super dull now. Like, brain-numbingly boring.'

I didn't think he was boring, but she is a teenager. Everyone is boring. Still, this is the longest sentence I've heard from her, and I notice that she has an unusual accent. I can't quite locate it, but it's definitely not local. It's a strange mix.

'You know Liam well?'

'Yeah. He's my, um, dad. Stepdad. Male authority figure. Whatever.'

Wow. I was not expecting that. She's got to be somewhere between fifteen and eighteen. I wonder how long Liam has been in her life?

She dismisses the whole thing with a wave of her hand and takes the offered mug of steaming hot chocolate. She sits on the edge of my bed, and I immediately wrap Bernadette's hand-crafted shawl around her shoulders. She glares at me for a moment, as though about to tell me off for daring to show some concern.

'Don't bother,' I say, beating her to it. 'I am impervious to your abuse. It just slides off me.'

'Impervious?' she says, raising an eyebrow at me. 'Does that mean you're not a pervert?'

'I suspect you know what it means, but for the record no, I'm not. Now, what the hell was that out there? And don't try to bull-shit me. I'm impervious to that as well.'

She snorts into her drink and shakes her head. The towel promptly falls off. She takes a nibble at one of the cookies, and nods. 'These aren't awful,' she mutters, which I suspect is a high compliment.

'Be still, my beating heart. Can I put that on my business cards?'

She bites back a laugh, because it's not cool to laugh.

'I wasn't trying to kill myself,' she says, staring into her mug. 'So don't go running off to tell Liam I was. You didn't need to come and get me. I swam at regional level; I know what I'm doing.'

'Maybe. But you might not know this coast as well as others. You have to respect the sea, the currents, especially on a wild day like this. And that was not just going for a swim... what's your name, anyway?'

'Bella. And okay, yes, you're right – I should have been more careful.'

'You shouldn't have been doing it at all. And if you were planning on sea swimming in December, then at the very least you need a wetsuit, and a buddy.'

'Well, you were my buddy, weren't you?'

Like all teenagers everywhere, she is desperate to win the argument and have the last word. 'I was not your buddy, no. I was someone trying to enjoy a walk on the beach who saw a young woman disappear into the ocean. With bloody headphones on.'

She grimaces and looks at the abandoned headset on the floor. 'He's going to kill me. They're my third pair this year.'

'That's for you to deal with. I'd guess they're dead, but who knows? How are you feeling now, Bella?'

She sips some more hot chocolate and bites the inside of her cheek. She is jittery, her knee rising and falling as her toes tap the carpet. 'I'm okay. Warming up. Please don't tell him.'

That all comes out in a jumble, and she meets my eyes properly. There is an imploring look in them, but also a hint of manipulation. I'd guess those big baby blues have got her a lot of leeway over the years. I shake my head.

'Impervious to that too. And please don't ask me not to tell him – I have to. I won't over-dramatise it, or claim I have any clue what your motives are or what you intended, but I need to tell him. Where are you staying? With Bernadette and Brian?'

The baby blues narrow a little, but she nods. 'Yeah. Some of the time. But I move around, stay with my cousins, and at Rosings sometimes.'

Rosings... the name is familiar, but it takes me a few moments to put my finger on it. Rosings Hall is the abandoned manor house that we used to hang out in as kids. It was a shell of a place last time I was here, but Bella is talking about it as though it's a place to live, so I guess that is yet another thing that's changed.

I am literally made of questions at this point, but I hold back. Bella is clearly a smart operator, and I feel like I have to stay on my toes around her. I remember better than most exactly how clever girls of that age can be.

'Right. Well, get yourself properly dried off. You'll have to wear some of my clothes for now.'

She looks horrified, and mutters a shocked 'No way!' I laugh out loud – her reaction is so genuine, so disgusted, that I have to.

'It's that or my dad's,' I reply, rooting through the wardrobe. I find a few things that got left behind in the move and throw them onto the bed. They're a bit dusty, but at least they're black and a bit more cool than my current outfits, at least to someone like Bella. She pokes the black jeans with one finger, but manages a smile for the Nirvana T-shirt with the yellow smiley face on it.

'I've got one of these,' she says, grinning, 'but it's a new one. This is, like, ancient.'

'Yep. It's vintage, like me. Come on, get yourself sorted. Then you can have the unrivalled pleasure of me driving you home.'

'Why will that be a pleasure?'

'I lied. It won't. I haven't ever officially driven in the UK – it will be terrifying. Just think of it as a theme park ride that could end in death.'

'Cool,' she says, sounding way too enthusiastic.

ELEVEN

I was hoping that my dad would have retired his ancient Aston Martin and replaced it with something more practical – ideally a tiny city car with automatic gears. No such luck. Queen Mildred, as he always called her, is still gracing the garage.

Bella's eyes widen as she runs her hands over Mildred's smooth curves, the silver paintwork shining, the roof thankfully up. It's not a day for cruising the country lanes in a convertible.

'This is even more ancient than you,' she comments, touching the famous winged insignia. 'It's kind of James Bond-y.'

'You're not wrong. This is a 1986 Aston Martin, and I was born in 1987. Not the most family-friendly of cars, but I have many happy memories of our times in Queen Mildred. To give her her full title.'

She nods reverently, and her eyes run over every inch of the car. Dad had given me the keys once I promised to treat her with the respect she deserves, and after asking me lots of questions about my driving experience. Not many people drive stick shift cars in the States, but I learned in one back here – in fact I learned in this very car, with my Dad. I was going to take my test here, but time ran out, and I did it in California instead. This, I tell myself as

I slide into the cream leather seats, will be fun, and I'm sure it will all come back to me.

It does, eventually. After a few stop-starts, and more than the occasional stall. Bella doesn't seem to care, or even notice. She's switched off again and is staring out of the window, tugging absent-mindedly at her lip ring. I don't attempt to make conversation – I recognise that look, and I'd be wasting my time. Plus it means I can concentrate on the driving instead. The roads haven't changed much, and there aren't vast amounts of traffic at this time of year. In less than ten minutes, I am taking Queen Mildred up the steep hill that leads to both Rosings and the more recently constructed Byrne house.

I park up outside the new build, realising that it has been built in the grounds of the older house. It's all on one level, sprawling in its own garden, which is filled with children's play equipment – swings and slides, a wooden climbing frame. A couple of abandoned footballs are scattered around, along with goal nets. I smile, imagining how much joy grandchildren will have brought to Bernadette and Brian's life. With eight kids of their own, I'm guessing the next generation will be plentiful. Probably enough for a whole football tournament.

I get out of the car, pausing to appreciate the serenity of the location. The hill looks down over the village and out towards the ocean. It is beautiful, surrounded by woods, the only sound that of birdsong. Until, that is, the world's biggest screech rends the air in two.

'Ellie de Vere, as I live and breathe!' Bernadette screams, her voice as loud and strong as ever. She is a tiny woman but has some kind of amplifier fitted in her lungs – she can make her words carry for miles. Maybe she was always like that, or maybe she developed it in response to raising so many boys. Whatever the reason, when Bernadette wants to make herself heard, the whole world listens.

She comes galloping out to us, followed by two blonde-haired children who look to be around five or six. They aim straight for

Bella, but look on curiously as Bernadette wraps me in her scrawny arms. She hugs me much tighter than you'd give her credit for, and I remember that while she has the looks of a sparrow, she also has the strength of a silverback gorilla. I laugh and hug her back, delighted to see her. She pulls back, pats my face, and proceeds to give me a thorough inspection.

'Gorgeous as ever, darlin',' she says.

'You too, Bernadette. You don't look any older than when I left!'

That's not entirely true – there are more lines, but she is still trim and spry and looks fantastic. The main change is her hair. When I left it was a vibrant red like Cara's, but now it is mainly white with a few strands of pale rose red mixed in. I have a dim memory of seeing her in the tiny bathroom of their own house using henna on it when I was younger, and her telling me that red hair doesn't go grey – it just fades until it's white. I guess she's in her mid-seventies now and has embraced the change.

She casts a look at Bella, who is shuffling at my side trying not to attract attention. Ha, I think – good luck with that. Bernadette Byrne notices everything. She's like the parenting version of a special forces soldier or a Navy SEAL.

'I'll be dealing with you later, Isabella. Go on in and get some breakfast now.'

I'm expecting a tirade, but Bella just nods and meekly does what she's told, the other two trailing after her. To be fair, I always used to do whatever Bernadette told me as well. She's just one of those women you don't mess with. As Bella goes in, Brian comes out – and I really can see the change in him. He is physically the opposite of his wife, tall and brawny, a former rugby player. I remember him as a giant in every possible way. Now, nearing eighty, he seems to have shrunk in on himself. He walks with a cane, and his hair is fully grey. The eyes, though, are exactly the same – sparkling with laughter as usual.

'Come and give an old man a hug now, will you?' he says, smiling at me. I fly towards him and, despite his obvious health problems, he still manages a fierce grip. I find my eyes filling up with tears at being with these people again. The people who were my second family, offering me chaos and fun and noise, and constant rounds of soda bread toast and mugs of tea.

I am ushered into the house and given the guided tour. I learn that Sean, their youngest, is still at home with them, and still 'playing the field' when it comes to women. Cara, as I already knew, lives nearby with her family. Liam is over for Christmas from Dublin, they tell me, which answers at least one of my questions. I get updates on the five older siblings, who I knew less well and was always slightly scared of. In total, Bernadette and Brian have twenty-one grandchildren, and three great-grandkids. I am shown more photos than I will ever be able to remember, plied with tea, and walked through every single room in their bungalow.

'It's beautiful,' I say, once the tour is done. 'So much space! And so much Christmas!' There are decorations on literally every available surface, and a tree in every room – even the small bathroom has its own miniature pine in a pot on the window-ledge. They always did go OTT at Christmas, which is natural with so many kids I suppose.

'Well, with all the wee ones coming over all the time, why not? Only twelve days to go, Ellie! As to the space... it was a shock to the system in the beginning,' Bernadette replies, looking scandalised. 'The old place was always good enough for us, but those stairs were deadly steep, and it's nice to have a bit of a garden around us, room for the whole tribe to play. All thanks to our Liam, bless him. Talking of which, darlin', how did you come to have Miss Bella in your possession? She either left the house very early this morning, or snuck out late last night...'

'That's awful behaviour,' I say, faking disgust.

Bernadette laughs and points at me. 'She's not a patch on you, Eleanor de Vere! You had more attitude in your little finger than my seven boys had all together!'

'I know. I was an arse, wasn't I? My poor mum! As to Bella, we, uh, bumped into each other down on the beach this morning, and I offered to bring her home.'

'Well, thank you for that. One less thing to worry about today. She told you Liam is her stepdaddy?'

'Well, I think she used the words "dad", "stepdad" and "whatever". I didn't press her on it.'

'That sounds like our Bella,' Brian responds, easing himself down into a comfy-looking armchair. 'The other two are Alice and Alex, Liam's twins.'

My eyes widen at the whole idea of Liam being a dad to three kids. I can't make it mesh with the old Liam, who wasn't even capable of keeping himself out of trouble, but the new Liam? The tall, calm, put-together Liam? That I can totally picture. I didn't get to see the children that much, but they must have their mother's colouring, with all that blonde hair.

'Wow. Twins and Bella. That's a handful. Is he around, or does he still stay in bed until midday?'

Both of them laugh. I suppose my information might be a bit out of date.

'He's over at Rosings, Ellie. You know, the big house. He bought it didn't he?' Bernadette says. 'Along with the land. He's doing it up, gets stuck in every time he visits.'

'Wow again. Last time we were there he fell through the rotten floorboards.'

'I remember,' his long-suffering mum replies. 'Came home covered in bruises, his hair full of ceiling plaster. How that boy ever survived into adulthood, I'll never know... why don't you head over and see him, have a gander? You could take him some breakfast, you could.'

I do need to talk to Liam, so I agree.

'No problem. Keep an eye on Miss Bella, won't you? She seems a bit... down?'

I have no doubt that she will be safe here under the watchful care of Bernadette, but I feel better for saying it. She nods, and replies: 'I will. I'll get her doing some chores with me. She'll complain and swear at me under her breath, but she's a good girl at heart and she'll go along.'

Within minutes, I am waved off with promises to return, with love for my dad, and accompanied by a big wedge of home-made toasted soda bread slathered in butter and wrapped up in a tea towel to keep it warm. I really must ask Bernadette to show me how she makes it. I've tried various recipes over the years but none have quite matched up. Maybe nothing ever does match up to things you fall in love with during your childhood.

The smell fills Queen Mildred as I drive even further up the hill, making my nostrils twitch. The aroma is so familiar, so reminiscent of simpler times. It calms me down, which is odd – because I really shouldn't be nervous. Liam and I have broken the ice, and hopefully things will be plain sailing from now on.

As I head down the long and winding drive to Rosings, I start to notice the changes. The woods are still dense and wild – light layers of snow starting to thaw on the ground, greenery peeking out – but the path through them has been cleared, allowing me to drive along without any impediment. In previous years, the whole place was overgrown, the vines climbing over the brickwork, the forest creeping right up close as though it was going to swallow the house whole.

I turn off the engine, and glance at myself in the mirror. I don't know why. It doesn't matter what I look like, I tell myself, even if I am about to possibly meet Liam's wife. I run my hands over my hair anyway, untangling a few little knots left by my impromptu swim this morning.

I get out of the car, and am immediately attacked by a blur of yellow fur. And when I say attacked, I mean jumped on, licked by, and woofed at. I crouch down to deal with the affection bomb, and straight away get knocked on my ass. This is okay by me – in fact it just reminds of Miley Cyrus back home. I vow to call Tyler as soon as the time zones line up.

The puppy in question here is a mix, I'd say maybe Golden Retriever and something much shorter. The body is all retriever, as is the head, but the legs are about half the size they usually are.

'Hey, boy,' I say, tickling his ears and enjoying a face bath, 'what's your name?'

'Ralph!' a voice cries, in the exasperated tone of a person who has to say the same word approximately seven million times a day. 'Sorry, Ellie!'

Liam appears above me, grinning as he tugs the dog away and offers his hand to help me up. He's wearing paint-spattered cargo pants and a thick cable-knit sweater that makes him look like a Hollywood version of a fisherman. Really, how did this happen – how did he get so handsome? And is it okay that I even notice?

'That's okay, no problem. Do you think, Liam, moving forward, that every single time I see you I'll be on the floor for some reason?'

'Who knows?' he asks, hauling me to my feet. 'We should probably do some kind of scientific study. So, this is Ralph. Named after Wreck-It Ralph for very obvious reasons.'

'Ah. My boyfriend's dog is called Miley because she behaves like a wrecking ball. We should introduce them. Maybe hire them out to construction crews when buildings need demolishing.'

I see him process the reference, and smile when he gets there.

'What happened to Ralph's legs?' I ask. 'Did someone steal them? He's like, half a Golden Retriever.'

'Yeah. His mum was a pedigree retriever from a long line of Crufts winners. His dad was a maverick corgi who broke into the garden at the wrong time and seduced her with his roguish charm and his fluffy tail.'

'Ah, I see,' I reply. 'A tale as old as time. I presume he brought his own step ladder?'

'Nature, as they say, finds a way... and although the litter won't exactly be winning best in show, they all went to good homes. Ralph is nine months old, so basically a bit of a teenager. And you know how much fun they are.'

I nod, knowing that I need to have a conversation with him about that very thing. I'm not really looking forward to it, especially because I see a hint of tiredness around his eyes. Maybe he had a sleepless night too. Back when we were kids, I'd have known exactly what was going on with him from one glance – but now, he is obviously better at guarding his feelings, as most of us adults are.

'You want to see the house?' he asks. 'And also, is that Mammy's soda bread I smell?'

'Yes, and yes. I can't believe you bought this place... did you win the lottery?'

He laughs and gestures me forward, grabbing up the treats from his mother first. 'It wasn't that expensive. The land was more valuable – you know what a mess the house was. When I started looking for somewhere bigger for my folks, this just came to mind. I always loved it here. Back then, it was because it was the perfect place for my daredevil lunacy. Now, I just enjoy working on it. Did you know it's been here since 1608 in one form or another? I found that out using my superior research skills.'

We reach the big wooden door, and he points up at the engraved stone archway above us. The date is clearly carved into it, now clean of the ivy and creepers that must have covered it when we were young. 'I see. It's amazing how you figured that out really. It's almost as though the date is right there for anyone to see.'

'I know. I should have been a detective.'

We walk into the stone-floored hallway. I stop and look around, frowning as I try to match my memories with the reality. 'And this is... amazing. It all looks original!'

'That's the aim,' he says, running his hands over the wooden panelling and grinning in satisfaction. 'Obviously it's not. There wasn't much left really. I think it was only the cobwebs holding it together. It's taking a while, but I'm in no rush. I'm doing a lot of the work myself, and Cara's husband, Ben, project manages when I'm back in Dublin. It'll probably take years, but that's okay. I need the distraction.'

He pats the panelling again, like he's communicating with it, and I wonder what he needs the distraction from – and whether my morning encounter at the beach might be part of it. There is a subtle undercurrent of sadness in him, and I desperately want to know why. But, I remind myself as I make appreciative noises about the work he's done, I have lost the right to probe. I walked away from him, from this place, and we both made our own lives. I can't expect to come crash landing back into his world like this.

'Come on, let me show you the big room... it should probably have a better name than that, really. This is where I'm hoping to have the gang round for Christmas. I need a tree, now I come to think of it...'

I follow him through, and stare at the sheer size of the place, the high ceilings, the pale winter sunlight filtering through full-length windows. The floors are made of stripped pine, and the walls are painted a perfect shade of pale green. 'Erm yes – like, the bloody massive room, maybe? It's gorgeous, Liam. It'll look brilliant with a tree in here, and I can just imagine it in summer, too. Show me the kitchen next – and make me some coffee.'

'Yes, ma'am,' he replies, giving me a salute. 'Would you be wanting a shot of Bushmills in that?'

'No, thank you – I drink a lot less now than I did when I was sixteen. Plus I'm driving.'

The kitchen turns out to be just as gorgeous as the other room, fitted out with Shaker-style cabinets and smooth granite work surfaces. It's kept a look of countryside charm that matches the age of the building, but I spot top-of-the-range appliances as well. This would be a great kitchen to bake in, so much space, so many clear surfaces. So much history too, I think, looking at the enormous fire-place. Definitely the kind that would have been used to roast a whole wild boar back in the day. The mind boggles at how many meals have been prepared in this room, how many conversations have been shared, how much laughter. It wasn't even recognisable as a kitchen when I was last here.

'It's so lovely,' I say, walking over to lay my fingers on the solid mantel, 'that you've brought it back to life like this...'

He is using a fancy-looking coffee machine, leaning back against the counter. The sunlight hits his hair through the window, highlighting the deep auburn tones, and I have a moment where I simply stop breathing. I am here, back in St Tilda, talking to Liam. It is something that would have sounded crazy a month ago, and now it feels so right. Like a part of me is opening up again, daring to allow this change.

'I know,' he says, smiling at my response. 'Turns out it was abandoned in the 1890s. Nobody seems to know exactly why, but the census records show that by then, nobody was living here. That's another project for the future – researching that.'

'There might be secrets,' I say, excited at the idea. 'Hidden compartments, false walls, family tragedies... it could be haunted! I always felt like it was!'

'I didn't get that vibe at all.'

'That's because you were an idiot child who was too busy figuring out ways to skateboard off a chimney. The only feeling you had time for was adrenaline and the odd broken bone.'

He shrugs and passes me a coffee. He unwraps the soda bread and we both take a slice. Ralph settles at my feet, staring at me intently with begging eyes.

'That is true,' he replies. 'Back then, I was a little bit crazy... I think it was having all those siblings, and being in the middle. I had to do some pretty serious shit to get noticed in the Byrne family. Amazing I survived. Though I'll have you know I don't do those things anymore. I've become much more risk averse. Can't even remember the last time I went on a roller coaster, never mind skateboarded off a chimney.'

Part of me is sad that he has grown up. Sad that I have too. We were so carefree and reckless back then.

'Yeah,' I say, wiping crumbs from my mouth. 'I have it on good authority that these days, you're super dull and brain-numbingly boring.'

His eyes widen, and then he laughs, deep and hard, the sound impossible to resist joining in with. It washes away that undercurrent, and leaves him just looking... happy.

'At a guess, then, I'd say you've met Bella?'

Much as I'm enjoying making small talk with Liam, I'm aware that we are both treading carefully. There is the banter, the familiar sense of mocking each other and challenging each other verbally, but we are both avoiding any subjects that might upset the delicate balance. And now, I know I have to do exactly that – it's why I'm here.

'I have. Look, can I talk to you about her? And is her mum here, or still in Dublin?'

A shadow falls over his face, and the smile falls from his full lips. He blinks once, slowly, as though trying to control his reaction, and nods. I'm guessing he has had to do a lot of talking about Bella with other adults.

'Come with me,' he says, 'and bring your coffee. I'll show you my hidden compartment.'

I follow him up the wide staircase, seeing that the upper floors aren't anywhere near as finished as below. I spot a can of paint and a room covered in dust sheets, and assume that's what he was working on when I disturbed him. Ralph gallops ahead and tries to lick a paintbrush, until Liam pulls him away. Dogs are so stupid. Maybe that's why I love them – they make me feel less stupid myself. I might make mistakes, but at least I don't lick paintbrushes.

'You know, Liam, I have to say I'm surprised to see you doing manual labour. You always loved your computers and your technology. I'd have expected you to have invented a robot servant to do all of this for you by now.'

'Ha! Don't think I haven't tried... I suppose I just figured out that I like doing this kind of stuff. I did a few years after uni working for a big tech firm in Sydney, but I was working on my own projects too. Websites initially, then apps when the technology was there. That's how I made my money, and how I managed to buy my first property. Another run-down place, but in Bondi, and significantly younger than this. Eventually, as my business expanded, I had a whole division set up for property development.'

'A whole division? Who are you, J.R. Ewing?'

Bernadette was obsessed with *Dallas* when we were growing up, and we absorbed her watching it on repeats in the background. When we were little, we'd act out famous speeches from the show, doing terrible accents.

'Better than being Lucy Ewing, which I seem to remember you made me act on several occasions...'

I laugh at the memory. 'I know. I'm sorry. In my defence it was funny, so that makes it okay. So, you have a whole property division?'

'I do. That's part of the business, but I also like to do projects myself. My work is all mental, but the refurb is physical – it's a nice balance. And these days, I'm all about the balance.'

'I don't believe it – Liam Byrne, all about the balance? Mr Daredevil?'

He pauses on the next flight of stairs, which is much narrower and maybe leads to an attic. 'Well, believe it or not, Ellie, some of us have changed over the last twenty-odd years.'

He's not kidding. Looking at Liam now and remembering Liam then, it's like the Before and After shots of Captain America. He continues on up, and I find myself staring at his jean-clad backside in a way that feels strange inside. Yes, he's changed, in all kinds of ways. He fills out a pair of Levi's very nicely for a start. I shake my head and tell myself off. They're only passing thoughts, but I still don't like them – I am with Tyler. Liam is married and a father of three. And anyway – didn't I learn my lesson about all of this years ago? Liam has never seen me in that way, and that is absolutely fine. I'm only flesh and blood, so I've noticed the way he looks, but that is where it stops.

'Where are we going?' I ask. 'Outer space?'

'Do you still make Uranus jokes?'

'Of course I do! The day I tire of Uranus, I tire of life...'

He laughs and shakes his head, then opens a creaking door at the top of the narrow stairs. I follow him through, and gasp in delight when I see that we are in one of the house's turrets. It's obviously a place he spends time, set up with a two-seater sofa and a dog bed for Ralph, as well as a mini-fridge.

The couch is covered in a multi-coloured blanket that I recognise immediately as Bernadette's handiwork. Speakers have been put up in the tiny alcoves, and a laptop sits on a small desk. There are framed photos of the children and a stunning blonde woman I assume is his wife, and a stack of books. Some are guides to restoring heritage properties, one is a history of the local area, and another seems to be a self-help manual that helps you find inner peace through carpentry.

I flash back to when he was stroking that wood panelling, and the genuine enthusiasm in his voice when he talked about the renovations. Being hands-on with this is obviously his version of baking. Meditation through action.

I don't mention that book. How Liam finds his inner peace, and why he needs to search for it, are his business. On top of the pile is a paperback copy of a crime novel, which seems like safer ground.

I pick it up and look at the blurb. A serial killer terrorising a small town, and a maverick cop trying to take him down. I pull a face. 'Gruesome stuff.'

'Yeah. I can't take risks myself anymore, so I read this kind of thing. Also, reminds me how good my life actually is. No serial killers.'

'That we know of.'

'True. I've always had my suspicions about Doris though. So, this is my office-slash-man-cave...'

The quirky room is not big, but when he pulls open the curtains, I see what makes it so special. It is the breathtaking panoramic view.

Liam rolls the small sofa on its wheels, and turns it to face the window. It's obviously something he does a lot, and it fits perfectly. I sit down and stare in wonder at the vista in front of me. I can see the woodlands tumbling down the hill past the bungalow, and the road winding into St Tilda. The little buildings curve around the village green, their rooftops dusted with snow. I see the smoke curling from the chimney of the inn, and vivid flashes of colour that mark out the bay – red and gold rock faces, yellow sand, the blue and white ripple of the waves. After that, infinity – the Atlantic Ocean in all her splendour. Endless and glorious, the unknowable space between my two homes.

I sigh at how beautiful it is, and how far it stretches – not just our little corner of Cornwall, but the whole coastline, curving around as far as the eye can see, a jumble of church spires and green fields and clifftops. It melts me, and any tiny scrap of reserve I had left disappears. I feel tears spill from my eyes, the weight of this moment swallowing me whole. My childhood. The way it abruptly ended. The break with Liam, which now seems so juvenile but for so many years has been emotionally choking. It's as though sitting here with this man, looking down at this magical landscape, somehow unblocks it all – and there is no way to stop those tears. I am crying me a river.

He glances over but says nothing. Just reaches out and holds my hand. It is so perfect, exactly like something he would have done all those years ago. He lets me cry, but gently strokes my fingers, letting me know that I am not alone. After a few moments, when I finally pull myself together, I look up at him apologetically.

'You all right, teenage dirtbag?' he says, infusing his words with the same mock-aggressive tone we used to use when we were kids. When taking the piss was the way we communicated our affection towards each other. That song was like our theme tune.

'Yeah, all good, pimple-face. Just… it's weird, but I feel homesick.'

'For New York?'

'No. For St Tilda. Even though I'm actually here. It's like this is all some weird out of body experience and I'll wake up in Brooklyn.'

He nods and doesn't call me a nutter – which is a sign of how mature we are these days.

'Nutter,' he says firmly, making me laugh. 'But yeah, I get it. I moved around a fair bit, and it gives you a kind of whiplash, not being sure where you're from and where you belong. Growing up in Ireland, then here, then Australia, then briefly Denmark, then Dublin.'

'Denmark?' I repeat, having not heard that part before. I suppose there's an awful lot I haven't heard before. I wipe my tears with the back of my hand, and it gives me the excuse to disentangle my fingers from his. It was starting to feel too natural.

He stares out at the view and is silent for a moment. Did I not say it out loud, I wonder?

'Anna, my wife, was Danish. She wanted to go home.'

'I suppose we all do, in our own way. It's just about figuring out where that is. What was it like, Denmark?'

It hasn't escaped my attention that he said his wife *was* Danish. I have no clue what that means, or if it was a figure of speech, and I wait to let it unfold.

'Nice. Friendly. Plus the language is frankly hilarious – you'd have laughed your arse off, and spent ages doing impressions of the Swedish Chef from the Muppets.'

'I would not!' I reply, outraged. 'That would be culturally inappropriate!' I pause for just the right amount of time, then add: 'Bork, bork, bork!' in a silly voice. Because his siblings ran in ages from Sean through to Cormac, who is in his mid-fifties, the Byrne house was a treasure trove of entertainment. It didn't matter what was in fashion, we watched whatever old VHS videos were available – and the Muppets was a particular family favourite.

'What happened?' I say gently. 'With Anna?'

'She died,' he replies simply, his voice rough with emotion. 'That's why she wanted to go home. It was almost four years ago now. We had our last Christmas together as a family in the town where she grew up, just outside Copenhagen, and we lost her in the January. We spent New Year's Eve in hospital, watching the fireworks from her room. The twins crashed out asleep on bean bags. Bella curled up at the bottom of the bed. Everyone pretending that they were enjoying it, all of us heartbroken. It was... dreadful, really, but it's one of the last vivid memories I have of her, you know? While she was still her. Before the pain and the drugs and the fading of the light took her away from us. She passed away two days later.'

It's my turn to reach out, and yet again we are holding hands. It still feels natural. It's like we were never apart. 'I'm so sorry, Liam. I really am. I bet she was amazing.'

'She was,' he replies, smiling at the memory. 'I met her in Sydney. She ran the PR company that represented my first business venture. She was nine years older than me, and already had Bella. Bella was six – the same age as the twins now. Her dad wasn't on the scene, never had been, and she... well, they came as a package deal, and I was more than happy with that. I loved being Bella's father, and Anna's husband, and then when Alex and Alice came along, it was perfect. The business was booming, we had each other, we had freedom and love and so much laughter... and then we didn't.'

I am doing the maths in my head; the twins were around two when it happened. When they lost their mum.

'The twins barely remember her,' he goes on to say, as though reading my mind. 'They didn't understand what was happening. It was awful, but sometimes I wonder if maybe it was easier for them because they were so young. They don't really know what they're missing, and obviously with my family there isn't exactly a shortage of love and support. Bella... well, that's different.'

Yes, I think. Very different. Losing your mum as a teenager is a vicious blow, and not the kind of wound you recover from overnight.

'How has she been since?' I ask, already knowing that the answer isn't *Great, thanks.*

'Up and down, obviously. I don't think there's ever a good time to lose your mum, but thirteen is definitely not it. We stayed in Copenhagen for a bit, then went back to Sydney. She was getting into trouble at school, dumped her friends, started getting into all kinds of scrapes. Some of it was the loss, some of it was just Bella being Bella – she's always been, uh, strong-willed? Which I don't say as a criticism, just as fact. She kind of reminded me of you actually.'

'Good Lord, she was that bad?'

He laughs, and we both needed it. A lame joke but one that at least breaks the tension.

'In the end we moved to Dublin – this was about a year and a half ago. Felt like we all needed a fresh start. I had offices there, not that I really need to work anymore, and it meant we were close to this place. To St Tilda, and my tribe. Being around all her cousins, being around my parents, is good for her. You know what Bernadette is like.'

'Like a fairy godmother and The Godfather wrapped up in one package.'

'Exactly. She's kind and big-hearted, but she also takes no shit, and Bella needs that. When did you meet her anyway?'

I realise that my fingers are still wrapped around his, and disengage on the pretext of patting Ralph's furry head.

'Unofficially last night, when I saw her hanging around the bus stops. Can you believe the youth of today?'

'I know. Bus stops? Disgusting! You'd have thought they'd have found somewhere better by now. And officially?'

'Officially this morning, down at the beach.'

Something in my tone must give me away, and he sighs, puffing out a big gust of breath. I can feel the tension in him, and it is contagious. 'Go on, Ellie. Whatever it is, I'd better know.'

I nod and give it to him straight. 'She walked into the water, Liam. She didn't know I was there because she had her head-phones on, and she walked right in. At first I just watched, but in the end I... Well, I kind of went in after her. Told her she had to come out, or I was staying with her. Once we were out, I took her back up to the inn and got her dried off, gave her a change of clothes. She insisted she was just going for a swim, and that she was a strong swimmer. By the time we got to your folks' house she seemed quiet but relatively okay.'

I leave it at that because, truthfully, that is all that happened.

There is nothing to be gained here by me giving my opinion or adding to his worries – he knows her better than I do, and he has lived with her since she was little. He closes his eyes for a moment, processing it all.

'Well, first of all thank you, Ellie. For going in to get her, and helping her afterwards. And she is a good swimmer, but that was still a stupid and dangerous thing to do. I don't think she's... looking to end it all or anything – but I don't ever really know. She's had therapists, and I try talking to her, but she's... Well, she's seventeen. Sometimes she opens up to me, sometimes she treats me like I'm the enemy.'

'Because that's how it feels to her, Liam. Even without losing her mum, she's going through that stage where she's finding her own identity, breaking away from you. It's completely natural and normal. But if you throw in the trauma as well, the upheaval, then it's even more difficult. I just wanted to tell you about it.'

He nods and pats his lap. Ralph jumps up on it and licks his face. 'Yeah, I'm glad you did. I'll talk to her. Any advice?'

'I don't feel I'm in a position to offer advice, Liam. I barely know her. Let's be honest I barely know you these days...'

He smiles, and it warms my heart to see how genuine a smile it is. The years melt away from us both, and this new, sensible, inner-peace-seeking Liam co-exists with my old friend.

'I'm not sure that's true,' he says. 'Yes, we have a lot to catch up on, but we've still got the same hearts. The same souls.'

It should sound corny, but somehow it doesn't. All I can do is nod. He's right. This all feels natural, the way we have picked up where we left off. He has changed, but he is still him.

'Okay. I'd say don't make a huge deal out of it, then, Liam. Be clear that she has to talk to you about it, and dig as deep as you can into what her motivations are, but don't let it escalate. You want her to open up, not shut you out. She'll be looking for any opportunity to make you the enemy, to close down, so try not to give her one. Don't get sucked into her drama, because she'll use it to deflect from what's actually going on.'

'A bit like the last time we spoke?' he asks, a gentle smile on his lips. 'When you goaded me into calling you names?'

'A moody cow, to be precise,' I say, sighing a little. 'And yes, exactly like that. I'm sure you're right, she wasn't trying to actually kill herself – but she was being careless with her own safety. She really didn't seem bothered about the potential danger she was in. Now, I know she's not your biological daughter, but you yourself know a thing or two about that – the crazy shit you got up to at her age? But that felt different. You did it because it gave you a kind of high. Bella did not look like she was doing this for a high.'

He listens and takes it all in, nodding as he cuddles the dog into his chest. I can't imagine how hard all of this is for him, navigating not only his own grief, but that of his own young children and a teenage girl.

'On the bright side,' I add, 'she does now have my old Nirvana T-shirt.'

'Your smiley face one? Oh, there's no way you're getting that back unless you do a ninja raid on her room.'

I frown, giving this some consideration. 'I think I could pull that off. It's a bungalow after all. But... well, maybe it's better she has it. It was just sitting in my old wardrobe gathering dust. Smelling more like mothballs than teen spirit. Right, I'd better make a move. I'm meeting my dad for lunch.'

Liam puts Ralph down on the floor, and we make our way back down all the stairs. I still can't quite believe what he's done with this house, and the way he has changed. It's not just Rosings that has been completely transformed.

'Did you know that Maggie's bakery now has a café in the back?' I ask, eager to share this wondrous knowledge.

He grins at me. 'I did. In fact I invested in it. Seemed like a force for good to have more of Maggie's cakes in the world. Especially her black forest gateau.'

'God, yes...' We both pause and pay silent homage to the glories of that particular cake. I can almost still taste its chocolatey cherry goodness. 'So, you built your mum and dad a new house, you bought Rosings, you're investing in bakeries... and you said earlier that you didn't need to work anymore. Can I ask, Liam – are you a billionaire these days?'

I raise my eyebrows as I speak, intrigued at the possibility that I am actually now meeting one for real. And he is definitely smoking hot. He is and always will be very firmly in the friend zone – in fact going on previous patterns once I go home I won't see him again for twenty years – but still, it's a fun idea.

'It depends on the currency,' he replies smoothly. 'But I've done okay for myself. What about you?'

'I'm possibly a billionaire if the currency is sugar granules. Or dust bunnies, I have a lot of those stashed under my bed. I'm... also okay. I have a job I don't mind. I'm also doing some baking, professionally, and really enjoying that. I guess I'm a work in progress. I, uh, got divorced a few years back.'

'I heard that,' he says, which kind of freaks me out. I don't know why. Just because I'm a psychopath who refused to hear news from home, not everybody had to be. 'I'm sorry.'

'Don't be,' I say, as he walks me outside. Ralph runs over and pees on one of Queen Mildred's tyres, then looks at us triumphantly. 'He wasn't right for me, and I certainly wasn't right for him... and it was a long time ago. Since then, I guess I've been a bit up and down. Came close to crashing this time last year, truthfully – for no reason other than cumulative fatigue and unhappiness. I cried into Santa's beard in Macy's and told him I hated my whole world.'

'Ouch. I'm sorry for that too. Not to sound like someone off a reality TV show, but life is a journey, isn't it? When you're young you think everything will be sorted when you're an adult, you think everything is simple. Then you get here, and it's actually even more complicated.'

He gazes off down the hill, and I want so much to hug him.

'What about now?' he asks. 'How are you now?'

I feel like a fraud for daring to discuss my own pathetic problems when he has dealt with such real ones, but he doesn't seem to feel like that. He sounds genuinely interested.

'Now, I guess I'm still trying to figure out what I want from life.'

'And what is that?'

I glance at him, and then at the spectacular view. The winter sunlight shimmering on the waves, the infinity of the ocean.

'I'm not entirely sure yet. Like I said, work in progress. But cake is a good a start as any.'

TWELVE

Maggie looks about a hundred years older than when I last saw her. Most people here have aged, but in a way that makes sense and speaks of a life well lived. Maggie, though, shocks me. It's not just the now completely grey hair, or the new wrinkles – it's the sense of fatigue that she gives off.

I've arrived early to pop into the kitchens to say hello. When I was a kid, I spent hours in these kitchens. Maggie looks like a baker should look – warm, round, always smiling, usually covered in flour. She smells of sugar and vanilla, and always had treats to hand. I'd help out with her baking projects, and when I was very small I'd do it all standing on a chair next to her. Even when I was going through my hating-the-world phase, I came here.

My mum is a good household cook, but Maggie is masterful. Over in New York I love watching *The Great British Baking Show*, which Dad tells me is called *Bake Off* here. It always makes me feel homesick, with its pretty pastel shades and countryside setting. Every time I watch somebody's showstopper fall to pieces or their cookies crumble, I remember Maggie telling me that things going wrong are all part of baking. 'It's an essential ingredient,' she used to say, laughing in the face of burned malt loaf, 'and besides, the wonky bits always taste the best!'

Today, though, she doesn't look capable of laughing in the face of anything. Naturally enough she already knew I was here, because this is a small village. Not a lot happens, and all of it is news that is eagerly chewed over by the locals. She greeted me with a big hug, but was so busy she could barely stop to chat. She constantly apologised, even though I told her there was no need – it's lunchtime, and you expect a café to be busy.

'I'll come back later,' I say, watching as she whirls around the kitchen, refusing my offers of help. 'When it's not so crazy.'

'Ha! Good luck with that. It's always crazy... I just can't keep up, love. I'm starting to think this whole expansion business was a mistake – the café might be new, but my knees aren't! It's wonderful to see you Ellie, and promise me you'll pop in again soon, and we can have a proper chat?'

I vow that I will, and head back into the conservatory to wait for my dad. It's a beautiful space, soaring glass arches flooding the place with natural light, pale wooden floors, the intoxicating scents of fresh home-cooked food. Tasteful Christmas decorations are draped from the rafters, and a chalkboard announces festive specials – lots of turkey and cranberry sauce, hazelnut hot chocolates, and steamed ginger pudding with brandy butter ice cream. It makes me salivate. That's all my Christmases at once. I'm planning on doing some home-made desserts at the inn, and that menu has inspired me – I imagine little individual ramekins full of nutty whipped mousse, or lemon and ginger posset, or tiny black forest trifles...

I go into some kind of food reverie until the waitress coughs politely. I look up in surprise. She is maybe in her late teens or early twenties, and has the beautiful auburn hair and pale skin that marks her out as a potential Byrne. My suspicions are confirmed when she smiles and says: 'You must be Ellie!'

'I am indeed,' I reply, 'how did you guess?'

'Well, you know what it's like around here – it makes the headlines if someone finds an especially fat frog in their garden pond.

Never mind the return of the prodigal daughter. I'm Lucy, by the way.'

'Nice to meet you, Lucy. Which one do you belong to?'

She looks momentarily confused, but then laughs and says: 'I'm Cormac's daughter, for my sins. I love your accent. I think you're probably the most glamorous person to ever set foot in St Tilda.'

Cormac. The oldest of Liam's siblings. He always used to scare the bejesus out of me. 'Glamorous? I don't think so,' I say, feigning horror. 'There's Cara for a start!'

'I suppose so, but she's my auntie so. I don't see her as glamorous, even though I know she is. Maybe I just mean interesting... not many people seem to leave this place, but you escaped.'

'It wasn't so much of an escape as a forced relocation,' I say, smiling as I see my dad outside, chatting to someone as usual. 'When I was younger I always dreamed of getting away, but then when I did, I realised how good I had it here. Is that what you want to do? Escape?'

She looks genuinely shocked at the idea and grimaces. 'Me? No! I like it here. I hate the big cities, can't even tolerate St Ives. No, this is the place for me, near the rest of the savages.'

It's a lovely thing to hear, and I wish I'd had her accepting attitude when I was younger. I spent so much time fighting over everything that I never had a moment's peace. My dad approaches, and Lucy immediately gives him a hug. She asks how he is, pulls a face when he says he's 'never been better', and takes our order.

'How are you, darling girl?' he asks. 'Had a pleasant morning?'

'Yes. I, uh, bumped into Bella, Liam's stepdaughter, down at the beach, and drove her home. Got a little tour of Rosings.'

'Ah, the divine Bella – I adore her! She reminds me so much of you at that age. But with less eye rolling. Liam is doing a great job on that old house, isn't he? It was such a shame seeing it slip into disrepair, used only for illicit teenage drinking sessions and ghost hunts...'

'Ha, I always thought it was haunted! I believe Liam has

invested in this place as well. It's strange for me, catching up on all of this in one big go.'

Our coffees arrive, and he waits until Lucy has finished before he says: 'I can imagine. But you were very insistent, dear, with both me and your mother, that you didn't want to hear about the goings on in St Tilda, and you especially didn't want to hear about Liam and his life. It's not been some big secret – it was your choice.'

'I know, Dad, I know,' I say, stirring my drink so hard it sloshes over the side. 'And truthfully, I'm a bit embarrassed about that now. It's like I somehow got stuck behaving like a spoiled brat of a sixteen-year-old. Who's watching the inn?'

I'm eager to change the subject, because my feelings about everything are still a little messy. In some ways I love being here, reunited with all these people, but there is also part of me that would quite happily crawl back into obscurity and avoid all of this emotional challenge. I mean, who likes a challenge? I know it's something people say in job interviews, but most of us are lying. Personally, the biggest challenge I want to face today is seeing how much steamed gingerbread pudding one woman can eat.

My father raises his eyebrows at me, clearly sensing my discomfort. I guess my dad doesn't like a challenge either, because he doesn't call me out on it.

'Nobody is watching the inn,' he says, sipping his coffee nonchalantly. Back when we lived here, there was always someone on duty – and there was always something to do. I know that after we left, he had an assistant manager called Edward. Edward moved to London, as many people do, and since then Dad seems to have had a string of part-time staff. Now, though, it is only him and Sean – and, at the moment, me. 'There's no need, Ellie. We don't open the pub in the day anymore, don't serve lunches. All of the guests have keys, and also my phone number so they can contact me if they need me.'

'But... isn't it hard? Doing it all on your own? Why don't you get more help?'

He pauses before he answers, and I get the feeling he is

weighing things up. Potentially preparing a nice lie for me. I so hope he doesn't. Or maybe I do – what if he says: *It's been unbearable since you left and you're the worst daughter ever?*

He shakes his head and sighs. 'Darling, I shan't sugar-coat it – I can't afford more help. I can't afford Sean. I can barely afford myself.'

I'd expected the reason to be less financial, and more logistical – like he couldn't find anyone he liked, or who 'fit' with the inn. It's not always easy finding good staff in remote areas, and he can be fussy – a leftover from his youth, when he was raised to be more discerning than your average bear. 'Oh,' I reply, frowning. 'I thought business was good?'

'I suspect I may have exaggerated that, sweetheart, because I didn't want you to worry. Truthfully, things have been difficult. Over the years I've had to take out business loans, and credit cards, and have accounts with the suppliers that needed settling. It's been even trickier since 2020. I've been keeping my head above water, but it's been a constant balancing act, moving money from one place to another, robbing Peter to pay Paul, then Peter threatening to sue me and Paul complaining that the cheque bounced... I'm tired of it all, Eleanor. If I'm being brutally honest, I'm tired.'

He looks it too, right now. Even talking about this seems to be taking its toll, and his hand trembles slightly around his mug. He is pale and hollow-faced, and sounds exhausted. I have questions, but now is the time for comfort. It has been good seeing him, but there is still a sense of awkwardness lurking just below the surface. As though we have missed too much, and are both scared of opening up too quickly. I reach out and pat his fingers.

'I'm sorry, Dad. I'm sorry it's been so tough, and I'm sorry you felt the need to hide all of this from me.'

'I shouldn't have really, I know,' he replies, managing a smile. 'It was my stupid pride. Plus I wanted you to simply be cracking on with your own life. Now you seem to have taken this very foolish decision to return, so I might as well come clean. I've been talking to Liam, and he's interested in buying the place. He's made an offer, and I've verbally accepted. I'm glad you're here, really, Ellie, so I can tell you face to face. I always had this pipe dream of passing it on to you, but you've never shown any interest – and besides, in the current situation, it's not exactly a dream inheritance – it's just a lot of debt and responsibility housed beneath a very pretty thatched roof!'

I feel a jolt of surprise at this news, and force myself to pause and think before I respond. Liam didn't mention this, and I suppose I understand – it's not his news to share, and also from the way Dad is talking, it's not even a done deal. I also feel a slight undercurrent of concern – does he really want to sell? Or is that the shock of his illness speaking?

'Are you sure?' I ask, frowning. 'I know it must have been a shock ending up in hospital...'

He pats my hand and smiles. 'It wasn't because of that, dear. Liam didn't visit me on my sickbed and persuade me to sign over my kingdom. In fact I approached him. I saw what he did for Maggie, and what he's doing at Rosings, and initially simply went to him for some advice. You look upset, and I'm sorry for that. Are you actually bothered about your inheritance? I know perhaps you expected more, and so did I. I was planning to set aside some of the proceeds of the sale for you, you know...'

I'm horrified at the idea that he thinks I'm sitting here fretting about money – that he thinks I'm doing mental arithmetic and calculating how much I might be losing. I have never wanted to be rich, or to seriously have a billionaire boyfriend. I just need enough to live comfortably and independently, hopefully doing something I enjoy. Give me a full heart over a full bank account any day. I know this about myself – but does he?

'Dad, no! Seriously, no – I've always kind of assumed that you would live forever. I've not once thought about what you might leave me in your will! Please don't think like that – and any money you make from the sale, if you go through with it, is yours and not mine. I have my own life and manage my own income; I don't want to siphon off yours.'

He stares at me intently, as though trying to tell if I'm being honest or not.

'I mean it,' I say emphatically. 'I'd rather you used it enjoying yourself. Take Sandra to Hawaii. Buy yourself a boat. Retrain at RADA and become the next Cary Grant. Whatever.'

He quirks an eyebrow at my suggestions, but some of the tension seems to leave him. 'I suspect I'm rather sensitive about this, darling, because of my own history. My parents were the first generation of our family to deal with financial strife, and I was the first de Vere son not to inherit the home that had been with us for centuries. I wanted better for you. I wanted to leave you some kind of legacy.'

'Dad, come on, please – I have zero interest in legacies! I was just worried that perhaps you felt pressured into selling. You always seemed to love running the inn, and I hate the idea of you being forced out of it.'

He nods and seems to accept this. 'I have mixed feelings I suppose. After you and your mother left, it was a lifeline really. I threw myself into it to fill the void. But in recent years, it's become harder and harder, and the pleasures have been outweighed by the problems. I must say I find the idea of all that pressure being lifted really rather refreshing. Plus I do quite like the idea of Hawaii. Or maybe the Scilly Isles, because Hawaii is very far away.'

I hate to think of his life being a void after we left, but I know it is true. I can't blame myself for that – it certainly wasn't my idea to leave, and whatever happened in their marriage is still a mystery. I have had moments where I have worried that I contributed, with my petty rebellions and teenage angst, but I genuinely don't think that's the case. I was a pain in the ass, but a normal teenage girl-level pain in the ass.

I want to ask him what happened. I want to ask him why he didn't fight for me. I want to tell him how much it hurt me, feeling like he didn't want me enough to even try, or to visit me in the States. But now is not the right time. He looks fragile, and I'm not sure I'm ready to hear his answers.

'Well, it's your decision to make, and yours alone,' I say. 'I am not a factor in this. I'm here now, and I'll help you run the place until you feel better or simply decide that enough is enough. Besides, with my god-like skills behind the bar, profits are bound to soar!'

He pulls a face and says: 'Oh dear. Must we really repeat that experiment?'

'We absolutely must! I will not be defeated! Now, come on, I have more important things to think about – like steamed ginger-bread pudding!'

THIRTEEN

As the next few days pass, I do actually get better at working behind the bar. Even the archnemesis is eventually mastered. Admittedly there's a lot of silent swearing, but I'm getting there. I've also swapped with Sean a couple of times and done the cooking instead, although it is mainly the type of cooking that involves putting frozen things in a deep fat fryer and operating a microwave. I can't help thinking it could be so much more, that this place has potential to be a foodie haven given its spectacular location – but that isn't my call to make.

When we lived here, there was a lot more genuine home-cooked food on offer – simple fare, but freshly prepared. These days he's even let his little fruit and veg garden grow over. I remember picking fresh lettuce and harvesting new potatoes in spring, all of which were used in the kitchens. We'd buy apples and pears from local orchards, meat from nearby farms, and Mum would take early morning trips to the harbour at Newlyn to buy fresh fish. It was hard work but in its own way wholesome and idyllic.

Now the menu is basic pub grub, with most of the meals bought in pre-prepared. I settle for doing some baking, supplying bread and fresh muffins for breakfast, and creating home-made desserts instead of the ones from the freezer. I've also started offering a selection of cakes to go with the coffees in the bar, and the lavish Victoria sponges and apple tarts sell out every time. That is always heart-warming, even if a room full of drunk people isn't exactly the most discerning of crowds.

If I had more time, I might look at changing things – but really, I don't. I live on the other side of the world, and anyway, it feels like my dad has made his mind up about not keeping this place.

That concept took a little adjusting to. I suppose I have frozen him in time as the dad I left behind. In my mind he is forever behind the bar or greeting hotel guests, full of bonhomie. Imagining him doing anything else is difficult, and even he doesn't seem to have a clear idea of what will be next for him. I just hope he's not making this decision too soon – which is of course easy for me to say. I'm painfully aware that I have helicoptered in after years of absence.

I feel like I am getting to know him all over again – the real him, and not the carefully curated version he has been presenting for all these years. We have spent a lot of time talking, and walking, and working together; it has been both fun and moving. As well as seeing so much more of my father, I've called in to see Maggie at the bakery, and paid another visit to Brian and Bernadette. Liam was there, locked in negotiations with a surly Bella about A-level coursework that she hasn't submitted. He'd rolled his eyes at me behind her back, and I'd stuck my tongue out. This is the secret that grown-ups keep from teenagers: we're not that grown-up at all.

This afternoon, I have been invited up to Rosings to help the Byrne family get it ready for Christmas – which is now only a week away. I decide to walk up to the big house, because the weather is still cold, dry and bright. We have had frost in the mornings, making the grass deliciously crunchy beneath my feet, and the very occasional flurry of snow – but nothing that has stuck. The light is so gorgeous that from the inside you could be forgiven for thinking it is spring.

I call Tyler as I approach Rosings, knowing he's working from home today. It's just after lunch here, and he will be up, dogs walked, and already in his office. It's been tricky navigating the time difference, especially given my evening duties in the pub, and I smile when he answers and his face fills the screen. His hair is still damp from the shower, and I can hear Miley Cyrus woofing in the background.

'How goes it, fair maiden?' he asks, doing a terrible British accent.

'It goeth well, hunky dude. I wanted to show you the view from up here.'

'Up where? You sound out of breath. You need to work on your cardio.'

He winks as he says it, but he's not wrong. I do a lot of walking in New York, but I'm not a gym person, and this hill is a lot steeper than it seemed when I was a teenager. Back then I floated up here on a hover board made of anger and rebellion. I'm almost there though, and I turn the phone screen to show him the panorama in front of me. I give him a little commentary, pointing out the village and the inn, and he is suitably impressed.

'Wow, that looks amazing,' he says, when we're back face to face. 'So beautiful. And you look... relaxed? Apart from the red cheeks that is.'

'That hill is steep, okay! That was like going for a hike! And yes, I think I'm settling into things. It's starting to feel a bit more normal, a bit more like home.'

There is a flicker of something on his face when I say this, quickly covered up, and I wonder if he is worried that I might never come back. In turn, I wonder if that would be as big an upheaval for me as it would be for him.

'Show me the house then,' he says, moving past whatever it was I was probably imagining. I turn the phone again, and show him Rosings, with its turrets and chimneys and golden stone. As I do, the door opens, and Ralph comes zooming towards me as fast as his short legs will carry him, followed by Liam on his considerably longer legs.

I crouch down low to let Tyler see the dog, because I know he will want to. Ralph obligingly snuffles at the phone and licks the screen, making sure he can't eat it before losing interest.

Liam mutters 'Sorry!' and proceeds to follow Ralph off into the woods. He's wearing a sweater decorated entirely with Christmas trees.

'Isn't he cute?' I ask, once I'm back.

'The dog or the good-looking guy dressed as Christmas?' Tyler replies. He has never struck me as the jealous type, and I am momentarily taken aback at the slight edge in his voice. I don't reply, and he quickly goes on to make a joke about it all, as usual.

'Personally, I think the dog was hotter,' he says, running his hands through his hair. 'It was all in the eyes. There was real chemistry there.'

'I'll give Ralph your number. What are you up to today?'

'Ah, you know, a roller-coaster ride of audit prep and spreadsheets. Nothing as fun as you.'

'Well, this part is fun, visiting friends and doing Christmas stuff, but later won't be so much fun – working in the pub is much harder work than I remember it being! Anyway, I'd better go...'

He nods, and blows a kiss at the phone. 'Okay, Ellie. I... uh, I miss you, okay?'

'You too,' I reply, before hanging up. I do miss him. I miss hanging out, I miss the dogs, I miss chatting about my day to him. I miss the cuddles and the kisses. But I've been so busy since I got back here that I haven't exactly been pining – I'm so tired by the time I fall into bed that I can barely think. What brain space I do have seems to be filled by my dad, his health, and his future. There isn't a lot of time left for yearning for my other half.

A flow of sadness runs through me, because I wish that I was missing him more. Yes, Tyler is a big part of my life – but I don't actually feel like my other half is missing. Maybe my other quarter. I miss him, but I don't feel incomplete without him. Will that ever change? And if not, what the hell is wrong with me? Tyler is fantastic. He's decent and kind and handsome, and he's made it clear that he wants to build a future with me. If this thing between us was right, that would make me feel ecstatic. In reality, it just makes me feel anxious – because I don't want anything to change. I don't feel ready to fully commit to him.

It's definitely a 'me' problem, I know. Maybe I really am just too broken to make a success of a relationship. This isn't a very festive train of thought, and luckily the door to Rosings opens again, and approximately seven thousand members of the Byrne family spill out to distract me.

There's Cara and a tall man I presume is her husband, Bernadette, Brian, a whole flurry of children between the ages of toddlers and teens, and Liam's kids too. Every single one of them is wearing a Christmas sweater. A quick glance shows me the designs include reindeer, elves, snowmen, polar bears, and even a few penguins. It is a dazzling display of multi-generational bad taste, and I love it.

Liam emerges back from retrieving the dog, and laughs at the stunned look on my face. 'Don't worry, there's a sweater for you inside. And I'm told they all light up. Welcome to the mad house!'

He places his hand on my back to usher me forwards, and I jump a little at the unexpected physical contact. He notices, and I feel like an idiot. It's Liam, and he didn't mean anything by it. I think I'm still a little bothered by my conversation with Tyler. I pass him the cake tin from my backpack, and he sniffs it, looking so much like the always-hungry teenage version of himself that I momentarily forget what he looks like now.

'Lemon shortbread?' he asks, nostrils flaring.

'Got it in one!'

'My nose has never forgotten the smell of your lemon shortbread, Ellie. Thank you.'

I'm then sucked into the whirlpool of Byrnes and swept into the grand room at the front of the house. I see a few of the older brothers are here too, along with Lucy from the café, and even more faces that I don't recognise. I am gripped by a familiar sense of both belonging and being apart. Again, I am the only child plunged into the family chaos – I always wanted to be around them, these people, but I also always felt so different to them.

'Here you go, Ellie!' Cara announces, presenting me with my own sweater. It's decorated with the face of my close personal friend Mr S. Claus. I slip it over my head, and Cara flips my hair out for me, smoothing it down with a slight tut. She looks spectacular, her hair shining and coiffed, her slim figure somehow managing to make her sweater look stylish.

Music is playing from a speaker, and a tray full of pastries and sandwiches has been set up on a table. Mainly, there is booze – endless bottles of booze. Wine, spirits, beer, Baileys. And from the faces of quite a few of the people in the room with me, they've already started. I accept a small glass of red from Bernadette, insisting I'll keep it to just the one because I have to work later.

'Ach, you work in a pub, Ellie, nobody will care if you've had a few wee glasses now!'

She's probably right, but I still feel the need to keep my wits about me. There's the walk back down the hill for a start. I see Bella sidling towards the drinks table and laugh as Bernadette fixes her with a soul-withering glare. The teenager wrinkles her nose and mutters something under her breath.

'Swearing in Danish is still swearing, Miss Bella!' she says, arms crossed over her narrow chest, her tone not one that a sane person would disagree with. I raise my eyebrows and shoot Bella a sympathetic look.

'You okay?' I ask, walking towards her.

'Well, I haven't jumped off a cliff or walked into the sea again, if that's what you mean.'

'That's a pretty low bar, but better than nothing I suppose. Bernadette is a hard one to fool, isn't she?'

Bella sighs in frustration. 'God, yes! She's unreal. I only have to think about doing something wrong and she gives me that look, you know? I really want to tell her to feck off but...'

'You're terrified of her?'

'Yes. And also I don't really want to let her down. It's a weird mix. I have your Nirvana T-shirt on beneath this reindeer.'

'Right. Well, you can borrow it for Christmas. My boobs are too big for it these days anyway.'

She stares at my chest, and nods. 'Do you want to meet the twins?'

It's an unexpected segue, but I nod and she calls them over. I don't know how they hear her over the music and the chatter and the laughter; it must be on some wavelength that only siblings can hear, like dogs and high-pitched whistles. The two youngsters run towards us, pushing and shoving each other in an attempt to get there first. Their blonde hair is wild, their blue eyes pale and piercing. Bella has the same eyes, and if I had to guess, I'd say she's probably a natural blonde beneath that black box dye.

'Alex and Alice, this is Ellie,' Bella says. 'She knew Dad when he was little.'

'Was he naughty?' Alex asks. 'Did he used to get in trouble?'

Alice remains quiet, but stares at me with interest.

'He did,' I reply. 'He was a bit of a daredevil. He liked skateboarding and climbing trees and doing things that his mum thought were dangerous. He ended up in the emergency room at the hospital at least three times a year.'

Their eyes go wide, and Bella snorts in satisfaction. I suspect I've just given her some ammunition.

Alice reaches up and slides her hand into mine. 'I like your hair. It's shiny. Do you want to help us decorate the tree now?'

And just like that, I seem to have passed some kind of test and been found worthy. She leads me away through the crowd to the corner of the huge room. The tree is magnificent, one of the biggest I've ever seen outside a shopping mall, and the space around it is littered with boxes full of baubles, tinsel and string lights. All of the children are involved, and so far the only discernible theme is 'chaos'. I laugh at the mismatched colours and the way that some branches are completely covered and some are almost bare.

'I know,' Liam says, appearing next to us. I still can't get used to how much taller he is than me these days. 'It's not going to make the cover of *Homes and Gardens* is it?'

'No, but who cares about that? This is my kind of tree! Alice, come on, let's get stuck in! I can hold you up so you can start on the bits higher up...'

She lets out a little whoop, and together we plunge right in. It's a lot of fun, and along the way I get to know the rest of the children, as well as some newly added Byrne family spouses who were after my time. My one little glass of wine turns into two, and the time passes quickly. As the kids and I tackle the tree, others get to work on the rest of the room. The music continues, and during the livelier tracks an impromptu dance floor springs up in the middle. Who'd have thought that you could do an Irish jig to the Black Eyed Peas?

I spot Liam off to one side of the room, a glass of whiskey in his hand, a slightly wistful look on his face as he watches what you would have to call 'the shenanigans'. I sidle over to him and bump him with my hip.

'Penny for them,' I say, wiping a sheen of sweat from my face.

'Not worth that much,' he replies, sounding sad. He's staring at the twins and Bella, who are dancing in the middle of the circle, surrounded by their extended family. Bella has tied tinsel around her forehead like a bandana, and the twins are holding her hands, whirling around her and laughing. It's a happy scene, but every Christmas without their mum must also feel bittersweet. He shakes his head, as though clearing it.

'Ignore me,' he says. 'I'm really pleased you came.'

'Me too. My dad told me about the inn, by the way. About you possibly buying it?'

'Ah. I was wondering if he would. And if you'd hate me for it.'

I frown, confused. 'I might be a moody cow, but why would I hate you? I'm assuming you made him a fair offer?'

'More than fair actually,' he says, grimacing a little. 'Something about this place over-rides all my business sense. It'll be years before I see a return on the café, this house is a money pit, and the inn... well. The inn has potential, but it's not there yet. Do you want to come out to the woods with me and Ralph? I think he needs a pee...'

'Wow, what a tempting offer. Can I watch?'

'No, you perv,' he replies, heading through to the back of the house, both me and the dog at his heels. 'He's a very private dog.'

He passes me a fleece that was hanging on the back of the kitchen door, and it makes my nostrils flare as I slip it on. Just like him and the shortbread. It smells of him, and it is very nice.

As soon as we're outside, Ralph cocks one of his short legs and lets out a powerful stream against a tree trunk. I swear to God he looks like he's smiling while he does it. I raise an eyebrow, and Liam laughs.

'Yeah, well. Maybe he's not that private after all. Walk with us?'

I nod, and we head into the woods that surround Rosings. It's still pretty wild out here, dense with gnarled roots and knotted branches, the ground scattered with patches of snow. In summer, when we used to illegally invade, there was such a thick canopy overhead that you couldn't even see the sky.

'I was thinking of staying,' he says, unexpectedly. 'Here, I mean. In St Tilda. Dublin has been great, but the kids are so much happier when we're here. Even Bella, although it might not look it. Or even if she's not happy, she's at least less alone, you know? Or maybe I just need the help, and I'm being selfish.'

'There's nothing selfish about needing help, Liam. The way you grew up – it was kind of great, wasn't it? Apart from the lack of bathrooms...'

He nods, and grins. Ralph attacks an especially dangerous-looking mound of earth, digging at it with his paws like he's searching for buried treasure.

'It was great. I was certainly never lonely. I always had someone around, even if they were holding me down and spitting in my face. Bella needs that – not the spitting, but the company. The distraction. Bernadette bossing her around. So do the twins.

And maybe... maybe so do I. Would that be weird, moving home after all this time?'

'Yeah,' I say, pulling a disgusted face. 'Weird and tragic. It'd make you a complete loser.' I complete the insult by making an L for Loser sign on my forehead with my fingers.

'I may be a loser, but you're an arsehole, Ellie de Vere.'

'I know. A massive one. It's a gift. And no, seriously, it wouldn't be weird. You know your children best. And what you need matters too, Liam. None of this can be easy for you. Raising them alone, missing her the way you obviously do... if coming home would help, then you should do it. I completely understand the appeal.'

He nods, and we continue on a little loop through the forest. I can hear the twitter of birdsong, and a flock of finches lifts into the sky above us in a flash of green and yellow. They're almost unbearably pretty against the pale blue, and I smile as I stare up at them.

'I've struggled, I suppose,' he says, as the birds disperse. 'I have my work, and the children, and the family. That's pretty much enough for any sane man. But being brutally honest, I've felt a bit hollow since we lost her. I'm keeping busy, and I have a lot to be grateful for, but still... None of this has been easy. It just feels slightly easier when I'm here, and they certainly seem happier. Though part of me wonders what will happen if I stop worrying about the kids.'

'Because then you'll have to start worrying about yourself?'

He rolls his eyes. 'Yes! God, that sounds so lame, doesn't it? You're right. I'm a loser. Let's stop talking about it before my ego shrivels up completely. What about you? Not tempted to give St Tilda another chance?'

'It was never my idea to leave, you know that. But now, my life is in the US. My job. My social life.'

'Your boyfriend with the dog?'

'Yes. Tyler.'

'Is it serious?'

I chew my lip and kick a pile of crinkled leaves up in a cloud. 'I don't know. I'm... I'm not great at these things. I suspect I may have issues.'

'Don't we all? Look, I know it was a million years ago, but I need to apologise.'

I look up at him, and those gorgeous hazel eyes of his are on mine. I'm still not used to it – seeing the eyes of the boy in the face and body of the man. 'For what?'

'For that night on the beach.'

I hold my cheeks in my hands and feel the blush creep over my skin. 'Oh, God. Please don't. I never, ever want to think about it ever again!'

He stands in front of me and gently pulls my hands away from my face.

'You have nothing to be embarrassed about, Ellie. I've thought about it so much over the years, you know? I'm glad it didn't happen.'

I nod, unable to formulate words. So am I, but I really don't want to rake it all up again.

'You were drunk and upset. You were looking for reassurance, not sex. I'm an adult now, and I see that – but I was a kid back then, and it scared the living hell out of me.'

'Scared you?' I ask, finally meeting his gaze. 'I was that repulsive?'

He is still holding my hands, I notice. I should probably do something about that.

'The opposite. We'd been friends for so long, hadn't we? Partners in crime, and not a hint of romance between us. Then that night, when you kissed me, I realised that I wanted so much more than friendship... in my own messed-up adolescent boy way, I realised I saw you as a lot more than a mate. And that's what scared me. You were leaving for America, and I knew you didn't mean it anyway. I was a spotty little kid with a crush, and I had no way of articulating any of it. I know I hurt your feelings and I'm so sorry. I'm sure you haven't given it a second thought in your new life, but I had to say it.'

Haven't given it a second thought? How wrong he is. I stand here with him now, as a gentle flurry of snowflakes drifts down through the bare tree tops, and I feel so many things all at once. It's too complicated to even try and explain. The reason I have blanked him out of my life for so long is because that rejection, at a time when I was so vulnerable, has stayed with me. I left this place feeling like the two most important men in my life – Liam and my father – didn't need me or want me.

'I have thought about it,' I say quietly. 'And thank you for the apology, even if it isn't necessary. I... I don't know what to say really. You did the right thing, but it did hurt. I'm sorry I cut you out afterwards. It was... well, I was going to say childish, but I think that's allowed isn't it? We were younger than Bella is now. We weren't wise or experienced. We were kids, feeling our way through a difficult time in our lives. We did the best we could. I'm glad this happened though, Liam. I'm glad I've seen you again.'

A fat snowflake lands right on the end of my nose, and he grins as he wipes it off.

'I'm glad too, Ellie. Now I'd better get you back inside before you turn into an icicle.'

There's no chance of that, I think. I'm feeling really quite warm.

FOURTEEN

I wake up the next morning refreshed after the most glorious night's sleep I have had since I arrived here. I stretch out as much as I can in my little single bed and smile up at the ceiling. It's amazing what a clear eight hours of rest can do for you. My mind and my body have finally relaxed into my new rhythms, it seems.

Plus, if I'm honest, my conversation with Liam has somehow lifted an invisible burden from my shoulders. It seems ridiculous that something that happened so long ago could still have affected me, but I guess I'm a ridiculous person. Now, we are friends again, and somehow everything in the world feels a little bit more right. It's like a missing puzzle piece has been slotted into place.

The entire Byrne family ended up decamping to the inn for the night, filling the bar with their flashing light-up Christmas sweaters and their bickering and their laughter. Bella sat in a corner with the other teens, annoyed at being asked for ID I knew she didn't have, but still managing to sneak a few drinks from her over-eighteen cousins and friends. I was laughing inside each time she poured an illicit vodka into her Coke. Ah, the joys of being a teenager – always thinking you're getting away with something. Liam caught my eye and smiled. It was just like old times, but with new faces. I'm sure she'd find it hard to believe how many drinks he snuck here before he was even her age.

My dad had a marvellous time, in his element with all the company, and also with a now semi-skilled daughter to help out behind the bar. We even video-called my mum in Florida, showing her the scenes of revelry as Brian, who loves a sing-song, serenaded her with an over-the-top version of *All I Want For Christmas Is You*. She laughed so hard she had tears rolling down her cheeks. I wonder if she misses it? There seems to be no animosity between her and Dad now, but she has never been back here. She has stayed in touch with a few people but never returned. She has embraced her life in the States, and been truly happy with Ethan. He has treated her like royalty for the whole of their marriage. So no, I think, as she waves us goodbye, she probably doesn't miss it all that much.

Sandra stayed over for the night, and offered to do the breakfasts – so I have enjoyed a rare and luxurious lie-in. I glance at my phone and see that it is eight thirty. Wow. Not that much of a lie-in then, but it felt good to wake up naturally and not to the sound of an alarm. I clamber out of bed and open the curtains.

It is a clear day, the frost shimmering on the cliff tops, the waves racing into the bay with little white toppers. A day for being outside, bundled up, breathing the fresh air and roaming all the wild corners. New York has plenty of green spaces, but at the end of the day it is a city. This is very, very different, and I feel elated at being here. At the freedom of it all.

I get dressed and head downstairs, where I help my dad and Sandra with the breakfasts, and then the clear-up. Only two rooms are now booked, by the almost-silent Mr Owen and a couple from Chicago who are visiting family for Christmas. It's fun to talk to somebody from my 'other home', and wonderful to hear how much they are loving Cornwall.

Once we're done with work, my dad and Sandra canoodle outside the bar for a few minutes before she heads off back home.

'You two are like a pair of teenagers,' I say when he comes back inside. 'Do I need to talk to you about safe sex?'

'Good Lord, please don't, darling! Sandra is sixty-seven; I don't think we need worry about that!'

He looks delighted with himself, and I shake my head in amusement. He's obviously had a tough few years, between his financial problems and his health issues, and I am secretly delighted that he has Sandra to misbehave with. I understand now how lonely he has been, and I also understand how damaging loneliness can be. It's an emotional cancer that eats away at you, keeping you isolated, preventing you from reaching out to those who might help. It's a condition I now suspect I've been grappling with for a lot of my own life. Seeing him here, right now, grinning about his girlfriend after a fun and sociable night in the bar, warms my heart.

'Shall we go for a walk, Ellie?' he asks. 'It's a beautiful day, and we should make the most of it.'

'You read my mind, Dad. Can we go to Kynance Cove?'

He checks the tide times, and agrees. We wrap up warm before heading out in Queen Mildred. He asks me to drive, which surprises me until he explains that he isn't allowed behind the wheel for a month after the stroke. After that, he gets assessed to see if it's okay.

'Why didn't you say earlier?' I ask, as I head the car along the coastal road. 'I could have done the wholesaler trips for you.'

'Sean has been carrying out that particular duty, darling. You've... well, you've been doing quite enough. I suppose I don't want to get used to you being here. It's already going to be very hard when you leave.'

He gulps slightly and looks out of the window as he says this. For all of his outward swagger and confidence, he is not a man who finds it easy to discuss emotional matters, I know. I give him the time to recover his composure, and realise that I am feeling a touch weepy myself. I work for a temping agency, so I can be flexible – but I will need to go back at some point. Back to Tyler. Back to

New York. Right now, I don't want to even think about it – it makes me feel sad. I've only just got used to being here.

My dad puts some classical music on the radio, and we chat about trivial nonsense for the rest of the journey. He fills me in on more village gossip, including Sean's outrageously playboy love life, and I tell him about my little baking business. We keep it light, we keep it casual, because we both need that.

We park up and make the climb down to Kynance Cove. It's a stunning place, packed in summer but empty now apart from us and a solitary dog walker. His spaniel is living the dream, galloping through puddles and sniffing at seaweed. Tyler's dogs would love it here.

The sand is almost white, the sea turquoise, the whole beach dotted with rock stacks and formations that make it feel other-worldly. It's like the kind of beach that adventuring hobbits would find while travelling on a quest, all twisted caves and snaking islands. You can get trapped here by the tide, but when it's low, all kinds of marvels are revealed.

I have always been mesmerised by this place, finding something new every single time I visit. Not to be morbid, but if ever I think about where I'd like my ashes to be scattered, it is always Kynance that comes to mind.

My father walks beside me, pointing out interesting shapes in the rocks, sheets of clinging barnacles, the rush and wash of water through gullies of sandstone. The sea birds cry and call overhead, the wind whistling around us as we explore.

We gaze out at a black archway rising from the water. 'Tremolite. Serpentinite. Bastite,' he says. 'Aren't they marvellous words, darling?' I repeat them, and smile as the breeze almost steals them from my lips. 'They are, Dad. When did you become an expert on geology?'

'Oh, you know, over the last couple of decades. I took a few courses in different things. Trying to keep myself busy. I can tell you rather a lot about rocks these days, and a fair bit about British butterflies too. And I have mastered the art of conversational Italian. Or at the very least, how to order wine in it.'

We walk on, and I smile even though there is a hint of sadness behind his words. Maybe this is the time, I decide. Who knows how much longer I will be here? He is not going to live forever, and I have questions I would love to know the answers to.

'Why did it all happen, Dad?' I ask, as we near the end of our circuit and perch ourselves on giant boulders. 'What went wrong with you and Mum? I'm a big girl now; I can handle it.'

He stares out at the sea, and I sneak a look at his profile. The proud nose, the strong jaw. The new lines and creases.

'It's not you handling it that I'm worried about, dear. It's you hating me. I don't like to talk about it because I'm selfish, and because I have always had a pathological need to be liked.'

I open my mouth to object but quickly shut it again. He's actually right, even though he has phrased it harshly. There is an element of my father that likes to perform, that likes to impress, that likes to receive applause, silent or otherwise. He had a complicated childhood, and it's not my job to figure him out – but yeah. I have to simply nod and accept that one.

'The need to be adored is part of what happened, truthfully, Eleanor. Your mother was – is – a wonderful woman. Kind, clever, funny, beautiful, loyal. She was everything a man could want. But she was also busy, bearing the pressures of running the business, of her own family, of being a parent. None of those things are negatives, but they meant that she ran low on time and energy. You were older, with a life of your own, and I was no longer the centre of your world either. Like the rather enormous baby I am, I started to feel neglected. It's not uncommon; men can be terribly juvenile creatures at any age...'

I raise my eyebrows. 'Well, I can't argue with that, Dad. Go on.'

He nods and continues. I have an idea where this is going to end, and wonder why I'm pushing to hear it – how will it help either of us? It's too late to change my mind now, though. He looks determined to see this through.

'So, long story short, sweetheart, I turned into that most despicable of clichés – a mid-life crisis on legs. I had an affair with a former colleague from London. It was meaningless, really, but it did go on for a long time. I think if it had been some silly one-night stand your mother might have forgiven me, but it was worse than that. It was over a year of me making up excuses to go back to the city. Buying trips, conferences, my sister. All fictional, as she eventually found out. I broke her heart, darling, and in doing so, I broke my own. I broke our whole family.'

I am not an idiot. I have known, deep down, that it must have been something like this. It was so sudden, so vicious. So irrevocable. I have always looked back at myself with pity, and at my father with sympathy for being left alone. I love my mother and Ethan, but I don't think I ever quite understood what she'd been through. She did a very good job of hiding all of this from me, of burying the pain he must have caused her. Of dealing with my tantrums and my abuse and holding steady and calm, even though she must surely have been screaming inside.

I watch the waves crash in against the rocks, wishing I could go back in time. Behave better. Show her that she was still appreciated. I have been cheated on myself, and it almost destroyed me. She must have felt even worse, with a child to consider, and a husband who had been unfaithful for so long. No wonder she has always adored Ethan, with his steady heart and his gentle devotion to her. To us.

'You're very quiet, Ellie. Should I not have been honest? It's not always the best policy...'

I pat his hand, and kiss him on his cold cheek. His voice is weak, and he is not a well man. 'No, Dad. It's okay. I can feel sorry for Mum and still love you, can't I?'

'Of course. You should also know this, though, because it might explain some of what happened, some of what you overheard. Even after she found out, I went on the offensive. Instead of apologising and begging forgiveness, I attacked. I always used to do that, when I knew I was wrong – and what I'd done of course was completely indefensible. It presented me with an image of myself that I very much did not want to confront, so I tried to shift some of the blame onto her. That was one of my many mistakes. That, and letting you go so easily. I'm so sorry, darling. I know how difficult it all was for you.'

I nod, because it was. There is no way to deny that, no matter how kind I want to be.

'Why didn't you, Dad? Fight for me, I mean? Okay, so maybe I get that you couldn't cope with raising me alone, I know I was diffi-cult – but why didn't you visit, or have me back for summers? It all felt so... final. Like you didn't want me anymore.'

Tears shine suddenly in his eyes, and he bites his lip. He squeezes my hand, and replies: 'Dearest child, it couldn't have been farther from the truth – I loved you desperately, then and now. You were the apple of my eye, from the day you were born. And you were not difficult, you were merely sixteen, and doing what comes naturally at such an age. I suppose I just... I don't think I felt that I deserved you, Eleanor. Ethan was quite clearly a better man than me, somebody who would cherish and treasure your mother in the way she needed – he would never squander such a gift, I knew. And he was decent, steady, willing to love you both and give you a wonderful life. I was, by that time, a complete failure in my own eyes. I had no right to either of you.'

He sounds so melancholy as he speaks, and I shed a few tears of my own. For him, for myself. For my poor mum.

'Once you were gone,' he continues, 'it seemed kinder to let you stay gone. I know you were angry with me, but it seemed kinder to leave you your anger, rather than let you miss me. I didn't want to keep dragging you home, making you choose. I wanted you to move forward, and embrace your new life. And honestly, in the early days, I was simply too sad to reach out. I had a few very bleak years, angel, and I didn't want to taint you with my bitterness and disappointment. Then over time, I suppose that simply become too entrenched, the distance had grown, and was totally my fault, but I couldn't find a way to close it. I never thought I would be able to, until now. Thank you, Ellie. For listening. For coming home. For giving me a second chance – because that's what this feels like, doesn't it?'

I nod, and give him a quick hug. Nothing that would breach his very English sense of decorum, but enough to let him know that he has not lost me. I am not thrilled to hear what he did to my mother, but I am aware that he is a human being not a saint. We have all made mistakes in life, and he has very much paid the price for his. She has forgiven him, and there is nothing to be gained by me making it all worse. I will think about it all later, once it has all sunk in. Until then, I will keep a lid on the emotions that are rolling through me.

We stand to begin the climb back up to the parking lot, the wind thankfully behind us to give us a shove. I am happy to go back to the inn. Back to the little room where I used to hide from their arguments, listening to my music and pretending a war wasn't raging around me. Now, I need to process everything that I have learned. I need to talk to my mum. I possibly need a bottle of gin.

We reach the car, and I glance back down at the cove and all its wild magic. He was right. This does feel like a second chance, and second chances are rare, for all of us.

Once we are cocooned inside Queen Mildred, he turns to me and says: 'One more thing to add, my love. It might seem obvious, but I must say it – I regret it all, enormously. Not a day has passed since that I have not regretted it. If I could go back in time, I would have done everything differently, and you never would have left.'

I nod, and manage a smile. I know he means it, but I know you cannot build life based on what-might-have-beens. Time machines are few and far between. All we can do is look ahead and make the most of all the chances that come our way, second or otherwise.

An image of Liam flashes before my mind, and I chase it away. He is my friend, and that is all he will ever be. I am with Tyler, and I have made the mistake of seeing Liam as more than a friend before. I might not have a time machine, but I can at least learn from that mistake.

FIFTEEN

I aim to stay busy for the next few days, which is a very easy goal. There is always something that needs doing around the inn. Not just the day-to-day tasks, but things I can tell have been neglected for a little too long – an inventory down in the cellars being among them. It was never my favourite of places, and only the fact that there was alcohol to be swiped ever tempted me down there. This time, Sean came with me and was flirting furiously until a big fat spider landed on his shoulder and he screamed like a five-year-old – that was the end of his attempt at being macho. Highly amusing, and sadly not caught on camera for the rest of his family to enjoy.

As well as that, I have deep cleaned the guest rooms that are empty, made the run to the cash and carry, and hand scrubbed the tiled floors in the kitchens. I've also stocked the cupboards with a few more ingredients, and carried on baking. That bit, at least, was a bit more fun. All of this is in addition to the usual routine of cooking, serving and servicing the rooms. There is literally no way my father could have done all of this alone, and I can understand why it all feels too much for him. Working hard is one thing – but working this hard and having nothing to show for it is soul-destroying.

I wonder what Liam will do with the place if he buys it. I

wonder what my dad will do. I wonder how it will feel when I'm back in New York, hearing about it all from a distance. It will be fine, I tell myself. I have lived apart from St Tilda and its people for decades, and I have a busy life of my own to step back into.

I have spoken to Tyler and caught up with his news, and I have chatted to my mum. She loves Florida, but has never quite accepted that sunshine on Christmas Day is entirely correct, so she and Ethan are taking a festive trip to Vermont instead. I have decided not to talk to her about what my dad told me, because really, I think that should be face to face. There might be tears, and there will definitely be hugs. I look back on the day I told her about my husband, Jason, and what had happened all those years ago, and the rush of pure love and sympathy that she drenched me in. I guess she understood a lot better than I'd imagined.

Keeping so busy has helped me work through some of it, at least. Nothing clears the mind like getting down on your hands and knees with a bucket of soapy water.

Although none of what he told me was easy to hear, I'm glad I heard it, and there is a positive. It was always painful to think that my own dad didn't want me, and the way I'd begged him to let me stay back then is a vivid memory that has left its scars. I begged, I cried, I cajoled – but his answer was always a sad and resolute 'No.'

Even after I was living in the States, I never understood why he didn't invite me back to the village to spend time with him, or take Ethan up on his offer to fly him over. In my teenage angst, I assumed that he simply preferred life without me in it. Now, at least, I have a slightly different perspective on that. One that doesn't start and finish with 'It was your fault for being such a cow.' It is amazing how much we can hurt the people we love, those wounds cutting so deep, enabled by a lack of communication. What if he'd reached out and tried to explain? What if I hadn't so brutally exorcised Liam from my life after one awful encounter? What if, as an adult, I'd insisted on coming back here and sorting it all out, with both of them?

It's impossible to imagine any of that. I suppose I just need to be grateful for the fact that some of those wounds might now have the chance to heal.

In between my bouts of extreme activity, I have spent a bit more time with Maggie at the bakery. She seems really worn down, and especially stressed about Christmas Day. She's planned a late afternoon event for people in the area as a thank you for supporting her new venture, not offering a full menu but instead providing a Baked Goods Buffet for anyone who wants to drop in. And really, I can't believe I haven't heard the words 'baked goods' and 'buffet' in the one sentence before.

'It seemed like a good idea at the time, my love,' she said, shaking her head at her own folly. 'But now I feel like I've been hit by a truck and I'm not even remotely looking forward to it!'

'I'll help,' I'd offered immediately. 'I'm much better than I was, I promise – people even pay me to bake for them these days!'

'Oh, I'm sure, sweetie, you always did have an eye for it... and thank you. Some of it's already done, the Christmas puddings and the fruit cakes, and some I can work on and keep in the freezer. It'll all be all right, I'm sure. I'm just feeling my age!'

'What, twenty-one?'

'Away with you! That and another forty-five years... I'll look into getting some more help in the new year. You know how it is, finding staff. I haven't seen my grandkids outside work for months, and I can't remember the last time Mike and I went on a date night!'

I remember Maggie and her husband always doing that, and obviously when I was a teenager I thought it was A, lame and B, gross. Now I think it's delightful to think of a couple in their sixties going out on date nights.

I made her promise to ask for my help if she needed it, and was then collared by Cara on the way past her boutique. 'Come in!' she said, dragging me over the threshold. 'We could give you a make-over!'

'No thank you,' I replied, looking around in astonishment at all the glitter and glamour and sequins. It's so sparkly in her shop that I feel like I need sunglasses. 'I'm not a fancy threads kind of gal.'

'That's because you've never needed them,' she said, 'being one of those horrifying naturally pretty kinds of gal. Even when you were heavy into the eye liner and had crusted-up puke on your top, you somehow looked cool... I so had a wee girl crush on you.'

'Thank you – I think. And I suspect that's just because you had no other girls to look up to. I was the best you had, poor thing. Still, you seem to have blossomed.'

'This is true,' she said, glancing at herself in the full-length mirror, flicking her gorgeous red hair. 'Now, I'll be seeing you tomorrow night for dinner, then.'

'Will you? And how will I be in two places at once?'

She waved away my objections, and assured me that her brother Sean would do an extra shift in the bar, and her niece Lucy would handle the cooking for a few hours. It seemed very much like a fait accompli, and yet again I was left to ponder the joys of having a family like theirs. Yes, it was crowded, and yes, they were noisy and seemed to be fighting all the damn time – but they always looked out for each other too. It's sweet that they are still doing the same as adults.

Now, I am waiting outside the inn, almost dressed up. Well, certainly more dressed up than I've been since I arrived. Cara persuaded me to take a plain black dress, the most ordinary thing in the entire shop. I felt like I was adopting the ugly puppy that nobody else wanted at the rescue centre. It's pretty in a Goth tea party way, with a V-neck that shows off a hint of cleavage, a thin belt around the waist and a full skirt. If someone more put-together than me was wearing it, it could probably look stunning – but I've matched it with a thick pair of tights and my black ankle boots, because it's not the weather for prancing around in heels.

I tug my coat tighter around me and turn my face to look up at the night sky. Smoke from the inn's chimneys is curling up into the moonlight, and the snow is falling in glittery tumbles. It settles on my hair, and tickles against my eyelashes. I can hear chatter and music coming from the bar, and it all feels superbly merry. In fact, it's beginning to look a lot like Christmas, with less than a week to go now.

I haven't bought gifts for anyone, because I had no idea if I'd still be here by now. I need to carve out some time for shopping, or at the very least last-minute ordering online. I'd already got Tyler's present, and left it with him to open on the day – a hoodie I'd had made up with a photo of all three dogs on the front. The designer had added crowns, and the words 'The Three Wise Labradors'. I think he'll love it.

I'm smiling as I think about him and the pooches, and I remind myself to hold that thought. To remind myself of what I have left behind. This has been like a vacation from my real life, but my real life is pretty darned good.

At that exact moment, Liam pulls up outside the inn in his sleek Audi SUV. The fancy clothes and cologne come with an equally fancy car, and yet again I shake my head in disbelief. I honestly don't think I've changed that much – I look like an older version of myself, I have the same sense of humour, and I haven't exactly done anything wildly ambitious with my life. Liam, though? This version of him is as far removed from the one I used to know as it is possible to be.

He opens the car window, and shouts out: 'Ready to go get hammered, teenage dirtbag?'

Well. Maybe he's not that different after all. I climb into the car, putting the cake tin I'm carrying on my lap, and see that the twins are in the back seat. Alex pokes his tongue out at me, and Alice says: 'You look very pretty, Ellie. That's the kind of dress that Wednesday Addams would wear to a funeral.'

I am momentarily taken aback by this, and Liam rolls his eyes as he starts the car. 'This is one of the problems with them having a much older sister,' he says. 'They sometimes go a little wild with the Netflix account. And you look great, by the way.'

'Thank you. The Netflix thing could be worse,' I reply,

winking at Alice. 'And anyway, I think Wednesday's quite the role model. What else do you like watching, guys?'

The twins quite happily chatter away as we drive to Cara's, which is a good thing. It distracts me from noticing exactly how fine their father looks tonight. He's wearing a gorgeous black suit and a plain white shirt – no tie, but formal enough to be delicious. I've always had a bit of a thing about a man in a suit. The right man in a suit, anyway. Like Tyler, I remind myself. He looks absolutely divine in a suit.

Cara lives a short drive along the coast, in what turns out to be a pretty spectacular barn conversion. She greets us at the door, elegant in a green silk gown and matching heels, holding her phone aloft.

'Photoshoot!' she demands, taking the cake tin from me and placing it on the doorstep. 'In the snow, now! It's *Christmas*!'

'No way, I'm freezing my... uh... toes off!' I bleat, feeling the sudden cold after the luxurious warmth of Liam's car heating. I'm pleased with the quick save to avoid almost-swearing in front of the kids.

'Resistance is futile,' Liam mutters. 'It's easier to do as she says.'

Cara directs us, getting us to pose in the middle of her snowy-white garden. Liam stands next to me, and the twins in front. It's all going well until Cara's own kids come hurtling out of the house, dressed in Marvel pyjamas and screaming with happiness to see their cousins.

Liam laughs as they all chase each other around with hastily assembled snowballs, Cara yelling at them to get inside before they 'die of a fecking cold'. So much for avoiding the swearing.

The evening is a pleasant one, although I'm surprised to find it is only the four of us adults there. I could have sworn Cara had said that Cormac was joining us, but she looks at me blankly when I mention it. She serves up lasagne and salad, matched with her own soda bread to give it all an Irish twist, and I have provided the pudding. It's a tiramisu layer cake, the sponge filled with masses of creamy mascarpone and possibly a little too much coffee liqueur.

The children are all content in the next room, playing games and watching TV, and the atmosphere is so nice. Laid back in every way apart from the clothes.

'She insists we dress for these little dinners,' Liam says, sipping his glass of fizzy water. 'No idea why.'

'Because you're all savages, and someone has to civilise you!' Cara retorts. 'Besides, I've seen your wardrobe in Dublin, Liam Byrne, and you have many a fine item hanging in it – don't be playing the eejit and pretending you spend your life in a tracksuit now!'

She sounds so much like Bernadette that we all laugh, and she feigns offence as she disappears into the kitchen for the cheeseboard. I follow after her, carrying some of the plates, and make admiring noises at the sight of the granite work surfaces and walk-in pantry.

'I've always wanted a walk-in pantry,' I tell her. 'It's one of my deepest desires.'

'Really?' she says, raising an eyebrow. 'Well now, that's just plain sad, Ellie – I'd think a woman in the prime of her life might have a few more interesting desires than that!'

She's looking at me in a way that invites gossip, but I'm saved by the arrival of Alice, Alex, and Cara and Ben's three boys, who range in age from three to ten. All of the kids make a beeline for her, all of them speaking at once. The only word I make out is 'sleepover'.

She hands them a tube of Pringles, and shoos them away, telling them she'll think about it. She leans back against the counter, and pours me another glass of wine from the open bottle. I should be keeping a more careful eye on my consumption, because Liam is driving, and I don't want to be the drunk girl in the car.

'I think we need to get Liam a drink,' she says, as though reading my mind. 'I'm sure he'd fair kill for a Guinness round about now, and he can leave the car here. I can run you both back.'

'But haven't you been on red wine all night?'

'Sadly no. Ribena. I'm off the sauce at the moment.'

I'm about to ask why when I see her hand go to her still-flat belly, and a small smile play on her lips. I smile back, and say: 'Really? Congratulations! That's wonderful news!'

'I'm sure it is, though I'm also a wee bit terrified. I don't know how our mammy did it. Even with three I feel like I'm being attacked by human baseball bats every day. Still, I don't suppose one more will make much difference... don't mention it to anyone in the village now, will you? Liam knows, and my mum and dad, but it's early days.'

'Mum's the word,' I reply, giving her a quick hug. 'I'm so happy for you!'

'What about you?' she says, tilting her head to one side. 'Have you never wanted kids? Any plans with Superman?'

It should feel intrusive, the way she so shamelessly delves right into the subject. Maybe I can't have children, or maybe I don't want them. There could be all kinds of reasons for my childless state, and questions like hers could easily cause upset without meaning to.

But even though it should feel intrusive, I find that I don't mind. It's just the way she is, and really, there's nothing to hide here. I shake my head and say: 'My husband didn't want children, and I was too young back then to really be bothered by that. And Tyler... well, I just don't know, Cara. He's great, he really is. And I always thought I'd have a baby, one day. But I don't know if I'm ready to make a commitment like that. I don't know if I ever will be.'

She turns this over, and I await her words of wisdom.

'That sounds shite,' she says simply. 'But don't give up. You're not that old now, are you? It's not too late. You could still meet someone special... maybe you already have. Besides, if all else fails you can come and borrow my boys whenever you like. That'd soon put you off. So. Let's be getting Liam a drink, will we?'

We do exactly that, and he does not argue. He is, in fact, as thrilled with a pint of Guinness as he was when we were fourteen and stole them from his dad's stash in the shed. The children talk the grown-ups into agreeing to the sleepover, and by the time we leave, Alice and Alex are both wearing superhero pyjamas too – but Batman and Superman rather than Marvel. All five of them are sprawled out on beanbags in the play room, one of the Despicable Me movies flickering on the big screen, all in various stages of almost-asleep-but-fighting-it. Alice comes over to give me a hug before we leave, and it is unbearably cute. She's so tired she almost falls asleep in my arms.

'She likes you,' Liam says, after he has kissed the twins goodnight and we walk out to Cara's car.

'Yeah. I'm very likeable. Pretty much on the same mental wavelength as a six-year-old. How's Bella, talking of people on my mental wavelength?'

'Good, I think. She's at home with Mum and Dad, catching up on her coursework. At least I think she is. Let's face it, she could be anywhere, doing anything, if she's at all like us.'

'Aye,' Cara chips in as we fasten our seatbelts. 'You two were proper terrors. Where am I dropping you? No reason for your night to end just because mine has. Liam is nowhere near drunk enough for my liking. Fecking embarrassment, he is. A betrayal of the Byrne bloodline.'

'I've been playing catch-up,' he protests. 'I've done my best! And anyway, it's... bloody hell, how did that happen? It's almost one in the morning!'

'It's the time flying when you're having fun thing, isn't it?' Cara replies. 'And I'll drop you both at the inn, will I? No such thing as closing time when your dad owns the pub.'

I meet Liam's questioning gaze and raise my eyebrows. I'm already pretty tipsy, but truthfully, I could go for a nightcap. He laughs and says: 'Some things never change, do they, Ellie? Go on then. One for the road.'

SIXTEEN

'This feels familiar,' he whispers, as we sneak into the inn. The lights are off, and I flick on the small ones behind the bar. I look around and see signs of a very good night – abandoned glasses, empty crisp packets, chairs and tables in disarray. I'd told Dad I'd do the clear-up so he could go straight to bed, and he's taken me at my word.

'I know,' I whisper back. 'Except now, we're being quiet because we're nice humans who don't want to wake anybody up, rather than being thieving little rats looking to score some illicit booze!'

'Speak for yourself,' he murmurs. 'I'm still up for some illicit booze. I don't get many nights away from the kids. My idea of fun in recent years has been lying awake anxious about Bella, and, if I'm really lucky, sanding a floor at Rosings. Everything is either work or worry.'

I feel a flash of sympathy for him. Being a working single parent is hard for anyone. Running a business empire where, I now know from Cara, thousands of people are reliant on you for employment, is even heavier. Add to that the grief for his wife, and I can't imagine how hard things have been for him. I lay a hand on his arm, and he smiles sadly and shakes his head.

'It's okay, I'm not going to be a morose drunk like my uncle Donal.'

'The one who looked like a sad clown when he'd had a few, and always ended up listening to country music and crying?'

'The very one. So, pour us a Guinness, will ya now, darlin'?'

He lays the Irish on thick, and I find two glasses. I show off my newfound bartending skills, and we settle in one of the corner booths with pints and some packets of dry roasted nuts. The very height of sophistication in our fancy clothes. He holds up his glass and says: 'Slainte!'

I return the toast, and we spend the next few minutes eating, drinking and making childishly appreciative noises.

'I have a cunning plan,' he says, wiping creamy Guinness foam from his top lip.

'Hit me with it, Dr Evil.'

'It's kind of stupid.'

'I'd be disappointed if it wasn't. As long as it doesn't involve jumping off a cliff or riding a skateboard, I'm up for it.'

He grins at me over his Guinness, and my heart does a little skip. I hate that it does that and feel horribly out of control for a moment. Liam was my best friend for so many years. He was my soul mate, my confidant, and also the first boy who kissed me so well I actually enjoyed it. But he is no longer a boy; he has grown into a gorgeous man. It is difficult to join the two parts, and it is confusing to be reacting to him like this.

'Let's go on a tour of our youthful haunts,' he says. 'For old times' sake. I'd... well, I wouldn't mind feeling young and irresponsible again, even if it's just for a few hours.'

I chew my lip as I think it over. I should say no. I should finish this drink and send him home. I should get myself to bed and sleep off the booze. I should do all kinds of things.

'Okay. I'll get some supplies,' I reply. 'You get the booze.'

We both jump up, newly invigorated, and he holds out up his palm for a high five. Then he disappears off behind the bar while I creep quietly upstairs. I needn't have bothered – my dad is still awake, in the kitchen making a camomile tea. This in itself is disturbing, and I stare at it in disbelief.

'I know, I know,' he says, dunking his tea bag. 'But I can't do the traditional end of night routine with a brandy and a cigar anymore, so this will have to suffice. Anyway, what time do you call this, young lady?'

'I call it "I'm a grown-up now, so it's none of your business" time, Dad.'

He laughs and pats me on the shoulder. 'Indeed. I don't think I ever said that to you even when you were a child. I was a dreadful father. Nice evening?'

'It was. And now Liam and I are going for a... uh, a walk. Down memory lane.'

'I see. Memory Lane. Well, do be careful down there, darling. Take a torch and look out for trip hazards. I shall see you tomorrow.'

He kisses me on the cheek, and I gather up a few items before meeting Liam downstairs. I pass him one of my dad's thick fleeces, which he puts on over his suit, and a pair of his wellies. I have an extra sweater for myself, and also a backpack containing a blanket and, yes, a torch. I've also tucked in a small packet of my home-made macadamia nut cookies in case we are at starvation risk.

'Wow,' says Liam, adding in a bottle of wine. 'Not bad. Definitely better prepared than we used to be. Why are there garbage bags in here?'

'To sit on so our arses don't get too wet. We're old now. We need to be aware of the potential to break our hips and suchlike. Is that a screw-top bottle?'

He nods, looking amused, and we set off into the chill air of the night. The snow has settled over the land like a wedding dress, and the stars are bright in the inky black sky. Without either of us saying a word, we both head towards the village. First stop, the oak tree in the middle of the green. The scene of many a before-times triumph – ball games when we were little, endless hours of tag with our friends and, later, picnics that involved hip flasks and cans of lager.

'Remember that time Lewis Jones threw a cricket ball at my face?' he asks, as we spread the garbage bag out and sit on it. The branches of the tree are above us, lit with Christmas lights that give a merry glow to our faces.

'I do,' I reply, accepting the wine and taking a swig. 'He really hated you, didn't he? I seem to recall him regretting it later...'

'When you marched over and kicked him between the legs, Ellie? Yeah, I think he regretted it! He should have learned really. You were always like my avenging angel. You were always fighting for me.'

I shrug and pass the bottle back. 'You were my friend. Plus he was a bully, and I just don't like bullies. Your brothers stuck up for you too, when they were around. I always envied that.'

'Really? You never seemed like you needed anyone to stick up for you – you were always ready to rumble!'

I cast my mind back, and nod. He's right. I was confident, I was fearless, I was capable of taking on the world for those I loved. Right up until everything fell apart. My father's perceived rejection, Liam's reaction to my clumsy advances, the trauma of being forced to move to the other side of the world... I haven't been that girl for a very long time. My marriage imploding hardly helped build me back up either.

'I know,' I say quietly. 'I was, wasn't I? I lost that, somewhere along the way, Liam. I was never quite the same after we left. Some of the fight drained out of me.'

'I'm sorry,' he says gently, his eyes meeting mine. 'And I promise you, I will return the favour. I will always fight for you, too. Just point me in the right direction, and I'll kick life in the balls for you. I'm a lot bigger than I used to be.'

In every possible way, I think. Not just physically, but in terms of experience. He has felt the joys of love, the sting of loss. He is a father to three. He is amazing, really.

'Thank you,' I say simply. 'Now, where's next on our reunion tour?'

He stands up, holds out his hands to haul me to my feet. 'It's got to be the bus stop, don't you think?'

Of course it has to be. We cross over the green, leaving boot prints in the virgin snow as evidence, and find our old hangout. I smooth the garbage bag down on the bench.

'That,' he says, pointing at the plastic, 'was a tremendous idea. Did we not mind our arses getting wet back then?'

'We didn't mind anything back then. We were untouchable. Even when you broke bones, you came back after as though nothing had happened. I saw Bella here, my first night back. She gave me the finger and looked very upset when I laughed at her.'

'I can imagine,' he replies, shaking his head. 'Little did she know she was messing with the master. I'll... I'll have a word with her though. I don't like the idea of her being rude to people.'

'Yeah, maybe so – Doris might catch her out!'

I shiver at the memory, and also because it's cold. That's another thing we never noticed back then I suppose. We often didn't even bother with coats on these grand adventures. We'd roll up at Bernadette's after hours roaming around and she'd take one look, then shoo us into the tiny living room, covering us up in one of her woollen knits and bringing us hot chocolate. Very few things in life cannot be cured by those two things.

Except, I think, glancing up at Liam, the pain that this man and his family have endured. He drinks down some of the wine and passes it to me. We've barely made a dent in the bottle, which is definitely progress – we'd have necked the lot by now when we were sixteen.

'I didn't come back for years,' he says, breaking our comfortable silence. 'Australia was a long way, and I was busy, and then I met Anna. I think I needed to really strike out on my own for a while, you know? I love my family, but we all had to fight for space, to be heard. For our own corner of the world. I found mine on the other side of the earth. I came back with Anna before we got married, and she loved it here. She'd have loved you, too. I'm sad you didn't get to meet her.'

'Me too,' I say, leaning into him. 'Imagine how much fun we'd have had ganging up on you? I'd have told her all your horrible teenage boy secrets...'

'Yeah. That sounds very plausible. She'd have enjoyed that. There's so much she missed out on... but it's been four years. I keep being told that I need to move on.'

He passes me the wine. 'Who tells you that?' I ask, horrified.

'Colleagues. Friends. My sister. In her case it's because she loves me, I know, and wants to see me happy. But it's not that simple. There are times when I feel almost okay. When life feels not just tolerable, but on the cusp of being enjoyable. And then the guilt kicks in, and I feel like crap again – because I'm scared of forgetting her. Being happy somehow feels like a betrayal. It's weird, and complicated.'

I slip my hand into his and squeeze his cold fingers. I should have brought us gloves.

'Of course it is. You'll never forget her, Liam. She lives on in your memories, and in your children. She'll always be part of you. And look, I never met Anna, but I bet she wouldn't want you to feel like that. I'm not saying you should move on, but maybe you should accept happiness when you find it?'

'Aye. Maybe that's true for all of us, eh? Anyway. Enough of this deep and meaningful stuff. Have you met Josh Hartnett while you've been living in the States?'

He needs to change the subject, I can tell.

'Well, would you believe it, Liam, but he bloody well lives in England! Isn't that typical? Plus, you know, married with children. I never got my chance with him.'

'I still feel the same about Sarah Michelle Gellar. These guys don't know what they're missing. Now, shall we move on? I know this is another sign of getting old, but I'm a lot more considerate of other people these days – I don't want to wake anyone up!'

'Where next? I'd say it would be "that crazy old haunted house up the hill", but you've gone and bought it.'

'Reckon you can manage the steps down to the beach? Or are you too much of a wuss these days?' he asks, a hint of challenge in his voice. His gold-flecked eyes are dancing with amusement, and I grab the wine from him and take a gulp.

'How very dare you! I'd say I'd race you, but I am too much of a wuss for that – you'd probably just dispense with the steps and jump off the cliff anyway.'

'Oh no,' he says, as we resume our journey. 'Not anymore. I'm definitely too much of a wuss for that. And I have too many people counting on me.'

I nod at that, understanding. He's a busy man with a lot of burdens. His life is on a certain path, and it is full in every respect. I am... well. I'm not really sure what I am. In a state of flux might be the best way of describing it. As we wander the still, silent streets of St Tilda, it strikes me that I haven't come very far since the last time we saw each other. Just in a really big loop.

I pass him the torch when we reach the steps, and he goes first. He takes it slowly, reaching out to hold my hand and help me down. My teenage feet would have flown down them, but my almost-forty feet are much more wary.

It's a beautiful night down here, and my breath is momentarily stolen. I had forgotten quite how special it is in this tiny bay, in the magic hours at night when the only light comes from the moon and stars, and the only sound is that of mother nature. The snow has started to flurry again, and I laugh as I spread our handy garbage bag on the ground.

'This is crazy,' I say, as we sit next to each other, the blanket tucked over us. I lie back and stare up at the sky, just like we always used to.

'It really is,' he replies, smiling down at me. The silvery moon catches his face, illuminating it like a painting in a gallery. 'Maybe we needed a bit of madness. Are you cold?'

'Bloody freezing!' I reply, laughing as my teeth chatter. He lies next to me and tugs the blanket close around our bodies.

'Can you see Brian, aka Orion?' he asks. 'Or Sirius the Bog Star, aka Sirius the Dog Star?'

'Probably. I never really knew what they looked like. I just liked the silly names, and being out here with you. We had such wild freedom, didn't we?'

'Yeah. We were lucky. I've missed this, Ellie. I've missed you.'

I take a deep breath, feeling suddenly nervous. Like we are on uneven ground, more perilous even than the steps.

'I missed you too, Liam. I tried to forget about you, but you were always there, lurking in the back of my mind.'

'Like a pebble stuck in your shoe?'

'Exactly like that, now you come to mention it. Do you ever wonder about how things might have worked out, if everything had been different? If I'd never left?'

'Of course,' he says, his breath warm against my skin as he turns on his side to face me. 'And the answer is, I have no clue. Maybe we'd have just stayed best friends, and maybe you'd have been my best man. Maybe we'd have fallen in love. Or maybe something else would have happened. It's impossible to know. And impossible to wish for, too, because if I changed anything, then...'

'Bella wouldn't be in your life, and the twins wouldn't even exist. Yes. I know what you mean. I'm just being a melancholy drunk. When I left here, when I lost you and my dad, it's like I lost my foundations, you know? I lost some of what anchored me down. I've been a little untethered ever since. Even when I was married, I think part of me was always expecting it to end.'

We lie next to each other on the sand, eyes locked, bathed in starlight, serenaded by the song of the sea. He smiles gently and places his hand on the side of my face. His skin against mine feels so right that I sigh out loud.

'I'm sorry you felt like that,' he says, his thumb stroking my cheekbone. 'How about now? How do you feel now?'

I know he means in general, in life. But all I can think about is this one moment, this one precious moment, lying here with him. The boy I've never forgotten, and the man who is unravelling me without even knowing it.

I have no clue if he feels the magic of this place, this time together. I have no clue if he wants to touch me in the way I want to touch him. If he wants to kiss me, the way I am desperate to be kissed. His body is so close to mine, his lips just a whisper away.

I have tried to ignore all of this. I have tried to deny these feelings, this need that I can feel rising inside me. Maybe it's a need that never entirely went away. He is Liam, and he is precious in every way. The reality of him is even better than the memory of him, and from the second he walked into the pub kitchen and back into my life, I have felt drawn to him. I have told myself it is purely platonic, but I was lying.

I look into his gorgeous hazel eyes, and know that I am on the verge of losing the battle that I am fighting with myself. I am so close to doing what I did all those years ago, and reaching for something that I cannot have, something I know he doesn't really want. Last time, he realised too late that he had those kinds of feelings for me. This time, he is clearly still in love with his wife, and I am with Tyler.

What can I say? Timing has never been our thing.

I hold his hand in mine and pull it slowly from my face. I smile to take away any sting from my words.

'Now, my friend, I feel like I really must go to bed. It's way too cold out here! Thanks for a lovely night. Will you... how will you get back to Rosings?'

I scuffle around and stand to my feet. He stays where he is, gazing up at me.

'I think I'll stay here for a little while longer,' he eventually says. 'Enjoy the freedom. Then I guess I'll walk up that hill of mine.'

'You'll be okay?' I ask, biting my lip so hard I taste blood. This has ended abruptly, and I never want there to be another misunderstanding between us like the last one. Now we are speaking again, I would like that to continue – and ironically, that means keeping some distance.

He nods and smiles at me. 'I'll be okay, Ellie.'

I nod back and turn to leave. I abandon the bag, the blanket, but hopefully not my dignity. My feet cannot carry me away quickly enough, and I trip near the top of the steps, landing with my hands palms down on the snow-covered grass. I recover, and scamper back into the inn. I hope my dad is asleep, because I don't want him to see me like this. Confused, upset, with tears on my cheeks that have no right being there. Nothing bad has happened. Nobody has hurt me. Why the hell am I crying?

I clamber up the stairs, avoiding the one that squeaks, and feel a sense of relief when I am finally alone in my room. My window looks down over the bay, and for a moment I want to sit in the cushioned seat and look through the glass. I want to see him, still there on the beach.

No, I tell myself. That is not a sensible thing to do. I need to sleep, and to let tomorrow take care of itself. Right up until the last fifteen minutes, this night was fun and friendly. It's not his fault that it changed, that the energy took a strange and uninvited turn. It's not his fault that I wanted more, that I wanted what I have no right to want.

Tomorrow, I tell myself, will be fine. It will all be back to normal, and I will never drink wine again. I go about my night-time ablutions, get into warm fleecy pyjamas, and climb under the duvet. Tomorrow I will feel all right, I repeat silently.

Tonight, though, I feel absolutely awful, for so many different reasons. I have never cheated on a partner, and I never, ever will. My father's affair destroyed his whole life and caught me and my mum in its blast radius, and my husband's unfaithfulness hurt me deeply. I would rather be alone than be the kind of person who cheats. For me, it is crossing a line that I would never forgive myself for crossing. Nothing happened between me and Liam – but I wanted it to, there is no denying it. Wonderful as Tyler is, when I was lying on the sand with Liam's lips inches from mine, I forgot that he even existed.

I did not cheat physically, but there are other ways to cheat. Other ways to hurt someone. If I could mentally discard my boyfriend so easily, then how strong can our relationship even be? Was I just carried away with the moment, or does this tell me something I need to listen to?

I have a lot to think about, but for now I need to rest. I need to switch off my mind before an emotional hand grenade goes off and blows me to pieces.

SEVENTEEN

I wake up with sticky eyes and a sore head, approximately three seconds after falling asleep. At least that's what it feels like. I drag myself into the shower, pop a couple of painkillers, and head downstairs in search of a restorative Diet Coke. As soon as I walk into the bar my heart sinks – I'd forgotten what a state it was in last night. I grimace and allow myself five minutes of wallowing in self-pity before I crack open my Coke, and get on with things.

I clear tables, scrub the bar, and replenish the fridge shelves, then pile the chairs up and vacuum, before setting them all back down. I fill and then empty the glass washer, and empty the trash and the recycling. By the time I've done all that, I frankly feel like shooting myself in the head. Every time I lean down, the pressure in my skull reaches maximum throbbing point, and the painkillers are not cutting it.

I rub my sore back, seeing that it's almost eight. Our guests will be down for breakfast soon, so I make a start in the kitchen. Dad emerges, looking disgustingly fresh for a man in his seventies who has recently had a stroke, and he gives me a quizzical look. 'Darling, why don't you go for a walk down at the beach? I can manage on my own for a while. One suspects you have a few cobwebs that need to be blown away.'

'Is that a polite way of one saying that I look like crap?'

He doesn't reply, the cheeky old so-and-so. I stay until the cooked breakfasts are ordered and prepared but am happy to leave him to it after that. For once the smell of bacon is not sitting well with me.

I drag my hair into a bobble, wrap up in my fleece, and take his advice. I have lost track of how many hangovers a walk on the beach has cured, and I do indeed have a few cobwebs. Physically, I do not feel fantastic – but mentally, I feel even worse. I still feel guilty for thinking about Liam in the way I undeniably thought about him last night, because it somehow seems like a betrayal of Tyler. I even feel guilty because Liam still seems like he belongs to another woman, a woman I never met, but who he clearly loved very deeply. I'm having a regular old guilt festival, without even having had any of the fun to justify it.

I would love to ignore it all, and the cleaning and cooking certainly helped me do that for a while, but I am an adult now, not a teenager. Ignoring problems does not usually make them go away. I climb carefully down the steps in the cliff-side, blushing as I remember Liam holding my hand on the way down just hours ago.

I amble towards the sea, standing to watch the waves as they tumble onto the sand, listening to the hiss and tug as they retract. It's a grey and threatening day, the sky the colour of ash and lead. The sun is trying to poke through the rain clouds, casting a dull yellow glow. It will rain today, and wash away some of the settled snow.

I walk along to one side, kicking at driftwood and stopping to stare at shells. I try to imagine Tyler here, but find I can only picture it because of the dogs. Tyler is amazing. He's funny, he's kind, he's super hot, and he very much wants me. He wants to build a future with me and give me everything I thought I was looking for. That should make me happy.

But the bitter truth is that it does not. Ever since he first started hinting at it, I have been scared. I worried that I was over-reacting last night, doubting my feelings for Tyler because of what had – or hadn't – happened with Liam. I didn't want to throw away a whole viable relationship just because of one moment. But now, in the very cold, dull light of day, I have to acknowledge that it is more than that. I am unsure whether he is the right person for me, or if there is simply no such thing as the right person for me.

I cast my mind back to when I met Jason, my short-lived husband. I was younger, more open perhaps. More invested in the concept of marriage and children, and having someone strong to help me steer my life. Did I ever feel butterflies in my tummy about Jason? Did I ever feel like I missed him as soon as he left the room? Did I ever feel desperate for his touch?

It's hard to see it clearly through the lens of betrayal, knowing how things ended up. I was devastated by what he did, and I was broken by the end of our marriage – but if I am brutally honest with myself, that was as much because it dismantled my life as because I loved him so deeply. Looking back with distance and clarity, I can say that I am now glad it ended. It wasn't right, and at least I won't have to wake up one day after sixty years together and think that.

None of this really helps. Thinking about Tyler now hurts, makes me feel like I've been punched in the heart. Whenever I think about him, I am consumed with guilt and regret – for what I wanted to do last night but didn't, and also for what I don't want to do, but know I must. I have to end things with him. He is too good a man to be anybody's second best. He deserves someone who is as certain about him as he weirdly seems to be about me. He says he will give me time, but I think I have come to realise that time will not change anything, and I have to set him free.

Of course, I might be wrong... I will miss him terribly, and what if time does change things? What if I just need to take a leap of faith, go home when my dad is well, forget about Liam, and really commit to Tyler? What if, what if, what if? What if, I think, viciously kicking the sand so hard it flies up in a wet clump and smacks me in the face, I just run away to a remote convent and become a bloody nun?

I carefully wipe the sand from my face, and almost jump out of my skin when I hear a voice behind me.

'What did that sand ever do to you?' it says.

I whirl around, and see Bella, her long dark hair whipping in the wind.

'It looked at me funny. Definitely gave me some side eye.'

'Right. Well, okay. Seems fair that you kick the shit out of it then.'

She gives the heap of dislodged sand a whack with her Doc Martens boot, and I nod in thanks. Teamwork's what makes the dream work.

Ralph is with her, and after a quick lick of my hands, he disappears off to run in big zooming circles around the beach, his little legs flying and his bushy tail streaming out behind him. It's very comical, and exactly what I needed. This is why the internet has succeeded – dog videos. Or cats, if that takes your fancy.

'How are you, Bella?' I ask her, as we stroll along the waterfront. The sky is so dark now, it almost feels like night-time.

'Well, I'm not down here to run into the sea, so there's that. And… well. I'm okay, I suppose. I really wasn't trying to end it all, you know.'

'I didn't suggest you were. But it was reckless and dangerous.'

She looks as though she wants to argue, but glances out at the waves, at the raw power of them as they pound into the bay. 'Yeah. It was. I just miss my mum a lot at this time of year, and I do stupider things than normal. I miss her all the time, obviously, but especially now. That last Christmas with her sucked, but at least she was here. My period started the day before she died, and that was one of the last conversations we had. Merry Christmas, welcome to womanhood, it's awful… She got one of the nurses to help me, because she was too sick to leave her bed by then. Obviously, not something you want to share with your stepdad at that age. Or ever.'

Her tone is so matter-of-fact, but it is a story that breaks my heart. How hard must that have been, to have gone through those formative years without her mum? Without anyone to turn to for help?

'I'm sorry, Bella. That sounds awful.'

'It was. And every Christmas and New Year, I get to remember it all over again. I know it sounds mean and selfish, but sometimes I'm jealous of the twins, because they don't even remember her. And worrying about Liam doesn't help.'

I frown, and ask: 'What do you mean, worrying about him? It's his job to worry about you!'

'I know that. But I'm going to make mistakes, aren't I? I'm going to do some stupid shit at my age – but every time I do, he reads too much into it and worries more than he needs to. And then I worry about him worrying, and I worry about him being lonely, and I worry about how either of us will ever stop bloody worrying...'

Ralph starts to dig a hole, his paws scrabbling at the wet sand. Oh, for the life of a Ralph, full of strokes and simple pleasures.

'That's a lot of worry,' I say, patting her on the arm. 'For both of you. Have you told him how you feel?'

'No, because then he'd worry about me worrying about him – you see? It's a mess! Sometimes I like it when we just fight about stuff like my coursework, or giving the finger to random passing strangers at the bus stop...'

I grin at her, and wink. 'You're welcome. The Ellie Dexter School of Etiquette is always ready to help.'

'Dexter? I thought you were de Vere?'

'Dexter is my married name.'

'You're married?' she asks, scrunching up her eyes in confusion. 'You don't seem married.'

'Right. How do married people seem?'

She shrugs and pulls a face. 'I dunno... bored?'

'That's just being an adult. And I'm divorced, actually. I think I might go back to de Vere, but it'd mean changing all my documents again, and then having to spell it all the time. At least with

Dexter, you can just say "like the friendly serial killer", and people get it.'

She laughs at that one, and it feels like a victory. 'Yeah. I understand. Liam adopted me when he and Mum got married, and Byrne is okay. We used to be Ostergaard, and that has way too many vowels. Anyway. Dad's up at the pub, looking for you. Something about dropping off a bag.'

I glance up at the cliff-side steps, and feel a sudden flash of nerves. I am probably just being stupid, imagining tension where there will be none. As I stare up, he appears, waving down at us. Ralph woofs and runs to meet him, rewarded with a scratch behind the ears. Liam looks nowhere near as washed out as I do. In fact he looks great, in battered Levi's spattered with paint, and a chunky knit navy blue sweater. He must have a whole section of his wardrobe for 'Hot Fisherman Knitwear'. His hair is curling slightly, maybe needing a trim, and his hazel eyes are bright and clear as he walks towards us.

'Liam, I'm going for a wander,' Bella says immediately. 'I'll make my own way back up the hill.'

He nods, but I see his gaze flicker over her face, as though he is searching for danger signs. The circle of worry she was talking about.

'Okay, but don't get into any trouble, okay? Bernadette has a stew on and wants us there for lunch. No escapades, please, Bella!'

She puts her hands on her hips and glares at him. 'Is that the cliff?' she asks me, gesturing along the curve of the coast.

'Is it what cliff?' I reply, confused.

'The cliff that Mr Sensible here used to jump off when he was my age?'

She doesn't wait for an answer, just harrumphs herself off in a cloud of 'take that!' I can't help laughing at the look on his face as she leaves.

'She has a point,' I say, amused.

'I know. That makes it even worse. Anyway, how are you this morning?'

'Fresh as a daisy. Assuming the daisy was buried in a compost heap.'

He grimaces, and pulls something out of his jacket pocket. It's a can of Diet Coke, and I laugh at the fact that he remembered. 'Thank you! I guess I'm still predictable after all these years.'

'Never,' he reassures me, as we follow Ralph on his wreck-it tour of the sea-line. 'Look, Ellie, I just wanted to clear the air. Last night... look, I was probably imagining things...'

'Yes, I'm sure you were! Nothing to discuss!' I say, dying inside. I so do not want to have this conversation. He raises his eyebrows, gives me a look and shakes his head.

'Not discussing things didn't work out so well last time. We had a moment, me and you. When we were down here on the beach.'

I continue to look blank, staring resolutely at my feet. 'You don't remember it?' he eventually adds.

Of course I do, I want to yell. It's burned into my brain. The touch of his fingers on my skin, his warm breath against my flesh. His body next to mine. How could I forget?

Should I pretend? Should I plead ignorance, and let us both off the hook? Maybe I should – but I'm obviously not that good a liar. I might be silent, but I'm also bright red with embarrassment.

'You do remember!' he says, pointing at my face. 'The cheeks don't lie!'

I speed up, walking quickly away to give myself some breathing space. He is much taller than me these days, though, and easily closes the gap.

'Yes, okay, I remember,' I say reluctantly. 'And it was just that, wasn't it? A moment? Nothing happened!'

'I know it didn't. And that's good, because... this is too messed up, isn't it? You're with someone, and I would never try and get in the way of that. Plus, even if you weren't, Ellie, I'm not ready. For you. For anyone. Part of me wants to move on, but part of me is frozen in time as Anna's husband, and even thinking about another woman that way makes me feel bad. I'm...'

Damn. Now I feel childish for trying to avoid the subject. He obviously needs to talk about it, to share this burden. I nod and wait for him to continue. 'You're what?'

'I'm being stupid, I know. I know it's not healthy, but it's the way I feel. Even if nothing happened, I was so freaked out. That's my problem, and I'm sure it will pass – but I also really didn't want me and you to get our wires crossed again, and leave it another two decades before we spoke. Because I meant what I said last night – I've missed you, Ellie, and I don't want to lose you again. Does any of that make any sense?'

I stare at him, taking in the flashes of gold in his eyes, the new breadth of his shoulders. The worried quirk of his lips. This is all too heavy. Too serious.

I shake up the Diet Coke can furiously hard for a few seconds, then before he can figure out what I'm doing, I pop open the ring pull, spraying him full in the face with chilled fizzy pop.

He jumps around trying to get out of my way, yelling and laughing and eventually managing to grab the can out of my hands. I squeal in protest as he wrenches it from me, and up-ends it – pouring the last few dregs directly on top of my hair.

'You... you Uranus, you!' I shriek, rivulets of sticky liquid creeping down my forehead.

'Ha, serves you right!' he replies, using his sweater to mop up Coke from his face. I catch a glimpse of golden flesh beneath, and avert my gaze. He looks down at me afterwards, grinning and shaking his head.

'You always were trouble,' he says firmly.

'Don't you forget it, pal. And yes, Liam – we're good. We're not the first two people to have an inappropriate moment when they're drunk. It's fine. It's great. It's nothing at all to worry about.'

He chooses to believe me, and we make small talk as we continue with our walk.

Now, if only I could do as good a job of convincing myself, and get rid of this sickening sense of yearning that is taking root inside me. I can yearn all I want – some things are just not meant to be.

EIGHTEEN

Christmas Eve arrives, and with it some serious snow. It started the afternoon before, coming down in thick flurries that lasted through the night, blanketing the whole village in white. It was worn down and trodden in as the day went on, and now it is actually pretty slippery out here. Even Cara has swapped her heels for flat calf-high boots, joining me for a late afternoon coffee in Maggie's café.

'I'm shut for the festivities now,' she tells me, tucking into a plate of lemon meringue pie, 'ready for the New Year's Eve rush...'

I wonder what a 'rush' looks like in Cara's shop. More than two people maybe? I know she has repeat customers who come to her for everything from wedding dresses to cocktail gowns, but they seem to come by appointment so the whole place always feels very serene.

'I suppose it's the opposite for you,' she continues. 'It'll be crazy busy in the pub tonight, won't it? Always a cracking night, Christmas Eve at the St Tilda Inn. I swear to God it was after one of your dad's lock-ins that I ended up pregnant with our Joseph...'

I laugh. I wouldn't be surprised if my dad's lock-ins were responsible for all kinds of things. Pregnancies, arguments, global warming.

'Yep, I'm half dreading it, half looking forward to it,' I tell her.

'There's no food on, which is a relief – so Sean can help out behind the bar at least. Will you be there? Is, uh, everyone coming?'

She narrows her eyes very slightly at me. 'And by everybody, would you be meaning our Liam?'

'No! Why would I mean that?'

She winks at me over her coffee mug, and I curse the blush I can feel on my cheeks. 'Just a wild guess. I always wondered if there might be something going on with you two...'

'Well, there isn't. We're just friends,' I say firmly. We are, I tell myself. There is nothing between us apart from friendship, and never will be.

We have seen each other in passing since our walk on the beach, and it has been relaxed and light-hearted between us. At least on the surface, in my case. I still feel more of a tug towards him than I want to, still notice more about him than I should. I wish it would go away, because it is making me uncomfortable. I am too old for crushes, especially on someone with whom I share so much history. Someone who has made it clear that any more 'moments' are not on the cards.

I have spoken to Tyler a few times, but haven't discussed anything serious with him. I have decided that I do need to end it with him, but it seems like an especially dick move to do it over the phone, thousands of miles away and just before Christmas. The time difference, plus the fact that we're both busy with work, has allowed me to keep our chats relatively short, and I hope that he hasn't noticed anything different. I am dreading hurting him, I really am, but I'll only hurt him more if I let this drag on any longer. Life is too short to waste on people who don't love you to the moon and back – that's what he deserves, and what I hope he will find.

Back here, Dad seems to be getting stronger with each day, and Liam is still eager for the sale of the inn to go through. He's said that while the paperwork and legalities are sorted, he's happy to start paying for extra staff. Extra staff will mean less need for extra daughters, so I will probably be able to leave for New York before too long – which is good, as my boss has very gently asked a few times what my plans are.

I sigh as I think about going back, and Cara looks at me pointedly. I realise she thinks I am sighing about Liam and I only being friends, and maybe part of me is – but it is bigger than that. My whole life feels like a giant question mark right now. As I open my mouth to speak to her, an almighty commotion goes up at the front of the café. Even over the Christmas music and the chatter of the customers, we hear a bang, a crashing noise, and a loud yell.

I jump to my feet, and see Maggie lying on the floor, surrounded by smashed plates and a now empty serving tray. Her foot is twisted in an odd direction, and she is white as a sheet.

'Maggie! Are you okay?' I ask, dashing over and crouching down next to her. Tears are shining in her eyes, but she nods and grabs my hand.

'I'm fine. Slipped on a puddle from all this snow! Help me up now, and I'll walk it off...'

Cara and I try to haul her up, but as soon as she puts any pressure on her ankle, she lets out an agonised wail and falls back down. Hmmm. That doesn't look good.

We share a worried glance, unsure what to do next. The café is busy, but sadly nobody rushes forward and offers their expertise. Luckily Lucy is more on the ball than the rest of us, and she dashes off, telling us to stay where we are. I hear Maggie muttering something along the lines of 'Well, I'm not bloody going anywhere, am I?'

Lucy is back in less than a minute, accompanied by a smartly dressed middle-aged woman holding a big white cake box.

'This is Dr Khan,' she says to me. 'She was picking up an order at the bakery, so I asked her to come take a look...'

The doctor joins us at ground level, immediately and with some authority dismissing all of Maggie's objections and her insistence that she's fine. She carefully examines the ankle, noticing her patient's attempts not to cry out.

'You're not fine,' says the doctor firmly. 'That looks like a fracture to me, and a possible dislocation. You will not be attempting to walk that off, Maggie, and you need to go to hospital. I'll call in now and see if we can get an ambulance. You'll need some pain relief.'

Maggie looks devastated, but then a thought seems to occur to her. 'Will there be gas and air? I loved gas and air when I had the kids...'

'Hmmm, your drug-seeking behaviour has been noted,' the doctor replies, smiling to show she's joking. 'And yes – they'll give you all the good stuff, don't worry.'

She disappears off to talk on her phone, and Maggie tries to persuade everybody else to go back to their cakes and coffees and chats. Obviously, nobody does – everyone loves Maggie and seeing her in pain like this is terrible.

Cara sits down flat on her backside next to her, stretching out her long legs. 'Pass us my coffee now, would you, Lucy?'

I join her on the ground, and ask for mine too. Within minutes, every customer who is physically capable is also sitting on the floor – sipping their drinks, eating their cake, and continuing with their conversations, but all on the same level as Maggie. Nobody has any intentions of leaving her alone, and Lucy does the rounds with refills and orders. She makes sure the music stays on in the background, and when new customers arrive, she explains what's happened and they invariably decide that they'd love to take their tea sitting on the pale wood floorboards of the café. Maggie shakes her head, smiling despite her obvious pain, and mutters: 'Stark raving mad, the lot of you...'

This is exactly the scene that greets the paramedics when they arrive half an hour later. They look around in confusion, taking in the sight of a café full of people ignoring perfectly good chairs and sitting on their bums instead. I'm guessing they've seen stranger, though, because they immediately get on with their jobs.

Maggie is assessed, blood pressure taken, and various questions asked. They encase her ankle in a kind of inflatable case that protects it as they move her, raising her up on a hydraulic chair and transferring her to a stretcher.

She is still alarmingly pale, and grabs hold of my hand before she is wheeled out of the place.

'Go and tell Mike, will you, love? Tell him not to worry, it's nothing serious. I'm sure it's just a sprain.'

The paramedic shakes his head behind her, and I'm guessing the X-rays will show otherwise. Toes really shouldn't point away from the feet at quite that angle.

'I will, Maggie. Don't worry about anything. Just take it easy, okay?'

She frowns, and I can see a million and one worries are going through her mind. 'Lucy knows how to close up here, doesn't she?' I say.

'She does, but what about tomorrow? What about the buffet? Half the village is coming...'

I squeeze her hand reassuringly. 'Everyone will understand if it doesn't happen, Maggie. Or if you like, um, I can do it? You said a lot was already done...'

Her eyes meet mine, and she looks so grateful – like I've just offered to donate a kidney, not bake a few cakes.

'Really, Ellie? Would you mind? It'd mean the world to me...'

'Of course. It's not a problem. I've been sneakily angling for it for days, didn't you notice?'

She pulls a face at me, and manages to find a small smile. 'Did you put that puddle there as well, you minx?'

I wink at her. 'I cannot confirm nor deny. Now, get yourself off to the ambulance. That gas and air won't inhale itself.'

She is finally wheeled away, to the sound of cheers and applause from a café full of her customers. She gives us a tired-but-regal wave, and disappears into the snow.

NINETEEN

Christmas Eve in the inn turns out to be pretty full-on. It feels like every single human being who lives in Cornwall turns up, along with the two guests who are staying here for the big day. They look a little bewildered as the place fills up, every table packed, every corner crammed, every space at the long wooden bar taken.

Sean, Dad and I pull endless pints, pour rivers of wine, and have to refill some of the spirit optics twice. The recycling bin is over-flowing with bottles that once contained beer and mixers, and the whole place is stripped of peanuts, chips and pork scratching. It's like a plague of fun-loving locusts have descended.

Empty glasses pile up along the bar, all three of us scurrying to load and unload the machine, tugging it open with vast clouds of steam in our eagerness to keep the drinks flowing.

A few of the Byrnes have brought guitars and banjos, and some of the locals are singing along – anything from Christmas carols to fishing shanties to Slade. People are jigging in a cleared space in the middle of the room, and the mood is high, cheeks bright pink from the roaring fire in the hearth and the sheer jollity of being alive and in such good company.

I have been dragged onto the impromptu dance floor a few times, and have had to swerve several villagers who have come brandishing their own mistletoe. My dad, the old flirt that he is, also has some pinned up at one end of the bar. I've insisted that I stick at the other end, because I am nowhere near drunk enough to want to lock lips with anybody here. Except one, of course, and he is also keeping a cautious eye on the roving kissing stations.

Liam is tucked away with the rest of his family, apart from Bernadette, who has stayed at home to look after all the small children. Cara's three boys are there, along with Alice and Alex, and a host of other younger grandkids. I can only imagine how high the excitement levels are in that house – not only are they all together, but it is Christmas Eve. That's crack cocaine for the under-tens.

Bella is here, along with her cousin Lucy and a few other older Byrnes. She's wearing my Nirvana T-shirt, and is minesweeping the tables when she thinks nobody is looking. She looks happy enough though, which is wonderful to see. Her story about her last Christmas with her mum has lodged itself in my heart like a splinter, and I have to fight the urge to run over and hug her. She wouldn't thank me for it, especially as I stink of spilled beer and exhaustion.

My dad rings the big brass bell that hangs over the bar at eleven o'clock, and shouts in his very best landlord voice: 'Ladies and gentlemen, last orders at the bar!'

There is a predictable rush after that, a human tsunami of customers. People double up, getting in extra rounds and whisky chasers and triple Baileys, and by the end of it there is not a single clean glass left in the building. I know a select few will end up staying behind for another hour or so, or even longer. I may have imagined it, but I'm fairly sure I remember coming downstairs as a kid one Christmas morning and finding the village postman still snoring in a corner, his feet propped up on a chair, surrounded by empty pint glasses.

Still, this is the last round that will be paid for, and I am almost trembling with relief. Sean and I exchange a look, and he grins at me. 'We did it!' he says, offering me his palm for a high five.

'We certainly did,' I murmur, feeling both wiped out and full of adrenaline. Working behind a bar is a kind of performance, in a way. You have to engage with so many people, exchange greetings and stories and listen to complaints, all the time giving the impression that there is absolutely nothing you would rather be doing right in that moment. It's why my dad has always been so good at it, and why I need to climb into an ice bath and sleep for a thousand years.

Tomorrow is going to be busy too. We have been invited to Sandra's for Christmas lunch, and to meet her daughter, who is home from London. But after Maggie's accident, I am going to duck out and head straight to the café. She's sent me a huge list of instructions on WhatsApp, followed by some very random emojis which possibly coincided with her drugs kicking in. The X-rays did indeed reveal a fracture, and she will be staying in hospital until she can have surgery to fix it.

Although I reassured her that I would be okay and that everything was absolutely under control, I am secretly terrified. Lucy has agreed to come and help, along with any able-bodied friends she can rope in, so I'm sure we'll be fine. It's a buffet full of cakes, not a gourmet Michelin-starred taster menu, and it will all be splendid. I repeat this to myself over and over again in an attempt to make it stick.

I pour myself a small glass of prosecco to celebrate the end of the working night, determined to stick to the one so I can be fully focused tomorrow. Or at least ninety per cent focused, being realistic.

I have only taken a few sips when Sean drags me off for a dance. The unofficial house band has launched into a spirited version of *Santa Claus is Comin' to Town*, everybody singing along in the chorus, a whirling group of us jigging around in a big circle. That segues into *Fairytale of New York*, and all of us screeching the words so loud my eardrums almost burst. Everyone seems to get up for this one, including the teenagers. A timeless classic.

Liam is in the mix too, screaming Shane MacGowan's insults at me as I scream my own back. This is familiar territory for us, a song that we have sung with each other countless times. I know my knees won't thank me for it in the morning, but it is such fun, bouncing up and down and yelling, and when it draws to a close we fall against each other, laughing and sweaty.

'Just like old times!' he says, steadying me with his hands on my shoulders. I gaze up at him with a big smile on my face, knowing I must look awful but not really caring.

'Yep, but with less booze – in my case at least.'

People are flagging after their exertions, and only a few of us are left standing as the music changes to a far more sedate choice – *Last Christmas* by Wham! Another classic, and it works surprisingly well on the guitar, Brian's melodic voice rising over the chatter of the crowd.

Liam reaches out and tucks a strand of my messy hair behind my ear, and even that small contact feels intense.

'I must look like crap,' I mutter, as he stares down at me, his gold-and-hazel eyes on mine.

'Never. You look like Ellie, and that was always a very fine way to look.'

Around us, a few couples are slow-dancing, draped over each other as they smooch. Liam and I are not dancing, not quite. We're just swaying, but I know we should stop. This is the kind of swaying that should come with a health warning.

I want to say goodnight, and run away up the stairs, where I will be safe – but somehow I can't. It's like I'm trapped here, in his orbit, unable to escape. Hot, bothered and completely undone by the gentle quirk of his lips, the look in his eyes. He opens his mouth to speak, but I don't get to find out what he was about to say – because Cara appears next to us, mischievously brandishing a bunch of mistletoe in her hand.

She holds it over our heads, laughing, and says: 'Come on now, you two! Don't be angering the gods of Christmas!'

It breaks the spell, shatters the moment. The moment that both Liam and I said would never happen again. I'm frustrated for a split second, and then relieved. We jump away from each other, both recoiling and looking a bit sheepish when we realise quite how close we had been. Cara has, unintentionally, saved us both from ourselves.

'Sorry, sis,' he says, grinning at her. 'The gods of Christmas won't mind! Right, I'd better check on Bella. She's just necked one of Patrick's whiskies when he wasn't looking...'

He walks away, and I watch him go with such a strange mix of emotions. I really don't have a clue what is going on here.

Cara raises her eyebrows at me, and says: 'You two need your heads banging together, you really do,' before she strides away in disgust.

I take a final glance around the still-full room. I smile at the madness – the banjos and guitars and the singing; at my dad telling a story with extravagant hand gestures; at the elderly man who has fallen asleep in one corner, a paper party hat wonky on his head. Familiar faces, new friends, old friends, all of them enjoying themselves. It's a lovely feeling, and I choose to hold on to the warmth of that rather than the whirling dervish of my feelings for Liam. My feelings for Liam are a black hole of confusion, and I don't have the energy to deal with it right now.

It is Christmas Eve in St Tilda, and that has always been a special time. I have missed out on so many, and now I am back, I should focus on enjoying it. I take a mental snapshot of the joyful chaos in front of me, before heading up to bed.

As I turn to leave the bar, I see a new arrival standing uncertainly in the doorway, gazing in. A new arrival who is wearing a sweatshirt decorated with a picture of three beautiful Labrador retrievers.

I freeze in my tracks, and stare at him in disbelief.

It's Tyler. And he does not look happy.

TWENTY

'Tyler?' I murmur, walking towards him. 'Is that really you?'

His eyes flicker over my face, taking in my flushed cheeks, my tangled hair, my less-than-pristine blouse. Then he looks back into the bar, at the revelry that is still in full swing.

'Yeah, it's me. Surprise!' he says. He tries to put a bit of humour into his voice, but I know him well enough to see that it's an effort. He looks wired and tense, which is not a normal thing for Tyler.

I reach out and put my hand on his arm. I feel a little curl of dread in my belly, and a wash of exhaustion. All I wanted to do was crawl into bed and remain unconscious for a few hours, but that is not going to happen. I owe it to this man to find the energy I need.

'Are you okay?' I ask, frowning. I know how he feels about flying, so this is a huge deal for him. It will, in fact, be only the third time in his entire life that he has been on a plane. The first two times provoked such a serious stress reaction in him that he vowed to never fly again. Now here he is, fresh from a long-haul flight from New York – all because of me. I am so not worth it.

'Well, I didn't die in a fireball over the Atlantic, so that's a plus. But I'm probably not at my best. Is it always like this?'

I glance back at the pub and see that several of the women have clambered up onto table tops to dance to a weird acoustic version of Beyoncé's *Crazy in Love*. Yikes. I'm not sure those tables were designed to deal with twerking.

'Um, well, it's often busy, but no, not like this. This is just a Christmas Eve thing. Do you want a drink? I can get you a beer. I happen to know the owner...'

This feels so strange, so horribly awkward. I feel guilty that I have not been missing him as much as he has obviously missed me, and annoyed that I cannot push past this stiff and uncomfortable version of myself. The man has flown halfway across the world to see me, and I haven't even kissed him! Belatedly, I wrap my arms around his waist, and give him a cuddle.

He gazes down at me and smiles, but it doesn't quite reach his eyes. 'Thanks, but no to the beer. My body clock's all messed up. Maybe a coffee, or a tea, now I'm in England?'

I nod and lead him up the stairs to the apartment. He dumps his case in the living room, and walks around the place, smiling at the photos of me as a kid. I make him a camomile tea, and one for myself while I'm at it. It's the closest to a chill pill I can come up with.

We both settle down on the couch, and he runs his hands through his hair and stays silent for a few moments. I have no idea how to handle this situation. I always planned on sitting down with him just like this, and being as honest and as gentle as I could be – but he has pushed the schedule, and we are both clearly feeling the tension.

'How was the flight?' I ask, breaking the silence. He grimaces.

'Every bit as delightful as I'd imagined. I thought they'd have to surgically remove me from the seat, I was gripping the arm rests so hard. But I wanted to come. I wanted to surprise you. Mission accomplished, I guess?'

I nod, and sip my tea. 'Definitely!'

I'm sure he was imagining this whole scene playing out a lot differently, and I wish I could give him what he expected. I'm still recovering from the shock of seeing him here at all. It's the last thing I expected him to do. I cast my mind back over our last few conversations, and wonder if he picked up on the distance I was starting to feel creeping in between us – I suspect this isn't just a 'Wouldn't this be a nice surprise?' visit. It's a 'What can I do to make this work?' visit.

'Was that Liam?' he asks, finally getting around to what I know he's been wanting to ask since he arrived. He's looking off to the side as he speaks, a sure sign that he is anxious. 'The guy you were dancing with?'

I have told him about Liam, the old friend I have reconnected with, and he even met his dog via the phone screen on the day we decorated Rosings for Christmas. I detected a flicker of jealousy then, and it caught me off guard. Turns out he was right, that maybe Tyler's instincts were a little more fine-tuned than mine. It seems like he knew there was a spark there even before I did.

I nod, trying to see the scene downstairs through his eyes. He's in the UK, late at night, in unfamiliar surroundings. He's just faced one of his worst fears, and is both stressed and exhausted. He was probably hoping his girlfriend would be thrilled to see him, that she would melt into his arms – which is not at all unreasonable. Instead, he walked into a bacchanal and found the girlfriend in question swaying in the arms of another man. I feel like utter crap.

'Yes it was,' I say slowly and carefully. 'And Tyler, you need to know that nothing has happened between me and Liam. I would never do that.'

He tilts his head to one side, and finally meets my eyes. 'It's interesting, though, that you say that straight away, Ellie. I haven't accused you of anything. I haven't even asked.'

'You haven't, but I'm not an idiot – I know that might have looked bad. I hope you noticed the bit at the end where we both swerved the mistletoe.'

'I did, yeah. But that came right after the part where you were looking at each other like... like people in love look at each other. Like I look at you. The way you never look at me. No, don't protest

– I've come a long way to see you; at least be honest with me. What's the score, with you and Liam?'

I sigh, and rub my sore eyes. I think about what he has said and know that he is right. He deserves honesty. I did not expect him here, I did not invite him here, and I am not mentally prepared for this conversation – but it looks like I'm going to be having it anyway. I should have gone for a coffee instead of the camomile tea.

'There actually isn't a "score" with me and Liam. I won't lie and say there is no attraction there, but I know that's at least partly based on our history together, the fact that we have a connection that goes back so many years. But nothing has happened, like I said. And it's not going to.'

He is staring at me intensely, as though trying to read my mind, and when he realises I am telling the truth a flicker of relief dances across his face. I shake my head, and reach out to hold his hand. It is so familiar, sitting here with him like this, the way we have done at his place or mine so many times over the last six months.

'Tyler,' I say quietly. He blinks rapidly at the sound of that word, and closes his eyes. Something in my tone, my gesture, gives it away.

'It's over, isn't it?' he asks, his voice sad.

'I'm so sorry, but I think it is. I swear I haven't cheated on you – you know how I feel about cheating – but the fact that it even crossed my mind tells me that things aren't right between us. I know you want more, and I know you said you would give me time, but I can't keep you hanging on for something I don't think will ever happen.'

'How can you be so sure of that, Ellie? Haven't the last six months meant anything to you?'

'Of course they have!' I protest, keeping hold of his hand. 'I've loved being with you! But the way I feel about you, Tyler… It's never going to be more than this. I like you. I respect you. And just to be clear, I really do fancy you. But I'm never going to fall in love with you, and you deserve better than that. You deserve the absolute best woman in the world – it just isn't me. I've tried, and I've thought about it a lot I promise, and I'm... well, I'm just never going to be your Lois.'

He manages a weak smile at that, but I can see the pain in his eyes. He rubs the bridge of his nose and sighs.

'I don't want this to be happening,' he says eventually. 'I thought I'd make this big romantic gesture, and we'd have this sublime Christmas together, and maybe we'd even get engaged... What was I thinking? I knew you felt this way, deep down. I knew, but I hoped it would change. I hoped I'd eventually be good enough for you.'

My eyes fill with tears, and I squeeze them away. 'Tyler, please don't say that – you are good enough for anyone! You're kind and funny and clever and gorgeous, and any woman would be lucky to have you!'

'Any woman apart from you?' he asks, a touch of bitterness in his words.

'Well, that's a *me* problem, not a *you* problem. I'm a bloody idiot. Always have been, always will be. It must be genetic.'

Maybe it actually is, I think. My dad blew up his marriage, and now here I am, breaking the heart of this decent man, who wants to do nothing more than love me and build a life with me. Maybe, like my dad, I just have too much scar tissue beneath the surface to allow me to make good choices. At least doing this now rather than later gives Tyler the chance to meet someone new. Someone better. I know he wants to settle down, have children – and I also know that I am not the right woman for him to settle down with, no matter how much he thinks I am. These things cannot be unilateral – he can't want it enough for both of us.

'I'm really sorry,' I say, wanting to put my arms around him and console him, but knowing that would be the very definition of sending mixed messages. 'I didn't know you were coming. I was planning to talk to you about it all face to face when I came home. I didn't want to ruin your Christmas...'

A shadow of annoyance appears on his features, but he quickly controls it. 'I know. I get that. I suppose I'd have done the same. And I love the sweater, by the way. Just to be clear, I'm not giving you your gift now. It was the type that comes in a black velvet jewellery box, and frankly I think I might return it. Use the cash to pay for therapy.'

'Ouch. I deserve that. This... this whole trip has probably cost you a lot?'

'In all kinds of ways, yes. I don't care about the money,' he says, looking me right in the eyes. 'I care about what's happening here. I care about losing you. Are you sure? I can wait; I've told you that...'

'Says the man who just flew across an ocean because he sensed me slipping away?'

He lets out a low groan. 'Yeah. Fair point. I did sense that, and I reacted in a real measured way, didn't I? Okay. So maybe I'm not as good at waiting as I thought I was.'

'That's all right. You're allowed to be you. I just can't make myself into what you need, Tyler – what you deserve. My life is a mess. I have no clue what I want from it at the moment, and coming back here has really done a number on me. But it has at least given me some clarity about me and you, and I don't want you to waste another minute of your time waiting for me to come to my senses. It's entirely possible that I have none.'

I see him biting down retorts, quashing his own objections. He knows, really, that I am right. He has probably always known, but was hoping that I would eventually end up on the same page as him.

'Look, we're both wiped out,' I say, hating seeing the pain I've caused. 'There's a guest room free, and you're welcome to stay as long as you like. I know this is difficult, but a good night's sleep will help. I have to run a Baked Goods Buffet for the village tomorrow; you could come along? Free cake?'

He smiles, and it almost breaks my heart. He is so good, so lovely and so right – what is wrong with me? Why am I rejecting this man?

'Thanks, but no,' he says softly. 'I can't stand the thought of listening to you try and let me down gently for another day. I can't watch you and hear you and be around you, knowing that it's over. I can't. I just can't, Ellie. I'm sorry.'

He stands up and gets out his phone. I see the screensaver photo – me in his yard with all three of the dogs – and feel a moment of panic. Am I making a terrible mistake?

'What are you doing?' I ask, as he walks towards the door.

'I'm ordering the world's most expensive Uber,' he says, tapping at his keyboard. 'All the way back to London. I'll find a hotel there that isn't haunted by the ghost of girlfriends past. I'm sorry, Ellie, I know you want to sort this out – to be friends. And maybe one day we can be. But right now, I'm not capable of that. I guess I'm not evolved enough. I need to leave.'

I want to stop him. I want to persuade him to stay at least one night. I want... what do I want? I don't suppose it matters. I can't be selfish here. What he wants has to come first. He is hurt, and I am the one who wounded him.

TWENTY-ONE

It takes a while for Tyler's driver to arrive, predictably enough on Christmas Eve, and it is a strange time we spend together. I can tell he would like to go immediately. He is hurt, possibly embarrassed, and wants to be alone. I get that, but we can do nothing but wait. I try to persuade him to stay, or failing that to eat or drink, but he resists me with a newly erected wall of politeness. I hate it, but I understand it. He needs to do whatever it takes to get through this.

When the car arrives from Penzance, its headlights casting a glow on our faces as we wait outside the inn, we share an awkward hug and I wave him off. I watch him drive away, my arms wrapped around myself against the chill of the night. Behind me, inside, the party continues. I hear snatches of music, laughter, all of the curtains drawn but light spilling around them. I could go back inside. I could have a drink and hide away from this.

I stroll towards the little bench that looks out over the sea, my boots crunching on the snow. No, I decide, I cannot do that. I can't pretend that nothing has happened. I clear a space on the bench and sit down. It is cold and damp and I don't really care. I stare out at the vast spread of stars, the twinkling gems that stretch as far as the eye can see. The moon is not quite full but casts a silvery light on the waves. The sound of the sea has always calmed me, and I concentrate on that now. I will keep on breathing, and the world will keep on turning. Everything will be fine.

Right now, I do not feel fine. I have hurt Tyler, and I know I will miss him. There is a little empty spot in my heart where he used to live, but I can't deny that there is also a tiny touch of relief – of pressure lifting now the horrible deed has been done. I hate that I feel that, but perhaps it does at least assure me that I've done the right thing. For both of us. He might not think that tonight, but he will, eventually. When he finds his real match.

As for me, maybe I simply need to give up on love. That sounds like a horrible idea, but I am exhausted by it all. Haunted by the remnants of my failed marriage; pained by my inability to make things work with Tyler. And, right in the middle of it all, the tangled knot of my feelings for Liam.

I have never really thought of Liam as 'the one who got away'. That implies a missed romance, and he was always so much more than that, really – he was my best friend, my other half, the person who just 'got' me. He was also the first boy who made my pulse race faster, and then the first to break my heart. It was all a very long time ago, but if my time here in Cornwall has showed me anything, it's that it still matters. Our friendship still matters. His rejection still matters. *He* still matters. And let's face it, my pulse still goes crazy whenever I'm near him. Even more so now.

I rub my face with my hands, unable to see a way out of this particular conundrum. I suppose I just need to keep on keeping on, and before too long I will be flying back to New York. To a job I don't miss, and to a life without Tyler in it. I sigh, because it doesn't feel like a lot to look forward to. I will miss this spectacular view. I will miss the village and all its eccentric locals. I will miss Dad. I will miss Liam, and his entire family. I'm not at all sure I'm ready to plunge back into life in New York, a city where you can be surrounded by millions of other people and still feel lonely.

I hear the crunch of footsteps behind me, and the slightest scent of his cologne. I know it is Liam before he appears, looking down at me with concern. Maybe I summoned him.

'You're shivering,' he says, slipping off his jacket and tucking it around my shoulders.

'Am I?' I murmur, as he sits on the bench. He leans into me, and I stare at his jean-clad thighs pressed close. 'I barely noticed.'

'That's because you've been numbed by cold. Your lips are probably blue.'

'Well, that's a hot look if you're a Smurf. How's things going in there?'

'Like a scene from the feasting halls of Valhalla, with more ale and swearing. There are going to be some sore heads tomorrow.'

'Not yours?' I ask, glancing up at him. His cheekbones are bathed in moonlight, his hair thick and dark. A small smile on his lips as he turns to face me.

'No, I've been sensible. Alex and Alice will show no mercy tomorrow morning. It's the first Christmas we've spent at Rosings, so I want it to be as perfect as it can be. The added value will come from them running into Bella's room and jumping on her bed at six am – she's been sneaking booze all night. It's like she thinks she's invisible.'

I laugh. We were exactly the same.

'Are you all right?' he asks. 'Apart from the cold. I saw... Well, I saw you with a man. He had a suitcase, and did indeed look a bit like Clark Kent, just like you said. And now you're out here on your own, and you look like Sad Smurf.'

'I am sad,' I reply, snug in his big jacket, only now realising how chilled I was. 'I... I ended it, with Tyler. It was the right thing to do, but right doesn't always feel good, does it?'

He slips his arm around me and squeezes me into his side. My heart beats a little faster at the proximity, and I wonder if he feels that too? Or is this all completely platonic for him? Just two old friends, helping each other over life's roadbumps? I am past clinging to that idea now. My feelings for this man left friendship behind some time ago. I can't lie to myself about that now – but I can lie to him, if that's what I need to do.

He drops a kiss on top of my head. 'No. No it doesn't. Why did you finish it, Ellie?'

'He wanted more than I can give him. I like him, a lot, but I was never going to be in love with him. I wanted to set him free, and I know it was for the best, but it still feels like crap. I still feel miserable. That will pass, hopefully for him too. It was the right thing.'

I repeat those last few words again in my mind, feeling the truth of them – but also feeling the loss. I let my head fall against Liam's shoulder, feeling the solid bulk of him, the reassuring warmth of his arm around me. Liam has always been a safe harbour – but he is also at the centre of some of my turmoil.

'I'm sure it was,' he says, wiping tears from beneath my eyes. 'And it will get better. I wasn't sure if it was... because of me? Because of us? Which I realise makes me sound like the world's most arrogant asshole, but there you go. Maybe that's what I am.'

I tense slightly, and have no idea how to answer him. Dismiss his comment? Make a joke? Tell the truth? I'm too tired for any of it. I'm physically and emotionally wrung out.

'You're not arrogant, Liam. You never were. And I don't know.'

'You don't know what?'

'Anything! But specifically, I don't know if you were on my mind when I ended it. It was having these *moments* of ours that made me realise what I had to do, but it's not like I've finished with Tyler in the hopes of something happening between me and you. So you're off the hook.'

I pull away from him, and look him in the eyes. God, he is beautiful – but he also clearly troubled.

'What?' I ask. 'You don't believe me? Maybe you are arrogant then!'

'Don't be pissed off with me, Ellie. I'm as freaked out by all this as you are, and I've been honest with you – I'm not ready for anything more. Having you back in my life has been a blessing, but I can't... I can't give you more, just like you couldn't with Tyler.'

I stand up, and tug off his jacket. I am suddenly really mad.

I've worked all night, I've had a big drama with a man who I never wanted to hurt, and now I am basically being rejected in advance by a man who is allegedly a friend. Happy bloody Christmas, Ellie de Vere.

I sling the jacket at him in a display of temper that I haven't felt for years. I ignore the slap of cold air on my bare arms, and glare at him.

'Liam, I never asked you for anything more! I never expected anything more! Why don't you just... get over yourself and feck off!'

I turn on my heel and storm away, the sad tears I was shedding earlier morphing into angry ones instead. I have one hundred per cent had it with this night. I never want anything to do with a man ever again. Who the hell does he think he is?

'Ellie, wait!' he shouts as I run across the snow-covered grass, desperate to get away from him. Desperate to be alone, to be able to indulge my misery and my fury in the privacy of my own room.

Why am I so upset? He *has* always been honest. Maybe it's because I was secretly, in a tiny hidden corner of my foolish heart, hoping for more. I did not part ways with Tyler for Liam, at least not rationally – but having him tread all over dreams I didn't even know I had is the final straw. I feel crushed, made entirely of fatigue.

I speed up to escape him, and I've almost made it to the door of the inn when he grabs hold of my hand. He spins me around, and I stare up at him, the tears running freely now. He pulls me into his arms, holding me so close I can feel his heart thudding against mine. I gasp as he presses me against the wall, his body trapping me there. His eyes are on mine, gold and hazel, and his hands come up to cradle my face.

'Don't cry, Ellie, please,' he says, his breath warm, his voice low and rasping. 'I'm sorry. I don't know what I'm doing around you. I'm a mess. I can't stop thinking about you. I can't stop wanting to kiss you...'

My palms are flat against his chest, my pulse racing, all

conscious thought chased from my mind by this intimacy. By the delicious pressure of his body close against mine.

'Then do it, Liam,' I murmur. 'Kiss me.'

His lips come down over mine, and his hands twine into my hair, and I forget who I am or where I am or why I am. All I know is this kiss, the one I feel like I have been waiting my whole life for. There is no hesitancy, no awkwardness, no doubt – just passion and need and the overwhelming urge to cling on to him and never let go.

My fingers find their way up to his shoulders, and my back is crushed against the wall as the kiss intensifies. He is suddenly everywhere: his lips, his hands, his sheer overwhelming presence. I melt into him, and for the first time in my life my knees actually go weak. His arm reaches around my waist, holding me upright and pulling me even closer.

We might have kissed for seconds. We might have kissed for hours. By the time we finally come up for air, we are both breathless, and I have lost all track of time. I keep my grip on his shoulders, not trusting my own legs just yet. He leans his forehead down so it rests against mine, and I feel him shaking slightly. I realise with a grin that he is actually laughing.

I can't help but join in, and we stand there, physically joined, both lost in the moment.

'Well,' he finally says. 'That was...'

'Better than the last time?' I suggest. He pulls his face away from mine, and smooths my hair back from my face. I twist my head to kiss the skin of his palm, and his pupils dilate in response. Yeah, I think. Definitely better than last time.

We are still wrapped around each other when the door to the inn bursts open, and a pile of people spill out in a cloud of noise and light. Before we can edge apart, we are surrounded by a small tribe of Byrnes.

Cara stares at us, bundled up in a faux fur coat, and breaks into a grin. 'About bloody time, you two eejits!' she announces. Brian walks past, giving his son a solid pat on the back, and his brothers follow suit. Bella takes one look at us and shakes her head.

'Disgusting,' she says, her voice slightly slurred but no signs of distress on her face. 'Kids today!'

I'm embarrassed but also can't stop laughing. I look up at Liam, who still has his arms around me, as though he doesn't want to let go either. He grins and gives me a quick kiss on the lips.

Cara, who hasn't been drinking, gets all the instruments loaded into her car, as well as her dad and Bella. The rest set off on the walk back up the hill to Rosings, singing and joking as they go.

'I don't want to leave, but I have to,' Liam says, his fingers tracing delicious circles on the skin at the side of my neck. Even the slightest of touches makes me tremble.

'I know,' I reply, leaning into him one last time. 'It's Christmas Eve. Go be with your kids.'

He reluctantly pulls away from me, and I feel the loss of our closeness. 'See you tomorrow?' he asks. I nod and promise that he will.

I watch him walk away with a heart crammed full of feelings, and a body that is still feeling way too hot for a snowy night in December.

He stops and turns around, gives me a final, butterfly-inducing smile, and disappears into the night.

TWENTY-TWO

I have two sensations when I wake up the following morning, one coming hot on the heels of the other. The first is sweet and sensual and makes me smile – the memory of Liam's kiss. Of Liam's warm eyes on mine. Of our promise that we would see each other again today. I feel as excited as a teenager at the prospect.

The second, chasing all that away, is guilt. I didn't only break Tyler's heart, I made a liar of myself. I told him that nothing was going to happen with Liam, and it took me just a few minutes to prove myself wrong.

I roll over in bed, torn between the two conflicting emotions. I drag the duvet over my head, and am glad that I have a busy day ahead. There is nothing I can do to change what has happened, and also, I don't want to. I don't know what the future holds with Liam, but I cannot regret that kiss. That magical moment.

I can regret hurting Tyler, but none of it was deliberate. I don't think I've behaved like a terrible person – I have always tried to be open with him, even when it was difficult. It would have been so much easier to go along, to say 'I love you' and not mean it, to let him believe that we would have the happy ending that he wanted. I never did that, though I know it doesn't exactly qualify me for sainthood.

I want to call him, to check that he is okay, but I'm not sure it would be appropriate. Can I be both the person who wounds him and the person who expresses concern for him? In the end I settle on sending a message. A simple one, that wishes him a merry Christmas, and tells him to stay in touch if he wants to. He might not, I know, and I will have to accept that. I cannot have it all my own way.

I stare at my phone screen for a few more seconds, wondering if I should also message Liam. But what would I say? Last night was amazing, but this morning comes with its own set of complications.

I find myself going round and round in circles, and eventually give up and climb out of bed. For once, I could have had a small lie-in, but I'm too tied up in mental knots to rest.

I go downstairs into a still-cold inn, wrapped in my bathrobe and wearing fluffy bed socks. The bar isn't as much of a disaster as I'd expected, because Sean and my dad had started the clean-up while the party continued. The pub isn't open today, so there is no sense of urgency anyway.

The couple who are staying as guests were up until the early hours drinking with my father and the rest of the locals, and had declared very forcefully that they would not be down for a cooked breakfast. Instead, I make up a tray for them. Some granola, a pot of honey and nuts, some fresh berries and milk. A couple of croissants and jam, yoghurt, and a cute little gift box that contains two pralines. I add two glasses of Buck's Fizz, because hey, it's Christmas.

I tiptoe past their room as I go to deliver it, not wanting to wake them up, and then make my way back to the apartment. My dad is still asleep, and I am happy to let him rest. I am not a little girl anymore, up early and wondering if Santa has been. I smile as I imagine the scenes at Rosings, and later at Bernadette and Brian's home. I know the plan was for the twins to wake up in the big house, open their gifts, then head to their grandparents' for one of Bernadette's trademark full Irish fry-ups. Then lunch back at

Rosings for all of the clan, and into the village for late afternoon cake and company.

I have my part to play in that, and I am looking forward to taking over for Maggie. I am looking forward to a lot – certainly more than I was this time last year. I shudder a little as I remember my sad, desperate trip to see Father Christmas in his grotto, and the dreadful way I felt about my life back then.

This has been a year of transition, and this will be a Christmas unlike any other. There is no exchange of gifts, but that is fine by me. My dad and I agreed not to buy each other presents, but instead to use the money to treat ourselves to a night out together in London before I finally go home.

Home, I think, as I get dressed. Where is that, now? I have never loved New York and have often thought about leaving. Then I started to build my little business, and I met Tyler, and things improved. But everything has changed now. There is no more me and Tyler, and I have no idea what is going to happen next. It is both exciting and terrifying.

If Liam and I lived in the same place, we would be able to let this thing between us develop organically. We would be able to see where it led. But he lives in Dublin, and I live in the US. He was already toying with the idea of coming back here more permanently, and truth be told, I am not repulsed by the idea myself. I have enjoyed being back in St Tilda, and could see a future for myself here – but how much of that is influenced by Liam? How much of my yearning to stay is built around being with him? That feels like a lot of pressure, for both of us.

I creep out of the house, and go for a quick constitutional on the beach. It has stopped snowing, but the temperature is brutal. Seabirds huddle in groups in the cliffs, their white feathers puffed out against the chill, and the roll and crash of the waves competes with the whistle of the wind. A pale wash of sunlight is battling through the clouds, and the air is fresh with the aromatic tang of seaweed and salt. It is absolutely beautiful.

I sigh contentedly, and pause to appreciate that. Contentment is a very under-rated quality.

After that, I set off for Maggie's café. Her husband, Mike, had called into the pub last night, passing me the keys and updating us all on her progress. He took a quick pint, but soon left – he was clearly lost without her, the sweetheart. He was invited to Rosings for Christmas, and probably several other places too, but politely refused them all – he is spending the day where he has spent every Christmas Day since they met, at Maggie's side.

The café and bakery are much warmer than the inn, with heating on a timer, and I appreciate the cosiness as I set to work. As Maggie had already explained, a lot of the classics were already done, Christmas puddings drenched in the smell of sherry, and rich fruit cakes crammed with plums and nuts. One seems to contain so much rum that I assume she's baked it for a sailor. Four big cheesecakes are already made and in the freezer, and I get them out and put them on the counter to start defrosting. Baileys, Tia Maria, cherry brandy and Champagne flavour – genius. I think we might need a whole table just for adults-only cakes.

I smile as I get going, relishing the well-stocked kitchen with all its flashy appliances. I find the supplies Maggie told me about, filled with edible Christmas decorations, icing, and little plastic snowmen, and go over her suggestions. 'But feel free to do your own thing,' she added to her messages.

I spend the first thirty minutes planning, taking into account bake times, chill times, and storage, and then I get to it, rubbing my hands in glee. I was on something of a high already, and the thought of spending the day in this kitchen just sends me even further into the clouds.

The next five hours are lost in a solid whirlwind of measuring, mixing, whipping, beating and rolling. Things go wrong, but as Maggie always told me, that's an essential part of the process. I thoroughly enjoy myself, and take pictures as I go to send to my baking mentor. No reply, so she's either conked out on the good drugs, or too horrified to respond.

Lucy arrives at about four, accompanied by Bella and their other cousin, Patrick Junior. Bella looks slightly weary, and I pass her a Diet Coke from the café's big fridge. She stares at it then shrugs and pops it open.

'How was your morning?' I ask, knowing she'll have been woken early. I find that I am eager to hear news about Christmas Day at Rosings, about the spectacular lunch that I'm sure was served up, about the presents and the fun and the shenanigans. Mainly, of course, about Liam. I still haven't heard from him – but then again, he hasn't heard from me either. I'm sure he's been busy, and he will be here later anyway.

'It was too early, and it was too loud,' Bella groans. 'But... it was okay, I suppose. Actually, it was good. I got some new headphones. And they're "definitely your last, young lady", apparently.' She says this in a mock Liam dad voice and makes me laugh. 'The twins were really excited. And Liam was happy, having the whole family around. Yeah. It was all right.'

I know that in teenager world, that is as glowing as it's likely to get. I nod, warm inside at the thought of Liam hosting his first Christmas in the big old house that was once our derelict playground. At the thought of Liam, full stop. Some of that must show on my face, because Bella grimaces, tells me it's disgusting again, and strides away swigging her Diet Coke.

Lucy takes charge of the crew, setting up trestles at one end of the café to serve from. Maggie had already planned this so well, and everything is pretty much ready to go. The tables and chairs are all dressed in pink and white, and big vases of roses in matching colours are placed around the café. Tiny confetti in the shape of stars is scattered on the table tops, and each one is decorated with its own miniature Christmas tree. The sun shines through the soaring glass ceiling, and the whole room looks splendid, dazzlingly pretty.

We set up one section for drinks, bottles of prosecco, beers and wine, as well as big flasks that we can fill with hot chocolate.

There's a whole table just for children, with soft drinks and juice boxes, and cupcakes I've decorated with snowmen and reindeer.

The young people help me carry all of the cakes and puddings out, and I slice the boozy cheesecakes. I've baked up chocolate Yule logs, gingerbread snaps, cinnamon cookies and a big layer cake in the shape of a Christmas tree. There is a black forest trifle, a selection of tray bakes, and individual little ramekins filled with cherry and chocolate mousse. I've iced a layer cake with tiny holly leaves, and added in some easier classics like carrot cake and a coffee and walnut sponge, all made more festive with sprinkles of edible glitter.

We add in jugs of cream and sauces, and I have custard ready to go when people arrive. I stand back and survey the end result.

'Do you think there's enough?' I ask the teenagers, suddenly nervous.

'There's enough to give the whole of Cornwall diabetes,' Bella snarks.

Lucy pats me on the arm. 'It's perfect. Maggie will be delighted.'

We take more photos and send them to the patient. She does reply this time – with more random emojis, including a hockey stick and a koala bear, and then a follow-up from Mike that says: 'She's on the morphine again!'

Patrick gets the Christmas music on the go over the sound system, and before long the first guests start to arrive. I know that people have deliberately had earlier Christmas lunches than usual just because of this, and I hope they're not disappointed.

Lucy steps up as the host, directing people to seats and greeting them, while I buzz around doing last-minute checks on the food, and setting the custard to gently warm on the hob. Within half an hour, the café is packed, and spirits are high.

I'm too busy to notice everyone who turns up, but I do spot Bernadette and Brian, along with most of the clan. My heart does a little tap dance when they walk into the room, and I take a few deep breaths as I carry out a quick and hopefully subtle scan. Alice and Alex run over to say hello, and I help them stack their plates high with cookies and cake. It's probably never going to win any nutritional awards, but it is Christmas.

I go over to their table with some wine, and see immediately that Liam is not there. I squash down the silly feeling of disappointment. He might be still on his way. He might be having a snooze. He might have been abducted by aliens. There are all kinds of valid reasons he isn't here, and his whole world does not revolve around me.

'Merry Christmas to you, me darling'!' Bernadette exclaims, getting up and hugging me. 'I have a scarf I knitted for you up at the house. Nothing special, but nice to keep up the tradition, eh?'

The thought of a new multi-coloured creation from Bernadette makes me smile. 'Thank you, that's so kind. Did you all have a nice time? At Rosings?'

'We did, my love. Are you wondering where the other fella is?'

She misses nothing, as ever. There's not even any point in denying it; she's like a human lie detector. She has a twinkle in her eye though, and does not seem at all displeased by the situation.

I nod sheepishly as I fill their wine glasses.

'The lazy so-and-so said he needed a rest,' she replies, taking a sip. 'Though why I don't know, all he did was peel the veg, it was yours truly who did the cooking! I'd say maybe he has a few things on his mind...' She gives me a mischievous wink, and I feel myself blush.

'Right. Well. I'd better go and see to my custard...'

I dash off to the kitchen and do just that. I pour it into two big jugs, and add them to the serving table. The cookie platters are looking depleted, so I top those up, and do a quick walk around checking if anybody needs anything. The music is merry, a collection of swing covers of Christmas classics, and as the daylight fades the fairy lights draped from the rafters start to twinkle. The whole of the room comes alive with silver and pink shimmers, and the kids *ooh* and *aah* and point upwards.

Everything goes well, and people seem to be having a marvellous time. My dad is at Sandra's, but messages to wish me luck and tell me that he'll be back in the morning. The guests have checked out to go and stay with family, and the inn will be empty when I finally go back there. How odd, I think, to have the whole place to myself – the first time that has ever happened. If only I had my old teenage partner in crime to share it with.

Liam still has not arrived, and I fight the instinct to over-think. He's probably just passed out in front of the fire, or taking a well-earned breather. We said that we would see each other today, and there is plenty of time for that.

Eventually, the buffet draws to a close, and one by one the various groups of family and friends leave to go back to their homes. Lucy makes a video montage for Maggie, gathering messages from them all as they leave, and I think it will really cheer her up. Not only did everybody have a great time, but they all miss her and send their love.

I dismiss my helpers as soon as the café is empty – they are young, it is Christmas Day, and they have spent it doing a favour for a sick friend. I'm sure Maggie will treat them once she is out of hospital and back on her feet, but for now, they have spent all this time here out of the goodness of their own hearts. Not a lot of teenagers would do that – I'm not entirely sure I would have done back then.

They disappear bearing boxes of leftovers, and in Lucy's case a nice Chardonnay. I have no doubt at all that Bella will be sharing it, but that is not something I can control.

It takes me over an hour to do the basics of the clearing-up. The whole café will need a proper clean before it reopens, but there is some uncertainty about when that might be. I can help out as much as possible, but realistically, I have no firm idea of how long I will be here, and I am already working at the inn. Much as I'd love to, I can't be in two places at once, or sustain spending a whole day in the café and a whole night at the pub. Maybe for a few days, but not long-term. Not that I'll be here long-term. Or will I? I just don't know.

The uncertainty isn't helped by Liam's no-show, and the fact that neither of us has reached out even by phone so far today. That is as much down to me as him, I know, but for some weird outdated reason, I feel like he should make the first move. I know that's stupid – I am a modern woman who is perfectly entitled to make any damn move I like. And yet, I don't. I think I am scared. The last day has been a rollercoaster. Seeing Tyler again, ending things with him, and then that kiss with Liam... Was that the start of something, or was that an accident? Was that something he is regretting now?

Uncertainty aside, all I feel when I think about that kiss is joy. Hope. Heat. It was everything I had always dreamt it would be, but maybe that's all it was. A dream.

I give the surfaces of the kitchen a final wipe over, and almost reluctantly leave the café. I switch the overheads off, but the fairy lights remain steadfast in their pretty twinkling. I grab myself a box of cheesecake slices and an open bottle of prosecco, and head back towards the inn. I will decide later if the prosecco is half full or half empty, depending on my mood.

I do a bit of cleaning in the bar, and put the bedding from the used guest room in to wash. Nobody is booked in until New Year now, so we'll have the chance to give things an overhaul. Or my dad will, or whoever Liam takes on to help him.

I fill in some time by taking a long soak in the bath of one of the guest rooms. They're nicer than the one in our apartment, and come with better toiletries too. I slather on some nice body creams scented with roses, and blow dry my hair. Maybe that's actually what I am, anyway – just a guest. Just a transient visitor, passing time here on my way to somewhere else.

I go back to the apartment and get dressed. I set myself up in the living room, finding *The Lord of the Rings* on one of the TV channels, and add cake and booze to the little side table. Well, I think, covering myself in a fleecy blanket, this is hardly exciting, but it is okay. There is plenty to like about this scenario, and I need to focus on the positives.

I have to remind myself that when I first arrived here, two weeks ago, I had shut Liam Byrne out of my life for years. Now, I am pining for him. It's ridiculous, and I need to snap out of it.

My phone pings, and I grab it up immediately. My heart sinks when I see that the message is not from him, but Tyler. And then I obviously hate myself for being so shallow and selfish.

'Having a surprisingly cool time,' he says. 'Made some friends in a hotel bar. Going back to NY in a few days. Good luck with everything, Ellie.'

It is hardly effusive, but it is perhaps better than I could have hoped for. Maybe there is a chance that one day, we could indeed be friends. I send a quick reply, and go back to Frodo and his magical adventures. He's about to leave the Shire for the first time.

'Don't do it, Frodo!' I warn him. 'Stay at home and find a nice hobbit girl with hairy feet and a warm heart!'

He doesn't listen, the impetuous fool. Just sets off to save the world, like the pint-sized hero he is. I remember sitting in this exact spot with my mum all those years ago, watching this on DVD. I was a little more adventurous back then, and would have been on my merry way as quick as a flash if I was a hobbit.

Thinking about my mum reminds me that I need to call her. She left a voicemail at what would have been breakfast time with her and Ethan, but was hours later here. I press her contact, and within a few rings she answers. Her smiling features fill the screen, and I immediately feel emotional as I take in the familiar lines and creases of her face, her pretty brown eyes, the silver streaks in her neatly bobbed hair.

'Darling, what's wrong?' she asks, straight away.

'Nothing, Mum, I just miss you. Plus I'm really tired, and I've eaten nothing but cake all day.'

'Ah. How did the buffet go?'

'It was great, Mum. I think Maggie was really pleased.'

'I'm sure she was, sweetie,' she replies, smiling. 'And it was very kind of you, stepping in like that on Christmas Day.'

I dismiss that, and reply: 'I enjoyed it, and Maggie has always been good to me. How is Vermont?'

She fills me in on their stay in a cute little B&B, and takes me on a small video tour of their room, then down to the restaurant and bar. It's late afternoon with them, and through the window I see that the land around the place is covered in snow, just like it is here.

'We have a meal out tonight,' she tells me, 'and then a drinks party for guests back here. What are you up to?'

'Well, actually I'm upstairs in our living room, watching *The Lord of the Rings.*'

'Just like old times!' she says. I am full of admiration for this woman, knowing what I know now. The way she held herself together through the aftermath of my father's affair. The way she has built her own life and has never once bad-mouthed him to me. She has a lot of class, and dignity by the bucket-load.

'Yeah, in some ways. Bit weird though, because I'm the only one here. Dad is away for the night, there are no guests, and the pub is closed. It's just me and Frodo.'

'And Aragorn, dear. Never forget him. So very dishy. Why don't you go out? I'm sure you could visit with Cara, or go and see Bernadette.'

Something must show on my face, and she picks up on it of course. I wonder if this sixth sense is something that comes about when you have children, part of the biological process?

'Why the long face, dear? What's going on? I can tell something's wrong, you know. Tell me all; I'll find out eventually. I know I'm just a silly old woman, but I do have some life experience. Maybe I can help, even if it's just by listening.'

'You're not silly, and you're not old,' I reply firmly. 'And... well. It's nothing, really. It's just that I... that we... that Liam and me...'

Her eyes widen in surprise as she fills in the gaps, but she keeps her tone neutral as she asks: 'Oh! What about Tyler?'

She has never met Tyler, but I have told her about him, and I understand better than ever now why she would hate the idea of me cheating on him.

'I'd ended things with him, Mum. He flew over to see me, and then he left, and then Liam kissed me, and then I did the cake buffet, and now I'm here with a bottle of prosecco, feeling a bit blue.'

'I see. Well, you have had a busy few days, haven't you? I'm glad that you and Liam have made up, Ellie, and I don't suppose I'm surprised this has happened. Even when you were seven, I started to think you might end up together. So, why feeling blue? Isn't it what you want?'

That, of course, is the big question, isn't it? That, and the equally big one – is it also what he wants?

'I don't know, Mum. I just don't know. There's a lot to think through, a lot to consider. It's not an easy situation.'

'Well, my love,' she replies, smiling gently. 'Nothing worth having ever is. Promise me you won't be afraid.'

'What do you mean?' I ask, frowning.

'You know what I mean, Ellie. Don't hide from it. Don't cower away from life as though it's always about to kick you. I know you've had some tough breaks, and I know you've been doing your best, but really... You used to be such a fearless girl. I want that for you again, sweetie. I want you to be fearless, just like you always used to be.'

She's right, as usual. The ins and outs of how I have changed so much are complicated, but I have. I want to be fearless again, too – but I'm not entirely sure how to go about it.

Halfway through my prosecco, the idea comes to me – as many good ideas do when prosecco is involved. I pause the movie, and go to get a notepad and pen from the drawer in the kitchen. The top page shows one of my dad's shopping lists, and his handwriting makes me smile. Whatever happens next, at least he and I have found our way back to each other.

I go back into the living room, and grab one of his old encyclopaedias to rest the notepad on. In tried and tested tradition, it is time to write a letter to Father Christmas. Okay, so it's a day late, but I'm sure he won't mind – and if he does, maybe he'll hold it over until next year. He's good like that.

TWENTY-THREE

I wake up not only without an alarm the next morning, but also without a sore head. I finished the bottle, but there were only a couple of glasses left in there. Not enough to do any real damage.

I roll over in my single bed, knowing it's going to be freezing cold once I'm out. As I do, I find the letter, tucked under my pillow. Again, not conventional, but it worked for me last year. I pick it up, and read it aloud. It doesn't take long, because there is only one request.

'Dear Santa, please make me more Frodo. I don't need to be fearless. I need to be brave.'

I smile at the words, and still mean every one of them. It's okay to be scared of things, and to be afraid of life kicking you, as my mum put it. But cowering? No. I won't do that. I will feel the fear, and... play basketball. As the old saying doesn't go.

I clamber out of the covers, dragging the duvet over my shoulders for the time being. I plug in the old machine, and am delighted when it lights up with a red neon display. Why haven't I done this before? What kind of joyless creature shares a room with a mystery basketball machine and never shoots some hoops?

I spend a fun ten minutes trying to beat my record of two in a row, and then turn it off again. So. That was that.

I get dressed quickly, and check my phone. It feels like a slap to the heart when there is still nothing there from Liam, but I grit my emotional teeth and take it. I have no idea what is going on now, and that isn't really good enough. If he has changed his mind, then I will have to deal with it – but I can't carry on in this will-we-won't-we limbo. It isn't fair to me, and as I seem to spend a lot of time trying to be fair to other people, maybe I should cut myself the same slack.

I make myself a slice of toast and a coffee, then grab my jacket and the car keys. It's time to take Queen Mildred out for a spin. If I don't do this now, I won't do it at all. I will have yet another day of waiting around, feeling like an extra in my own life. Waiting for somebody else to tell me what happens next.

It's raining outside, a fine grey drizzle that soaks everything within seconds, and the snow is turning to mush underfoot. I scoot quickly into Mildred's comfy surroundings, and off we go – out of the village, up the hill. Past Bernadette and Brian's new house. All the way to Rosings.

When I pull up outside, Mildred's wheels crunching on gravel, I see that I am not the only one taking action this morning. Rosings is quite the hive of activity. Liam's jeep has its back open, and a big black roof box attached to the top. He is currently stacking a big suitcase into it. The twins are wrapped up in raincoats and wellies, chasing Ralph around through puddles, and Bella is lurking in the doorway of the house, glaring at the world in general and Liam in particular.

I take a deep breath and get out of the car. I ignore the fact that it feels like I've been hit by a sledgehammer, and find a smile for Alice and Alex as they run over to greet me. Ralph does the same, but luckily he's the only one who sniffs my bum.

'Off on an adventure?' I ask, my eyes darting from the suitcase and back to them. Liam's face is set in stone, dark marks under his eyes from a sleepless night, his hair unruly in the drizzle.

'Yes! Daddy's taking us to the big toy shop in London, and then we're back to home in Dublin,' Alice announces very seriously. 'I'm going to write to you, though, I promise, so don't be sad.' She is such a sweet girl, and her tiny hand in mine, her words of consolation, are almost enough to make me cry.

'That would be wonderful,' I reply just as seriously. 'I never get proper letters anymore!'

They both give me a hug, then Bella stalks over to us. Her hair is bundled up beneath a beanie hat, and her expression is thunderous.

'Come on, Alice, Alex,' she says. 'Let's walk down to see Nanny and Granddad with Ralph.'

The kids squeal in excitement, and she turns to me. 'Thanks, Ellie. For being cool. And for the Nirvana T-shirt.'

'I never said you could keep that,' I point out, grinning.

'Possession, law, tenths. Deal with it. I hope I see you again some time.'

Without a word to Liam, she turns on her heel and sets off down the hill with her siblings and the dog. If I could see auras, I think hers would be entirely black right now, maybe with a crackle of red.

I look at Liam, who is fastening up the roof box. He is soaked now, his T-shirt plastered against his body in a way I really don't want to notice but do anyway.

'You want to come inside?' he asks. No, I think. I want to run all the way down this hill, and away from you. Away from whatever it is you're about to say to me. Away from this kick that I just know life is about to aim at me.

I nod and follow him through. The place has obviously been cleared out of the detritus of everyday life. The coat stand is empty, the curtains closed, and inside the big room, Christmas decorations are packed in boxes, the huge tree standing bare and forlorn in the corner. I tear my eyes away from it, and we walk into the kitchen. It's the same in here – counters cleaned, plugs switched off. Everything shut down.

'I'm sorry, I can't offer you anything with milk in it,' he says, picking up the kettle and going to fill it. 'The fridge is empty.'

He doesn't meet my eyes as he goes about his business, and I can tell he is using it to buy himself time. He is as switched off as the plugs, as closed as the curtains. How have we gone from that kiss, that promise, that potential, to this?

'I don't want a coffee, Liam. I want... some honesty, maybe? You're leaving?'

He leans back against the counter, and nods wearily. 'Yes. Today.'

'Right. And you weren't going to tell me? Or even say goodbye?'

'I was going to message you later, when we were in London.'

That, I decide there and then, is not something that sits well with me. If I hadn't come here, he would have simply disappeared from my life with no explanation.

'That,' I say quietly, caught somewhere between angry and sad, 'is a shitty thing to do, Liam.'

His nostrils flare slightly, and he rubs his face with his hands. He looks and sounds exhausted, and a flash of sympathy worms its way into me.

'I know it is, and I'm sorry. I'm a coward. I knew that if I saw you, I might change my mind.'

'About what?'

'About everything. I can't do this, Ellie. That kiss... that was a mistake.'

It hurts to hear him say that, and it is a hurt that is horribly familiar. This is not the first time that Liam Byrne has rejected me. Not the first time that he has pushed me away. I have a flashback to being sixteen, standing before him begging his forgiveness. Him staring up at me from the couch, shaking his head and telling me to go. Telling me to leave him alone. Telling me that he didn't want me.

I am not sixteen anymore, but I feel the same sharp tang of that pain. All my confidence comes crashing down around me, and I am suddenly an insecure teenager again, feeling unwanted and unloved. I gulp back the sob that wants to escape, and blink away tears that I will not allow to spill.

That kiss was a mistake, he says. That kiss that I have thought about endlessly since. The one that I now realise showed me for sure that Liam Byrne is not just a friend, and will never be just a friend. Liam is the man I am in love with.

The irony of realising this now, as he tells me it is all finished before it even began, is not lost on me. I search his eyes, seeing the regret that lies in them, but also seeing his determination. I would not be able to talk him out of leaving even if I wanted to, even if I was willing to abandon my pride. No matter how brave or fearless I become, I will lose – because Liam has made his mind up.

This is over.

I nod at him, once, before I leave.

'Okay,' I say simply. 'I'll... see you after the next twenty years, then.'

TWENTY-FOUR

I have baked myself a cake, to mark my first weekend back in New York. It is a nice cake, chocolate fudge, and it is still warm from the oven.

I push a spoonful around my bowl, but have no appetite. It's been the same since Christmas now, but still I persist. I will not fall into the black hole of despair I was in last year, or start stalking Macy's Santa. I will treat myself kindly, as much as I can. That seems to involve making myself good food, and then only eating half of it.

'I'm sorry, chocolate fudge cake,' I say out loud. 'It's not you, it's me, I promise.'

It is the second week in January, and I have been back in work for the last five days. It has felt strange, being in my Brooklyn apartment, commuting to the office on the subway, living my little New York life.

I have been walking as much as I can, strolling the magnificent parks and waterfront spaces of the city, but it still feels so enclosed compared to the wild Cornish coast. There is beauty in the city, in its glorious architecture, its history and its vibrant culture, but it is not the same. For me, it will never be the same. I miss the clifftops and the green fields and the never-ceasing sound of the waves outside my window. Now, I am trying to readjust to the sound of traffic outside my window, the hum and rattle of the Fourth Avenue Line and the early-morning delivery trucks.

I spent my final evening in the UK with my father in London, as we'd planned. We saw a show, had a late dinner in Chinatown, and talked away the whole night in our hotel room.

'You know you don't have to go, don't you, darling girl?' he'd asked. 'You know you could stay.'

'I know, Dad. I just... it's time. I need to get back to work. But don't worry, I won't leave it so long next time.'

His health has steadily improved, and Sandra has agreed to help out. The sale is still going through, and Sean has also signed on for extra shifts. He will be fine, I tell myself – even though I know he will miss me, he will be fine.

Maggie had her surgery, and was home the day after in a cast. Next it will be an orthopaedic boot, and then hopefully back to normal. She's opening the café part-time, with Lucy and Bernadette's help, and I wouldn't be surprised if she finds a way to keep her hours down. 'It's all been a bit of a wake-up call,' she told me. 'I was so tired. There's more to life than work, my love.'

My final night in St Tilda was bittersweet, a farewell party held at the inn. Everyone was there, including Maggie in a wheelchair, and the vast majority of the Byrne family. All apart from one, obviously. Liam had retreated to Dublin, and much to his sister's disgust, had decided to stay there. I never got more of an explanation from him, nor did I ask for one. Dealing with life's kicks is one thing – actively seeking them out is another.

Truthfully, by then I was more than ready to leave. Every corner of St Tilda reminded me of him. The cliffs he jumped from. The bus stop and the village green. The beach. Even the inn itself, and that one amazing kiss. He might have physically left, but for me, he was still absolutely everywhere. I managed to hide my pain from my dad, I think, and hopefully from everyone else. I pretended I was fine, that life went on as normal.

I was not fine, though, and life was far from normal. My poor battered heart needed to be away from the memories, from the ghosts of what we had and what we never will have. It will be hard enough to get over it all as it is, but it would be impossible if I stayed there.

Tyler and I have exchanged a couple of messages, but neither of us has suggested meeting up. I think that is the right thing at the moment. If he feels even a fraction of the heartbreak that I do, then he needs time away from me like I need time away from St Tilda. I hope that one day we can be pals, but that will have to happen on his schedule, not mine.

So now, here I am. Celebrating surviving my first week back at work by not eating chocolate fudge cake. I clear the plate, and make myself a mug of tea instead. It is Friday night after all – a girl's allowed to go crazy.

I take it through to my tiny living room, and try to settle down to watch the TV. Nothing quite captures my interest, though, which is another familiar feeling. I am struggling to focus, to lose myself in a book or a movie like I used to. Every night here so far has felt endless.

Maybe, I think, I should finally stop waiting for someone to get me a puppy, and find one of my own. My mind immediately trips me up, and loops me into memories of Tyler's Labradors, and Liam's Ralph. I squeeze my eyes shut and try to block them out. I cannot get a puppy. For a start, my lease does not allow me pets. Also, I work full-time and it wouldn't be fair. Maybe I could sneak in a gerbil or a guinea pig though. Food for thought.

I flick through the channels, avoiding anything related to the news or current affairs, because the state of the world is never going to cheer you up, is it? My mood is low enough already. In fact, I admit to myself as I sip my tea, I'm miserable. I have been miserable since Liam left St Tilda, and I am ashamed of myself for being so soft. When will I finally grow the kind of hard shell you need to survive this life?

My channel hopping takes me to a repeat of *The Great British Baking Show*, Paul Hollywood both smirking and twinkling as he offers a delighted contestant a handshake. Maybe I should go on *Bake Off*. It's the one thing I seem able to do successfully these days.

I'm actually starting to snooze off when there is a knock at my door. This is unusual, because I don't know anybody well enough for them to call round to my apartment unannounced. Which means it is either a neighbour, a sales person, or possibly an evangelical Christian looking to save my soul. I might invite them in and give them chocolate fudge cake.

I smooth my hair back, and decide that it doesn't matter if I'm wearing my pyjamas. It's my own home, and I'll lounge if I want to.

I keep the little security chain on as I open the door, and when I see who is outside I immediately slam it again. I lean back against the door and consider barricading it with the bookcases. Maybe climbing out the window and down the fire escape into the icy streets below.

'Ellie! It's Liam!' he shouts. I suck in a deep breath, telling myself to calm down.

'I know who it is!' I reply. 'That's why the door's still locked – go away!'

I realise that is a childish response. Rude, even. But I am not feeling quite myself tonight. I have no clue what 'feeling myself' is anymore. Losing Liam a second time around was even more painful than losing him the first time, and I cannot simply switch that off because he has turned up on my doorstep. I'm wearing my PJs and look like crap, for a start. What is it with the men in my life flying across oceans without warning, anyway? Though of course he probably hasn't flown across the ocean to see me. Probably he has an office here, or he's buying Queens, or he's engaged to a Manhattan socialite supermodel and he wants to tell me in person.

Ha – I'm definitely not letting him in! He knocks again, and says: 'I'm not going anywhere until I get to talk to you, Ellie!'

'Well, you'll have a long cold night in the hallway then, Liam, and also my neighbour might call the police. I have nothing planned all weekend. I'm staying in here.'

Wow, I think. That made me sound really cool. He is quiet for a few moments, then: 'Okay. I get it. You're pissed off with me. How about you at least open the door so I can talk without raising my voice? I feel like a fecking eejit out here! Please, Ellie!'

Against my better judgement, the corner of my mouth quirks into a smile at that one. He sounds frustrated, which I find weirdly satisfying.

'Okay,' I eventually reply. 'I'll do that. But I'm keeping the chain on, and you've only got ten minutes. I'm busy.'

'I thought you weren't going anywhere?'

'I'm not, but I'm still busy. Time is money. Now, what do you want, Liam?'

I open the door, and looking at him properly almost undoes me. His hair is a mess, ploughed into rows by his fingers, and his eyes are... Well, they are intense. I struggle to look away, and fear he may somehow be mind controlling me. I move to the side of the door just in case.

'I want to apologise. I want to beg your forgiveness. I want to tell you that I was wrong, and I've regretted it every single minute since. I want to tell you that I miss you like crazy, Ellie.'

Huh. That's not a bad start, I think, a rush of emotion running through me. What the hell is happening here? Am I hallucinating? Is this even real? Have I wished for this so often that my subconscious has conjured it up?

'Are you still there?' he asks. 'And, please, can I come in? I'm baring my soul here, Ellie, and it would be so much better if I could do it face to face.'

I don't know what to do. Part of me is joyous, ecstatic, floating on a cloud of happiness and relief. But the other part of me is more cynical. It has started to grow that hard shell, and it is not sure that Liam deserves a second chance. That he deserves my trust.

'It was Bella who made me realise,' he says, continuing when he realises I am not opening the door any further. 'She was so angry, and I thought it was just because I was taking her back to Dublin when she wanted to stay in St Tilda. And she was angry about that, too – but mainly she was annoyed with me for being what she very graciously termed "an absolute arsehole". She told me I needed to get my shit together. That I needed to open my eyes and see what was right in front of me. Then she added in some charming stuff about how she wouldn't be around to look after me forever, and I needed to find someone else to take care of me when I inevitably lost my teeth and went senile. Which, she seemed to think, was going to happen in about five years' time.'

I can't help but laugh as he talks. Bella, bless her. All that piss and vinegar and grief and angst, but all wrapped up on this occasion with a solid dollop of good advice.

'Did you ground her or send her to her room?' I ask, trying to imagine the scene playing out between them. The father-figure being lectured by his wild stepdaughter.

'Neither. I cried on her shoulder. Then she cried on mine. And basically we spent the whole night bawling together. It was very cathartic. I felt like an honorary woman.'

'Sexist. So, when did this happen?'

'It happened on the third of January. The anniversary of Anna dying.'

That hits me hard. I hear the pain in his voice, but I also heard the genuine regret when he apologised earlier. This is not a simple situation, and it probably cannot be solved through a closed door. I need to put on my big girl pants and deal with this.

I slide the chain off and open the door fully, gesturing him inside. He reaches out to touch me, and I ward him off with my hands.

'No, please don't, Liam. I'm barely holding it together here. Please, just sit. Say what you need to say. I'll listen, I promise.'

He nods and takes a chair. He looks insanely big in my tiny apartment, and the smell of his cologne fills my senses. His eyes flicker around the room, and he smiles at what he sees.

'This is nice,' he says. 'Cosy. Can I stay?'

'What? Can you stay here, with me? No, you cannot! You can afford a hotel, I'm sure.'

I keep my voice firm, but my body isn't quite so sure that the answer is no. The idea of Liam staying, of him sleeping next to me in my bed, is making my heart beat annoyingly faster.

'Yeah, of course I can. Sorry. I didn't even mean to say that, and I wasn't talking about sex... I just want to be near you, Ellie. I don't feel right without you. I've booked a week out of the office, and my mum and dad are staying with the kids in Dublin. I wanted to come here and show you I was serious. To show you this was real.'

'Serious about what? I'm so confused, Liam! You made it perfectly clear the last time I saw you that it was over. And I only got that much because I forced it. You blanked me. You tried to sneak away without even having the balls to talk to me face to face. It hurt, Liam – it really hurt! Even if you'd decided you didn't want anything more to happen between us, I thought we were friends? Friends don't treat each other like that!'

He groans and buries his face in his hands. I have tears in my eyes, and I don't even try to hide them. He came here to show me he was real? Well, this is real. Me, crying, in my pyjamas, struggling to eat because I'm so sad.

'I know,' he mutters. 'I know, you're right, about all of it! Look, can I explain something?'

'You might as well. You've come all this way.'

'That kiss.'

I nod. That kiss. I remember it well, the way he reduced me to rubble, my knees weak, my pulse racing. I couldn't get enough of him. It unravelled me.

'That kiss was amazing,' he continues. 'And it was the first time I'd kissed a woman since Anna died. When it happened, all I could think about was you. I was full of you, Ellie – intoxicated. I couldn't wait to see you the next day. Except, when I woke up, it was Anna who was on my mind. I felt like I'd betrayed her. Like I'd abandoned her. Especially at this time of year, everything is so raw, and I... I'd forgotten all about her. While I was kissing you. That whole night. I forgot about her.'

His pain is so raw, so deep, that I cannot even formulate a

response. I cannot mock this, or make a snappy comment, or even argue with it. This is his truth, and it is a hard truth.

'I see. That sounds terrible, Liam. I'm so sorry. I'm sorry you went through that. But, you could have told me. You could have explained, and I would have accepted that. I'm not an ogre.'

'I know that. You're kind and understanding, and you would have got it. It was me I was worried about, not you. Bella told me I was holding on to my grief as a way to hide from life. I suspect she might have a point. She's very wise for a girl with so many facial piercings.'

I smile. Bella is also, I know, part of Anna. They both lost her, and that gives Bella the right to speak her mind – to tell him what she thinks without the fear of him dismissing her. Bella telling him to move on is not Cara telling him, or a friend or colleague. It is Anna's own flesh and blood.

'Do you think she's right?' I ask gently. The anguish is clear on his gorgeous face, and there is no way I cannot respond to it. To this man, who I have tried so very hard not to love. I have failed, it seems, because all I want to do is take him in my arms and comfort him.

'I think she might be. Losing Anna almost broke me. It was only having the kids that got me through it. So maybe when I started to realise how deeply my feelings for you ran, I got scared. Because if you love someone, there is the chance that you can lose them, like I lost her. And I do love you, Ellie. I know this is messy. I know it's complicated, and the geography of our lives makes it even more so. But I love you, with all my heart, and I'm willing to do anything it takes to make this work between us.'

He stands up and holds out his hands.

'Please,' he says. 'Give me another chance, Ellie.'

I stare up at him, still not quite believing what I'm hearing. I take his hands, and he pulls me to my feet. He touches my hair, and gazes into my eyes, and his proximity is as confusing as always.

'I can't think straight when you're that close to me,' I say, stepping away. He looks crestfallen, and I quickly add: 'That's not a no,

Liam. I just... I need to think. Do you want some hot chocolate fudge cake?'

He looks momentarily bewildered, but quickly recovers. He knows that my love language is confectionary. Behind him, on the muted TV screen, the *Baking Show* contestants are unveiling their showstoppers. I shake my head to clear it, and walk through to the kitchen. He follows me, and I slice him some cake and pass him a spoon.

He takes a mouthful, and a sound comes from his lips that I'd associate more with a blue movie than with cake. Job done, I guess. I watch him as he eats, making fresh tea, letting his presence here in my little apartment sink in. Letting his words sink in. Letting his offer become a real thing.

After a few more moments, I pour us both a drink, and then I take the bowl from his hands. I place it down on the counter, and I walk towards him. I wrap my arms around his waist, and he pulls me close, hope in his eyes. I stand on tiptoes and kiss the corners of his mouth. Just when I thought he couldn't get any better, he now tastes of chocolate.

'I love you too, Liam. And the answer is yes. I'll give you another chance.'

He kisses me then, properly – and yet again, nothing in the world exists but him. I have no idea what the future holds, but I do know what this moment holds, and for now, that is enough.

I stand at the end of the aisle, feeling a sudden rush of nerves. It looks like an awfully long way to the altar, and everyone is staring at us. What if I trip over my dress, or break a heel?

I glance at the rows of people inside the church, the familiar faces and the friends. Bernadette and Brian. Cara and her new baby boy. Maggie, now completely recovered. My mum and Ethan, here visiting. And right at the front, looking impossibly handsome in his tailored navy blue suit, Liam. His eyes meet mine and he gives me a little smile, and a wink that promises me that everything will be okay. I immediately feel better about everything in the entire world.

My dad glances down at me, my arm linked into his, and gives me a beaming smile. 'You look beautiful today, Eleanor – utterly radiant. Very rude of you to steal my thunder, you know.'

'I think you'll find the thunder belongs entirely to Sandra today, Dad, and it will be impossible to steal. Now come on, let's make a respectable man of you.'

He nods, looking very slightly overwhelmed, and we slowly stroll up the aisle. I am an unconventional choice of best man, but I am happy to play the part. We arrive at the altar, and within a few minutes, the bridal music begins. Everyone, including us, turns around to see the bride making her own way towards us.

Sandra has her crazy curls pinned up, and looks stunning in a blush-pink dress. Her eyes find my father's, and the two of them look blissfully happy. My dad ended up staying on at the St Tilda Inn as the manager. Liam technically owns it, and he's invested in a lot of improvements, but my dad still runs the place – with Sandra by his side. She's as good a hostess as he is host, and they have formed the perfect partnership in all aspects of their life. He popped the question over the summer, and I couldn't be more thrilled as I watch them take their vows. It really is never too late to find love.

After the service, there is a celebration back at the inn – because if it's not broken, why fix it? The two of them are heading off on a mini-break to a stately home hotel called Bancroft Manor in the Cotswolds tomorrow, but tonight, it's all about the party.

The place is packed, and Maggie has outdone herself on the catering. She seems much happier now she does less hours at the café – mainly due to her new co-owner, yours truly. I always hoped I could make a living from doing something I loved, and it turns out that I can. The café is always bustling, and the bakery business is booming. Professionally, things couldn't be going better.

I watch as Alex and Alice tear up the dance floor in their posh togs, joined by Cara's boys and their other little cousins. I see the Byrnes sprawled out over several tables. I see friends old and new. I spot Bella, who still seems to prefer stealing drinks even though she is now old enough to legally buy them. She sees me watching her, and holds up the remains of a pint of Guinness in a mock salute.

Liam is across the room from me, chatting to Sandra's brother, but I feel the connection between us just as strongly as if he was right next to me. We live together at Rosings now, the whole bunch of us, and I couldn't be happier. He looks up and over, as though he has sensed me looking at him. He smiles, and it is a smile that is only for me. He mouths the words 'I love you', and I feel a blush spread over my cheeks. The man still has that effect on me.

Cara appears at my side, and offers me a glass of Champagne. She looks from me to her brother, and shakes her head, silky red tresses swaying over her shoulders.

'Look at you two,' she says. 'Love's young dream, the pair of you. It's sickening, so it is.'

I know she doesn't mean that. She was almost as pleased as I was when Liam and I got back together. She offers me the Champagne flute, but I shake my head.

'No thanks,' I reply, giving her a wicked grin. 'I'm off the sauce.'

She stares at me for a few seconds, dumbfounded, then seems to put the pieces together. My hand is resting on my belly, and her eyes fill with tears.

She wraps me up in a hug, and whispers: 'Congratulations! I told you it wasn't too late didn't I?'

'You did,' I whisper back. 'But don't tell anybody else just yet.'

She makes a vow of silence, but I'm not entirely sure I believe her. She looks way too excited as she makes her way through the throng and back to Ben and the baby.

Liam joins me, and slides an arm around my shoulder. He drops a kiss on my cheek, and says: 'You okay?'

'Yes. Just looking at all those kids on the dance floor, and wondering how we're going to cope with having four in the house.'

'We're going to cope just fine. We can teach them to jump off cliffs, and skateboard, and smoke and drink to excess. We'll be the model parents.'

'Oh God,' I say, throwing my mind forward a few years. 'What if they're like us when they're teenagers?'

'Then we'll deal with it. But for now, could I tempt you to a dance? I've made a special request with the DJ...'

Just then, the music begins – and *Fairytale of New York* fills the room. I laugh as we are swept into the middle of the room, jumping and yelling and feeding off the energy that is all around us.

New York never held many fairytales for me. St Tilda, though?

That's a whole different matter. St Tilda is where I began, and now I am back – living my happy ending.

A LETTER FROM THE AUTHOR

Dear reader,

Huge thanks for reading *Christmas Wishes and Irish Kisses*. I hope you were hooked on Ellie and Liam's journey. If you want to join other readers in hearing all about my new releases from Storm, you can sign up here:

www.stormpublishing.co/debbie-johnson

You can also sign up to a newsletter that I send out myself – you'll be the first to hear all my news, book gossip, and more – there will be giveaways, free samples, and short stories. It's totally free, I won't send so many your inbox hates me, and I promise it will be fun!

debbie-johnson.ck.page/32bc38fdb7

If you enjoyed this book and could spare a few moments to leave a review that would be hugely appreciated. Even a short review can make all the difference in encouraging a reader to discover my books for the first time. Thank you so much!

Thanks again for being part of this amazing journey with me and I hope you'll stay in touch – I have so many more stories and ideas to entertain you with!

Debbie Johnson

KEEP IN TOUCH WITH THE AUTHOR

facebook.com/debbiejohnsonauthor

x.com/debbiemjohnson

ACKNOWLEDGEMENTS

As ever, so many people need a big 'thank you' in this section – mainly my family and friends. I couldn't do any of this without you. I'd also thank my dogs for helping me stay sane, but they're really rubbish at reading!

Thank you to my agent, Hayley Steed, and her team at Janklow & Nesbit, and to the Storm squad – in particular my fabulous editor, Kathryn Taussig.

Mainly, thank you to you – the reader who got to the end of the book! I can't tell you how much I appreciate your support.

Printed in Dunstable, United Kingdom

70950962R00140